D0732238

Also by Jim Knipfel

These Children Who Come at You with Knives, and Other Fairy Tales

Unplugging Philco

Noogie's Time to Shine

Ruining It for Everybody

The Buzzing

Quitting the Nairobi Trio

Slackjaw

The Blow-off

Jim Knipfel

Simon & Schuster Paperbacks
New York London Toronto Sydney

Simon & Schuster Paperbacks
A Division of Simon & Schuster, Inc.
1230 Avenue of the Americas
New York, NY 10020

This book is a work of fiction. Names, characters, places, and incidents either are products of the author's imagination or are used fictitiously. Any resemblance to actual events or locales or persons, living or dead, is entirely coincidental.

First Simon & Schuster trade paperback edition July 2011

Designed by Meredith Ray

Manufactured in the United States of America

10 9 8 7 6 5 4 3 2 1

Library of Congress Cataloging-in-Publication Data

Knipfel, Jim.
The blow-off / Jim Knipfel.
p. cm.
1. Journalists—Fiction. 2. Crime and the press—Fiction. I. Title.
PS3611.N574B56 2011
813'.6—dc22
2010050194

ISBN 978-1-4391-5413-7
ISBN 978-1-4391-5901-9 (ebook)

For Dave Read, who knows a thing or two about our monsters

A man could spend the rest of his life trying to remember what he shouldn't have said.

—John Garfield, *Force of Evil*

The Blow-off

One

"Inside this tent! You will SEE . . . before your very eyes! This beautiful, luscious young lady transformed into a snarling, hideous, three-hundred-pound gorilla! . . . ALIVE! ALIVE! ALIVE! . . . You will SEE the clothing fall from her young and supple body! You will SEE thick black hair sprout from her tender bare flesh! The long black hair of a GORILLA covering her entire body! Her teeth will grow into dripping yellow fangs! She will—before your eyes!—become a BEAST of the jungle! But don't worry, folks. All the while she will be confined within an iron cage lined with reinforced steel bars! Only the bravest of the brave are invited inside! So step right up and buy your tickets. . . . ALIVE! ALIVE! ALIVE!"

The recording started once again from the beginning.

"No," was all she said.

The limp and faded banner hanging over the entrance to the

tent featured a screaming, bikini-clad beauty held loosely in the clutches of what appeared to be a twelve-foot-tall gorilla who, likewise, was screaming about something. His (as promised) wicked yellow fangs were dripping blood. Behind them, for some reason, stood a single palm tree.

"C'mon," he said, his voice distant, his eyes fixed on the crudely painted banner. His legs were already moving toward the tent, and he was tugging at her immovable arm like a Jack Russell terrier who'd just spotted something in the gutter. A slice of pizza or the severed wing of a pigeon.

"*No*," Annie repeated more firmly. She leaned back, digging her heels into the blacktop, which had softened in the unbearable heat of the past three days. She wrenched her arm free from his sweaty grip. There was no question or hesitation in her tone, no opening for negotiations. She folded her arms and waited for him to turn around and meet her unwavering gaze.

The heavy air around them reeked of burnt sugar and sweat and howled with a collision of warped calliope music, classic rock, and screams. Where they stood, they were hemmed in on all sides by thousands of dancing and whirling and throbbing pinpoint lights.

Hank's eyes snapped away from the banner and back to his wife, his confusion deepening. "No? Whaddya mean no? It's a *Girl-to-Gorilla* show." He spoke the term as if merely uttering it aloud would clarify everything.

"*No.*"

"Look, sweetie—Annie—like the tape says, there's nothing to worry about. It's in a cage. I've seen this show a dozen times and it gets me every time. Great little trick. It's done with mirrors, you know." He stared at her expectantly.

"That's great, Marv. Really. But no."

"Marv was your first husband," Hank gently corrected. He bit his lip, his eyes drifting involuntarily back toward the ticket booth outside the Girl-to-Gorilla tent.

"I just don't see the attraction."

"Fine, I can accept that," he said. "But would you mind if I went in? You can wait out here, and I'll be back in ten—"

From inside the tent came the squeal and crash of a metal cage door torn from its hinges and tossed to the ground. Annie jumped a step closer to Hank as, at that instant, the piercing shrieks of half a dozen teenage girls erupted inside. One of the tent's nylon side panels billowed outward, went taut, and focused nearly to a point before a small, almost delicate black fist punched through the orange fabric. The screams from inside the tent were growing more frenzied. There was a tearing sound as those same girls, blind with panic, ripped their way through the tent wall and poured out onto the midway, stumbling over one another, still screaming and laughing, before scattering in half a dozen different directions. Hank watched a few of them go, shaking his head in quiet, resigned amusement, knowing for certain there was now no way in hell he'd get Annie into the show. "They're a superstitious people," he explained. "They always overreact to these things."

"*Shhhh.*" His wife glowered at him and pinched his arm for the third time that night. There was nothing playful about it.

Hank winced and pulled his arm away. "All right, then. Let's move on. We'll see the gorilla show later. Great show. Trust me. Used to see it when I was a kid."

She took his arm and they moved down the midway away from the ripped tent, weaving their way through the thick Jersey crowds, trying to avoid the dropped ice-cream cones and puddles of cotton-candy vomit as they went.

The rides they were passing grew more rickety and treacherous with each passing year. Or maybe, Annie sometimes thought, she and Hank were just getting older.

"Why do you suppose they call that one the Black Hole?" Annie shouted into his ear in an effort to be heard over the tedious, thumping rhythms of the ride's soundtrack—some insipid pop tune or another—blasting at jet engine levels. The "ride" itself appeared to be nothing more than a small wooden shack capable of holding no more than five or six people at a time, so long as none of those people moved. Yet there was a line of ticket holders twenty or thirty long, eagerly awaiting a chance to step inside.

"You'd be surprised," he shouted back.

The Saturday night crowd was a swamp of hairy arms and soiled logo T-shirts, wailing children, haggard sundresses, drooping bellies, body odor, and cigar smoke.

"What's with you, you hit your head on something?" Annie asked once the noise had faded to tolerable levels. She'd noticed his face and it worried her. At first she thought he might be having a stroke.

"What's wrong?"

"You're *smiling*."

Hank stopped walking to assess what his face was up to, examining it with his free hand. She was right. The smile dropped away.

"Sorry," he said. He looked around. "C'mon, let's find a beer stand. Maybe that Chinaman who was here last year's still around someplace." She twisted the flesh of his upper arm again. She wasn't fooling around.

"*Ow! Christ,*" he yelped, yanking his arm away and rubbing the point of assault. "Why do you keep doing that?"

"Don't use that word in public." Her whisper was fierce. "Take a look around you. You shouldn't even use it at home."

"*What* word? That's the fourth time tonight and I don't even know what I'm saying."

Despite the repeated attacks, Henry ("Hank") Kalabander was in his element. It might have been his second or third element in terms of priorities, but it was without question one of the top five. He brought Annie to the Meadowlands Fair every year. Before Annie, he'd brought his first wife. And before his first wife, he brought whoever was handy. Or he came alone.

Annie had caught him smiling the first year he'd brought her here, too. It was the first time she'd seen him do that in public.

"But you hate crowds," she'd pointed out back then.

"Yes . . . yes I do. But I live in New York."

"And you hate New York. So why do you like it here? It's more crowded than Midtown, and you haven't been to Midtown in seventeen years."

"I'm not so inflexible that there can't be exceptions to the rule."

"Bullshit."

"Okay then, I'm not so inflexible that there can't be this *one single* exception to the rule. More going on here than in goddamn Times Square."

"I might almost accept that," she finally conceded.

That was some seven or eight years back. He knew in his heart it wasn't a real explanation, that nothing had been settled, and that he'd be back the following year and the year after that (as he had been ever since), trying to figure out the answer for himself.

"Where's that fuckin' Chinaman?" He was swinging his head from side to side, peering through the crowds, the rides, the game booths with each futile pass in search of a beer shack.

Annie refrained from pinching him this time, afraid she might do some real damage. "Hank, we talked about this a few months ago, remember? It was on the news. They don't sell beer here anymore. Some kind of statute—like they did in the city with the street fairs."

His head stopped swinging and he stared at her with deeply saddened eyes. "You're kidding."

"I'm pretty sure it was passed. Too many people were getting shot. Or having fun, something like that. If we see one, we'll stop. I just don't think you should get obsessed with finding one if it's just not here." She looked at her watch. "They close in an hour and a half. What else do you want to see?"

He gave her a weak smile. "You're right, kid," he said, lightly crossing her chin with his fist. "Let's see what they got at the back end this year. Maybe we'll grab a couple corn dogs on the way. I'm trusting they haven't banned those yet."

She raised one eyebrow. "You know what your doctor said."

He took her arm and headed toward one of the far corners of the midway, past the balloon race and the Billy the Drug Addict exhibit. "My doctor says a lot of things, most of them involving the terms 'heart attack,' 'stroke,' and 'death.' Which is why I prefer not to talk to him much anymore. C'mon, let's see if we can find a Chinaman who'll sell us a couple corn dogs."

Ten minutes later they turned a corner and Hank slowed to a stop. In front of them was another orange and yellow striped tent. Hanging along the side were ten fifteen-foot-tall banners, obviously painted by the same artist responsible for the Girl-to-Gorilla banner. In this case, things were a bit harder to figure out. There was a banner for Zumelda, the Egyptian Mummy Princess, and another for Monster McGee, King of the Sea, featuring a giant, snarling polar bear snatching up a paw full of tiny Eskimos. At the bottom of each were two round red logos promising that the creatures in question were both "Real!" and "Inside!"

The banner that caught Hank's eye was to the far right of the line. The central image was of a hideous creature, part ape, part wolf, it looked like, with shaggy hair, pointed ears, a long snout, and dripping, bloody fangs. In one bloody claw it clutched a disemboweled sheep. The legend across the bottom identified the horrible beast as Giles Goat Sucker.

"Oh, that's too good for a place like this," Hank said with quiet admiration.

Another warped tape loop was blaring a pitch through speakers poised above the entrance.

> ***". . . collection of marvels will astound you and confound you! Confuse you and amuse you! And they're all guaranteed one HUNDRED percent real! Get close enough to touch Monster McGee, King of the Sea. IF . . . YOU . . . DARE! You will never be the same again! And if you can prove beyond a doubt that any of the wonders you see inside this tent aren't as REAL as YOU and ME—I will personally pay you ten THOUSAND dollars in cash! So come inside, folks, and SEE the Egyptian mummy! SEE the world famous CHUPA . . . CAAAHBRAAA! The terror of Mexico! SEE—"***

Hank's eyes drifted down to the ticket stand and focused on the short, bald man who ran the show. He wore a glittering purple vest and red and white striped pants. To take a wild guess, he might have been in his late fifties. Or he could've been a lot older or a lot younger. It was hard to tell with someone that short. The face was squashed and heavily lined, and the nose, flat and askew, seemed to have been broken more than once. He was chomping on a long black unlit cigar.

"Well, I'll be damned," Hank said. "I thought I recognized that voice."

"You know him?" Annie asked, moving closer, casting a doubtful glance at the little man.

"Fortunately or unfortunately, yeah. Name's Rocky. Rocky Roccoco."

"Why does none of this surprise me?"

"His real name's Archie but he's gone by Rocky for as long as I've known him. Ain't seen him in years. Eight or ten at least. Always figured he was dead." By way of explanation, he leaned down and whispered into Annie's ear. "He's not really a midget but he keeps trying."

"Isn't the more correct term nowadays 'little person'?"

"Yeah, probably. Something like that, anyway. That's why he's trying to be a midget."

Annie looked up at Hank, trying to read his face. "So is he someone you want to say hi to or someone you'd rather avoid?" With Hank, she knew, it was usually the latter, but it was always good to check first.

He paused a moment in deliberation, considering the banners. "I can't honestly say that you'll *want* to meet him yourself? But I think he's someone you *should* meet. If that makes sense. He's . . . yeah, he's really something." She saw a mysterious and mischievous flicker in Hank's eyes, and that always worried her a bit. "Besides, I really want to see his show. C'mon, we'll help him turn the tip."

"We'll what?" She hesitated.

"Don't worry," he assured her. "No gorillas'll grab you in here. It's a museum show. C'mon." Before she could ask what a museum show was, he took her hand and began dragging her through the smelly, slow-moving crowd toward the ticket stand.

There's that Jack Russell again, Annie thought. There was nothing in his mind or his field of vision but that tent, and nothing was going to stop him from reaching it.

Above them, the recorded pitch rolled on. " . . . *will make you quiver and shiver and shrivel your liver! You will SEE!*"

They joined the drunk, the bored, the nostalgic, and the merely curious and took their spot at the end of the line. Hank winked at Annie. "I wanna see how long it takes him." Annie looked at Rocky, who didn't seem to be looking at anyone. His eyes were on the till and he chewed furiously on that cold cigar while mechanically repeating, "Two George Washington dollars, folks, that's all it takes . . . Two George Washington dollars . . ."

When it was their turn Hank slid four singles toward the short bald man. "That's exact change there, stubby. You can try that drop counter on some other sucker."

"Never heard of such a thing, officer," Rocky said without looking up. He snatched the bills away. "I run a straight-up operation here."

"Aw, c'mon there, short stuff, you ain't run a legit operation since before you was swimmin' around in your daddy's balls."

Rocky looked up only when he noticed this jackass wasn't moving. The gnarled face squinted at the man who was grinning down at him like some godforsaken half-wit. It took a moment before his eyes widened in recognition.

"Why you yellah rat bastard," he said, removing the cigar so he could sneer. "Whaddya dirtyin' up my air for?"

Hank hissed out a small laugh. "Don't want to hold up the line, newtling. We'll be inside. Pop in, you get a chance. And if not, go fuck yourself." He turned to Annie and pointed her toward the tent flaps.

"*Don't count on it, asshole!*" Rocky shouted behind them.

Annie had never seen Hank in this mode before. It was a little disconcerting.

"Should we be sticking around here?" she asked. "He didn't sound too happy to see you."

"Just wait," Hank replied as he led the way inside.

The interior was illuminated by four overhead strings of bare incandescent bulbs stretching the length of the tent, together with a handful of small spotlights trained on the individual roped-off exhibits. The floor was covered with an inch of sawdust. The moist air smelled of mildew, urine, and popcorn. Fifteen other curiosity seekers milled about, younger couples mostly, thin, rodent-faced boys with halfhearted mustaches and blank-eyed, gum-cracking girls clutching small, cheap stuffed animals. They were shuffling slowly through the sawdust from exhibit to exhibit, saying little, their expressions impassive. Too young to be that dead, Hank thought.

The sides of the tent were lined with meager displays, mostly poster-sized black and white photos of classic sideshow freaks of yore: Johnny Eck, Chang and Eng the Original Siamese Twins, and Percilla the Monkey Girl. One glass case held a stuffed perch covered in rabbit fur. Another, according to the hand-lettered placard next to it, held the three-thousand-year-old mummy of an Egyptian princess named Marcella.

"Was that the name on the poster outside?" Annie asked. "It isn't, is it?"

"Dunno," Hank replied. "But Marcella was the name of Rocky's second wife." He leaned in closer to the glass, trying to get a better look at the face. "With all that makeup, can't tell if it's really her in there or not."

Annie took a closer look herself. "Not unless his second wife was plastic."

Next to Marcella was a six-foot-tall stuffed polar bear, looking only vaguely ferocious. The once white fur was yellowed and reeked of cigar smoke. It was thinning in patches, leaving the stitching down his belly and around his mouth clearly visible. Next to him was a sign reading, simply, "Monster McGee, King of the Sea."

"I don't get that at all," Annie confessed.

"Ah, very simple," Hank said, turning to her. "Let me try to explain. Now this guy here, see," he gestured at the bear, "this guy here is Monster McGee. And he's whatcha might call King of—"

"All *right*," she cut him off. "Just shut up."

Hank glanced around again and saw what he was looking for on the other side of the tent. "C'mere," he said, taking Annie's hand and leading her through the sawdust.

The posterboard legend on the easel next to the aluminum cage read:

GILES GOAT SUCKER

(Chupacabra)

This legendary beast has terrified farmers and ranchers in South America for generations! For killing and eating livestock and devouring the blood of animals! Scientists say the monster never existed, but this one was captured in the Yucatán in 2001, while eating a live sheep, but it soon died in captivity!

Inside the cage was propped a department-store mannequin draped in a shabby, ill-fitting gorilla suit that gathered at the elbows and ankles. In place of the head was a stuffed wolf's head, its lips stretched back to bare the fangs. Strapped to each of its hands was a leather glove equipped with four long blades—a favorite Halloween costume accessory in the late 1980s.

Hank shook his head and sighed.

"What," Annie asked, "you expected them to have a real live monster in here?"

"No." His voice was oddly sad as he scrutinized the piecemeal creature in the cage. "Not really. Suspension of disbelief problems, I guess. I've always been a sucker for sideshow banners. They promise so much, and they get me every single goddamn time. Ever since I was a kid."

The tent flap flew back and an unmistakably nasal voice burst in their ears. "Well, if that ain't the home cookin'! As I live an' breathe, it's ole Hank Kalabander-Rhymes-With-Salamander!"

They both turned and saw Rocky Roccoco marching toward them, cigar in hand. "Hey Salamander, you ole so-an'-so. You with it and for it?"

"You know I am, Rock."

Rocky drew within a few inches of Hank and glared up at him as all the good humor suddenly drained away into the sawdust. "No, you're not," he scowled, replacing the cigar in his mouth. "You're just a *chump.* A lugen. Come here every year, get your fill in a couple hours, then go home to the suburbs with your lawns an' your clean sheets. You're no different from the rest of the townies."

Annie looked at Hank, nervous, not knowing what to make of this. She saw the hurt pass across his face, but it was gone in an instant. Hank took a step closer to Rocky and bent down, grabbing the front of his shirt.

"Better watch your step there, Rochester," he said. "Remember, I can still pick you up, turn you upside down, and shake you like a fish."

"I wouldn't suggest it," Rocky shot back, removing the cigar again, drawing out a thin string of spittle from his lower lip to the stogie's slick, well-chewed end. "Not with your back, old man. Liable to land you in traction."

Hank cocked his head slightly to the right and released Rocky's shirt. He turned to Annie. "I think he has a point." He straightened himself. "Rock, want you to meet my wife, Annie. We got hitched . . . ah . . ."

"Six years ago," Annie said.

"Yeah. Like she said."

Rocky stuck out a rough hand. "Annie, pleased to mee'cha." His bloodshot eyes scanned her up and down in an obvious and less than gentlemanly fashion.

"Roccoco's the name, and any wife of Hank Salamander's a wife of mine. But I'll tell ya, toots, you're wastin' your time with this mug. He's old and he's slow and he's a *nasty* bastard."

"I know that already," she countered.

"See that Rock? She knows already." Hank was beginning to recall why he hadn't bothered talking to his friend for almost a decade.

More rubes were drifting in through the tent entrance, and as they did most cast Rocky a curious look before moving on to Marcella.

"So," Hank said, "I had no idea you were with this outfit. Haven't seen you here for the past few years. Last I saw you, you were with Serpentine Brothers, weren't you?"

"Probably." Rocky was keeping an eye on the newcomers just to make sure none of these damn kids started messing with his attractions.

Guessing it might not be the time to push for details, Hank moved on. "Nice show you got here—and I gotta hand it to you on this." He waved at the sign next to the Chupacabra cage. "Very literary of you. Postmodern, even."

"What the fuck are you talking about?" Rocky looked at the sign, then back to Hank.

"Just the name, I mean."

"What about it?"

"Well, there's a novel by . . ." Then he thought better of it. "Yeah, never mind. Kind of a shoddy job on the presentation, though, don't you think?"

Rocky's face tightened. It was apparently Hank's turn to jab a sore spot.

"What the fuck do you expect? Three days before season opens, you got a banner, you got a legend, but you got no Chupacabra. Let's see *you* pull something outa your ass, Einstein. I had to improvise. Still got you in here, didn't it?" He glanced at his watch. "I gotta get back out front, make sure that pinhead ain't pocketing too much of the take. But hang out for a while if you like."

"Maybe let's grab a drink after you close up?"

Rocky nodded. "Solid, Jackson. Gate closes at ten. I could be outa here by ten-thirty. We'll go cut up a few jackpots."

As he turned to leave, Hank stopped him. "Heya, Rock. What's your blow-off this season? If it's Miracle of Life, I'll save my fifty cents."

Rocky looked confused for a moment, then the contempt returned. The cigar came out again. "Only get blow-offs with live acts, *dummy*," he said, before adding, "With it and for it, my ass." He turned and stepped through the tent flaps, out into the thump and scream of the dark midway.

Two

So what's the scoop, Winnie the Poop?" Rocky asked as Hank set three drinks on the glass-topped table: Annie's gin and tonic, Rocky's Grant's double, straight up, and his own Whatever Lager They Had on Tap. They were seated around a front table in a blessedly quiet lower Manhattan bar called Hanuman's. Strange to find a place so quiet on a Saturday but they'd done it. None of them had ever been to Hanuman's before, but it seemed almost empty from the outside and that was all they needed to know. A few silent eyes turned to consider them (especially the bald man in the purple vest) but soon gave up and drifted away.

"I'm sorry sir," the stiff young bartender had said when they entered. "But there's no smoking allowed in here."

It took Rocky a second to register what the hell the kid in the bow tie was talking about. He removed the limp black cigar stub from between his brown teeth and waved it about. "This thing look like it's smokin' to you, chum?"

With a resigned grunt, he nevertheless tucked the stub safely away in his vest pocket.

Upon first catching sight of all the brass, glass, and abstract art,

Rocky and Hank shot each other a glance and mouthed the words "fag bar" (well, at least Rocky mouthed them), but they decided to stay anyway.

"You first, half-pint," Hank insisted, holding up his glass in an implicit toast. "Last time I saw you, you were running a ten-in-one with Serpentine Brothers. That was some flea bag outfit, by the way. Now you got a museum show with some other flea bag outfit."

Rocky took a sip of the whiskey and gave a small shrug. "It's Fielding Blount's operation. He's a screwhead. Wish it was a better story. Moved from operation to operation as each one folded. Flea bag or not, Blount's about the only one left nowadays—at least on this scale. This is our first season at the Meadowlands 'cause nobody's left who could fill it. And I'll tellya, it's a helluva lot cheaper running a museum show than havin' to pay fire-eaters and keep Willy the Human Whale in spareribs. A lot classier than runnin' a flat store. So I run a museum show, and you should just shut your big yap about it."

"Hey, whatever happened to Willy anyway, now that you mention it?"

Rocky rolled his eyes. "He kicked. Funny story, though. After Serpentine folded, doc tells him he's gotta drop six hundred pounds or he's gonna die. So what's the stupid fat fuck do? He can barely stand but decides to start *jogging*. First day, right? Steps outside and *boom*!" He clapped his hands. "Gets hit by a fuckin' cattle truck."

"Oh, that's terrible," Hank said. "That poor man." Then both he and Rocky roared with laughter. Annie couldn't understand half of what they were saying but said nothing. Hank seemed almost happy, so she figured it best to let him be.

"You still live in Gibtown?"

"Off season, yeah, but even that's dying. Everyone, I mean.

Trailers emptyin' out, no one around to fill 'em. I'm a youngster in this business, remember." He shifted in his seat. "So what about you? Last I saw you, you weren't doin' much o' nothin' at all."

Hank's laughter dwindled. From the speaker mounted near the ceiling came the sound of a bleating tenor saxophone, giving the bar that film noir air, in spite of all the polished brass. Drinking in Manhattan at midnight with an aging, near-midget carny didn't hurt. Through the plate-glass window behind Rocky, Hank could see clots of sweating youngsters out in the streets in a desperate search for *fun*, hooting and barking and playing grabass as they went. As each group came into view, Hank squeezed his fists beneath the table, praying they wouldn't come in, replaying images of a distant and frightening world he wanted no part of.

Annie noticed his sudden silence and the increasingly malignant look on his face. This wasn't the carnival anymore. "Oh, Hank's been up to plenty in the last few years," she told Rocky to break the silence. She nudged Hank under the table. "Haven't you?" She knew the look. It always came on quickly. If Rocky hadn't been there she would have assured Hank that he was safe. She knew he hated coming into Manhattan and avoided it whenever possible. But it was Rocky's suggestion, so there they were.

Hank, meanwhile, couldn't tell from her tone if she was giving him a boost or trying to humiliate him for keeping her out this late with a would-be midget in striped pants.

"Yeah, guess I have," he said, looking at the table. "None of it lasted, though."

"That sounds about par," Rocky said. "Like what?"

Hank took a breath, deciding to make the best of it. "Well . . . starting when, eight years ago? Let's see, I washed dishes at that Greek joint in Times Square, you know, over on Eighth Avenue. Across the street from Show World."

"Screw the ladder an' start at the top, eh?" Rocky said. "You were, what, fifty at the point?"

"Forty-eight. Then I hacked for—"

Rocky stopped him again. "Hold on a sec there, Rochester. When'd you manage to get a driver's license?"

Hank gave a quick shake of the head. "Never bothered."

"And you drove a cab."

"They never asked."

Rocky set down his drink. "You are fuckin' batshit, my friend, and I'm tempted to give you a hug."

"Yeah, well," Hank said without looking at him. "Just keep it in your stripey pants, there, Marlene. Let's see, I was a bartender for about two weeks—"

"But no one saw any good reason to leave him any tips," Annie added. "Then he got the job as an elevator operator at Macy's."

"If you say the job had its ups and downs, swear to god, I'll head-butt you through this window," Rocky said.

"I can usually count on other people to dust that gem off for me. But if you won't oblige, I guess we can move on." Hank could feel the fatigue seeping into his guts. It had been a long day. Or maybe it was being in Manhattan and dredging up all these failures. Or maybe it was the booze. Hell, it'd been only one. "So as you can see I was a loser."

"Some things never change, eh?" Rocky said before turning to Annie. "Hey, doll. Hank here ever tell you how us two met?"

Annie shook her head. "Hasn't told me too much about his past, no. I've had to do a lot of guesswork."

"No? Wow, you're a gutsy dame. Guess I'll leave out that stretch in Sing Sing then, hey Hank? *Hah!*"

"That might be wise yeah. Otherwise you'd have to tell her how you were passed around like currency. Now just go ahead and tell your damn story, Petunia." Hank groaned quietly inside.

Rocky took another swallow of the whiskey, which was nearly gone. Hank tried to catch up, in part to keep things balanced, in part to numb himself. "All right," Rocky said as he leaned closer to Annie. "So this all happens back in the late seventies, see? Seventy-eight, seventy-nine, I think. This was before Serpentine. I was with Spike Burr's outfit, runnin' a little ten-in-one. More a five-in-one, really, but they were all wha'cha call nowadays multitalented."

Annie nodded, but didn't ask. "Anyways, see, we're parked in north Philly for a week, and show's goin' pretty smooth for a Philly stand. Weather's holdin' up. So in comes this kid, right?" He took another sip. "Now you gotta picture this. Kid comes in and he's in this full getup, see? Torn jeans, mismatched shoes, leather jacket, safety pins, hair all cut like a rooster." He raised both hands, fingers splayed, to the top of his head to illustrate. "The works. And I thought *I* had all the freaks in town." He gave another sharp cackle and looked over to Hank, who didn't join in. "So kid says he's lookin' for work with the sideshow, right?" He laughed loudly again. "Kid doesn't wanna run away with the *circus*. Nah, this one here, *he* wantsta run away with the goddamn freak show." He paused. "It's pretty common nowadays—guess the little fuckers think it's cool—but back then it was a new one on me. Mostly we just got junkies and guys just outa stir."

"Maybe I should give her a little background," Hank jumped in. "Don't want to give her the wrong idea, *do* you?"

"Yeah, you do what you need, sport. I'm gettin' another drink. Anyone?" He looked around the table as he stood. Annie shook her head. Hank nodded, then drained his glass. "Got it. Now you go on with your sob story." He turned and headed for the long bar, his purple vest twinkling under the track lights.

"I'm sorry," Annie whispered once Rocky was far enough away. "I had no idea he'd be such a dick to you."

Hank shook his head. "He's not. Just Rocky being Rocky. Midgets can get that way. And wannabe midgets are even worse. Bitter, spiteful little bastards." He looked to the bar to check on Rocky's progress. "So anyway, this story." He sat back. "I was in my early twenties at this point. Felt like an outsider most all my life, right? Like most white boys with half a brain at that age. We're romantics that way."

"Sure," she said. "It wasn't just boys, either."

It was a speech he'd made to himself a thousand times over the years. "A lotta kids, fourteen, fifteen years old, came to recognize their own alienation reading *Catcher in the Rye*, right? Maybe they still do."

"Of course," she nodded.

Hank shook his head. "Not me. I recognized my own alienation after seeing *Willard*. I had nothing in common with that snot-nosed whiner Holden What's-his-name and all his private school crap. I recognized myself in Willard and his rats."

"That suddenly makes a lot of sense," she said. It was a revelation that helped explain why, to date, he'd made her watch the movie five times without any explanations.

"Then punk rock comes along. Greatest thing in the world for someone like that, right? A whole fucking subculture designed for half-smart fuckups. So I start going to shows around Trenton and Philly, and up here when I could afford it—Ramones, Damned, Dictators, anyone I can see."

"That explains the record collection, too."

Hank paused and listened to the sound coming out of the speakers. The noir sound track had vanished, replaced with what sounded like Alban Berg, or one of those other abrasive European types. Maybe it had something to do with his mood. He frowned. It was appropriate, in its own way, but not something you hear in bars too often. "Yeah . . . anyway. So I start going to these shows with others of my own kind, and what happens?"

"What?"

"They beat the shit out of me. Every single goddamn time, these other punks jump me. Complete *strangers*. This isn't lighthearted joking around, either—I'm not talking about slam dancing—these guys were letting me know that I was not welcome in their club. But I kept going back."

"My god," Annie said, sounding honestly concerned. "Were you hurt?"

"*Hurt?* Of *course* I was hurt!" He held up his twisted hands. "My fingers didn't grow this way naturally. These were big guys. In combat boots. Little kids in combat boots, too, thirteen-, fourteen-year-old brats jumping on me. Girls. It didn't matter."

"Hank, why don't you tell me these things? I want to know."

"Never came up. But the point's this—"

Rocky returned with the drinks. "You about wrappin' this up, Johnny Alibi?"

"Yeah, Rock, thanks, have a seat." He turned back to Annie. "The point is, when you find yourself outcast from a society of outcasts, well, where do you go from there? What's the final refuge for the outcast's outcast?"

"The freak show?" Annie sort of guessed.

"Where else?"

"Yeah," Rocky took over. "So Mr. Discontent here shows up on the lot one night, wantin' to join up. Pay's shitty, accommodations are shitty, food's shitty but he doesn't care. He wants to be part of the freak show. That's just jim-dandy for me—we can always use an extra pair of hands, right? But then comes the kicker, see? 'Cause punkinlilly here didn't realize—never *occurred* to him—that when he signed on to work he'd actually be expected to *work*. Not just sit around all day eatin' fried dough an' being all existentialist an' mopey. There's heavy lifting." He gave Hank a look Hank knew all too well. "Goddamn hippie with a chicken haircut is what you were."

Annie looked at Hank, smiling. She was finally in on one of his secrets. "So how long did you last?"

"About three hours," Rocky answered.

"Five," Hank corrected. "There was a lunch break in there."

"Five, then. That's how long it took ole Salamander, clever monkey that he is, to decide that college might be an easier row to hoe. Pussy."

Hank turned his attentions out the window again. "Don't wanna push it there, Rochester," he said. "Remember I have a few stories of my own to tell."

Apparently taking the threat seriously, Rocky focused on Annie, shifting gears fast and smooth. "So hon, I gotta say, I like you. You're a helluva lot more fun than Hank's first wife. She was . . . a trip, weren't she Hank?"

"Yeah, that she was, Rock." He was still staring out the window at the slowly dwindling crowds. They were finding some place to go or they were giving up.

"What about you?" Annie asked. "Are you married?"

"Me?" Rocky pursed his lips and sputtered sharply. "Not no more. Was, couple times. No big deal. Now I got a skirt at every jump. Makes things easy."

"That mummy in your show," she said. "Hank says Marcella was your wife's name."

Hank's face showed no reaction but, below the table out of view, his foot snapped out and kicked Annie in the ankle. She bit her lip but didn't make another sound.

"Yeah . . . I guess it was. Hadn't thought of that before."

"May I ask what happened to her?"

Hank kicked her again. After all the pinches he'd received earlier that evening, he felt it was only just. Rocky gave Hank the briefest of looks before answering.

"She died a long time back. Same way as Hank's first wife."

"A car accident? I'm sorry. That's so awful."

Rocky's eyes cut momentarily, but his face remained unmoved. "Yeah. Truck sideswiped her. Went through the windshield. Took her head off. But hey." He clapped his hands. "Enough of that shit, right? We didn't get along anyway. This is a *party.* Old friends, new friends, all that happy horseshit . . . So what about you, sweets? How do you support this layabout?"

"Me?" she asked, spinning the half empty glass around between her fingers. "Well, now I run a little used and rare book store in Red Hook. There aren't too many of those left in New York these days."

"I can imagine," Rocky said, nodding. "That helps explain what you see in this big lug." He jerked a thumb Hank's way.

"What the fuck's that supposed to mean?" Hank asked, picking his head up. He'd been awfully glad when Rocky changed the subject, but now he wasn't sure where this was going.

"Oh, nothin' . . . nothin' at all, killer. 'Cept that you're old, you're a little worn around the edges, there's some yellowing, you smell musty. Oh, and your spine might crack if you ain't careful."

Hank's glass was halfway to his mouth but he stopped and considered this. "Y'know, that's actually cleverer than I would've expected from you, shorty. Had no idea you knew what a book was."

"I've picked up a few one-handers here and there."

"I prefer to think of Hank as rare, not musty," Annie said.

"Yeah, but he *is* worn at the edges. No denyin' that."

"I think 'endangered' is more like it," Hank concluded.

"On that note." Annie pushed her chair back. "I'm sorry, boys, but I think I need to head back to Brooklyn. It's almost one, and I need to open the store tomorrow morning. But you two sit here and get caught up."

"You sure?" Hank asked.

"Sure." She leaned over and gave him a quick kiss on the cheek, then stood. As she did, Rocky jumped from his chair.

"Where the hell are you going?" Hank asked him.

"Nowhere. I'm *standing*. You're supposed to stand up when a lady does."

"Since when?"

Rocky sneered at him. "You're such a lummox."

Hank shrugged and remained where he was. "Maybe, but face it, Rock. In your case it just don't make that big a difference. Standing, sitting, it's all about the same." He reached out and squeezed Annie's hand. "Get home safe. I'll see you when I get there. After I get Tom Thumb here headed in the right direction."

After she left, Rocky got them another round and returned to his seat.

"Car accident," he said so Hank could hear the quotation marks. "That's smooth."

"Didn't see much point in getting into it." He raised his glass again. "Thanks for covering, Muttley."

Rocky raised his own glass. "That's what freaks are for. She's a good woman. Puts up with you, anyway."

"Yeah, but I couldn't get her into the Girl-to-Gorilla tonight."

"That'll come in time," Rocky assured him with a cock of the head. "Right?"

"Probably."

"So what *are* you doing these days, ya pigfucker—livin' off all them mountains o' used book money?"

Hank looked toward the door and half-smiled. "Ahh, you'd be

proud of me, Rock. I found me some gainful employment at a local newspaper. Been there about a year an' a half now."

"What, you're a paperboy now?"

"Ah, shut your pie hole. I'm a reporter."

"A reporter? Jesus. You don't have any background in that."

"They never asked."

Rocky barked that laugh of his again. "Well, look at Mr. Fancy Schmantzy reporter there. What's your beat then, yer majesty? Fashion?"

Hank shook his head and looked down. "Crime," he said.

"Crime, he says!" Rocky nearly squealed. "Who woulda thunk it? You went from elevator operator to big city crime reporter like that?" He snapped his fingers.

"Pretty much, yeah."

"Crime," Rocky repeated. "That's the place to be . . . Y'know I used to tour with a crime wax museum. Now *that* was a moneymaker."

"I remember. That was a good show. Till people forgot who Richard Speck was."

Rocky was much more excited about this than Hank had expected him to be. Or maybe he was just drunk. "So where you at, one o' them jobbies on the Internet?"

Hank shook his head again. "Nah, it's a real honest-to-goodness paper. With print and ink and pages and everything."

Rocky's increasingly bleary eyes narrowed. "Really," he said incredulously. "I didn't think any of those still existed."

"In this town they do. Who knows for how much longer?" He thought about it a moment. "Guess it means we're both wrapped up in dead industries." Rocky threw back what was left in his glass, slammed it to the table with a startling crack, and wiped his mouth with a dramatic draw of the sleeve. "Now *that*, my friend, calls for a drink."

Three

Goddamn that dwarf, he thought. *Should've known.*

He was fighting to keep his eyes open, and his head upright, but was losing both battles. He couldn't even read the hands on his watch. The rocking of the train was throwing everything off, but it was strangely soothing.

Work's gonna be . . .

An insistent hand was shaking his shoulder. The voice sounded like it was coming from within a deep cave.

"Buddy? Hey, *buddy*! Wake up. This your stop? Gotta hurry—door's gonna close. Don't wanna miss your stop."

Hank's eyes snapped open and he saw the subway doors across from him. A man was seated next to him. He forced himself to his feet without thinking, head swirling, and careened across the aisle, bouncing off a pole and diving through the doors just as he heard the bell and the doors began closing. He felt a flash of victory and relief upon realizing he'd made it and was standing on the platform. Behind him, the train chuffed, groaned, and pulled away. He shook his head in an effort to focus.

The stairs weren't where they were supposed to be. That was

okay. They were always doing work, messing things up in the stations. He saw some stairs at the far end of the platform. Struggling hard to keep his toes pointed forward and not step off the edge onto the tracks, he paused several times to adjust his bearings.

There was a bench up ahead—a scarred wooden bench, with vertical slats every eighteen inches or so to keep bums from sleeping there. Good idea. If he sat down even for a minute he knew he'd be out. He hated falling asleep on the train. Hadn't happened in a long time. At least he hadn't ridden to the end of the line. He should've thanked the guy who woke him up.

He reached the stairs and with painful, leaden steps began pulling himself up to the next level. He was far too old for this shit.

It was only after he bumbled through the turnstile that his brain slowly started to register that nothing in this station appeared to be where it was supposed to be. The stairs were in the wrong place. The turnstiles were in the wrong place. And now where was he? There was supposed to be another flight of steps right there leading to the street, but it was gone. Wha'd they do with it?

He looked back through the turnstiles and saw the fake mosaic sign on the wall. CARROLL STREET, it read.

"Oh fuck me," he groaned aloud. There was no one around to hear.

That son of a bitch. How could he have fallen for that tired gag? Hell, he'd done that to old drunks and junkies himself when he was younger. Always good for a laugh. He immediately slapped at his pockets. Wallet was still there. At least the bastard hadn't gone that far. *Dumbass.*

He leaned against the wall, dropped his head, and considered his options. He could waste another fare and go back down to wait for the next train. Or he could hoof it. How long would it take? Half hour? Forty-five minutes? Depending on whether or not he could figure out how to get home from here. This hour, who knows how long it would be before the next train showed. Plus the night air might help clear his head before he had to face Annie and explain why a man his age had been out all night drinking with a sort-of midget.

Having made his decision he began looking around for a way out.

It took some time, but at least once he reached street level he thought he had some idea where he was, more or less.

The night was warm and humid, but not warm enough to explain why Hank was sweating as much as he was. He stopped walking as a third wave of nausea swept up from his guts to his head, then back again. He placed a hand on a nearby tree and doubled over, waiting. He coughed twice but nothing happened. Wasn't anything left, he figured. He felt bad about those steps he'd puked on a few minutes earlier, but at least they'd never be able to pin it on him. He slowly stood upright but was wracked with a violent hacking fit that ripped through his chest and drove the blood into his already pounding skull.

When he continued walking, he stumbled briefly again. He wanted to blame the sidewalks, as narrow and treacherous as they were, the slabs of slate jutting against each other at awkward angles and the tree roots beneath them that grew toward the row houses.

He told himself he'd make it. He was almost completely sure he was headed in the right direction. The stench was getting worse, anyway, and that was a good sign. He knew he had to get across the Gowanus Canal to get home. In the distance, silhouetted against the dirty orange sky, he could see the wooden water tanks poised on their spindly rooftop legs like Wells's alien machines. If he headed toward those he'd find the canal. If he found a way across the canal he could find his way home.

As he stumbled past each narrow intersection, the trees—silver under the quivering streetlights—were growing sparser and more barren. That was a relief. He didn't know how many he'd bounced off of already that night. Trees, garbage cans, fire hydrants. More things he didn't even see. His shins and shoulders ached, but he'd live. Just had to be—

Near a darkened corner Hank slammed into something hard enough to knock the wind from his lungs. He belched loudly and gasped. He took an unsteady step back and tried to shove the thing out of his way. It was pliable. Under the dim light of a distant streetlamp he caught a flash of orange. Orange and white. It was all he could see. One of those plastic traffic barrels? He found himself tangled up for a few seconds, the thing wrapping around him almost as if it were fighting back. Muttering and snorting angrily to himself, Hank pulled back and turned away before the thing could fall on him.

"*Christ.*"

Massaging his ribs, he reminded himself that if he didn't start watching where he was going he might not get home alive after all. He was already a wreck as it was. At least that woke him up a little.

There was a sound—a nearby whining or a distant scream, he couldn't tell. It echoed off the buildings around him. No matter, he thought. Probably a bird.

The more he tried to focus as he limped along, the more everything seemed to vibrate.

In the silence some blocks away, he heard a pack of dogs barking. He hoped they hadn't caught his scent. Gowanus dogs were bad news. Apart from the dogs, the only sound he heard now was his own wheezing breath and the scraping of his feet on the dirty pavement.

As he walked farther the brick row houses and their cramped

front yards gave way to black warehouses, and empty lots, and chain-link fences topped with tight coils of razor wire.

Not too far ahead he saw a single dead smokestack rising against the unnatural glow in the sky. He'd always wondered where that glow came from but wasn't going to go looking for any answers tonight.

The smell—the reek of oily industrial sludge, of sulfurous chemicals that should never have been manufactured—was beginning to seep into his nostrils and his clothes, making his already hesitant stomach churn once again.

Behind the chain-link fence surrounding one of the empty lots he passed, six enormous pill-shaped chemical tanks lay side by side. In another lot, cement trucks and delivery vans were parked three deep against the side of an unmarked and windowless steel building.

He stared through the fence, transfixed for reasons he couldn't identify. He knew he had to keep moving—the bridge couldn't be that much farther.

The few remaining trees he passed now were dead and gray. He passed a fireproof-door company and an abandoned tattoo parlor. One block before he reached the foot of the bridge he heard the dogs howling again. They sounded closer than before. To his left, a stark and imposing monolith stood alone. It seemed to absorb all the light around it. Across the street to his right was a desolate block-long warehouse.

Yeah, this whole neighborhood's really comin' around, he thought as he aimed for the right side of the bridge. Even as he thought it, he seemed to forget what he was thinking. All he knew at this point was that he better hold on tight to something.

After taking a few steps onto the narrow bridge he stopped, squinted, and looked around. Something was different. Last time he'd been across here, he remembered vaguely, the bridge had been made of black iron. Since then, someone had slapped a sloppy coat of cheap concrete over the whole thing. It was already cracking and crumbling away, once more exposing the metal beneath. Or maybe it was a different bridge? Fuck if he knew. Atop the guardrail they'd added an extraneous stretch of aluminum tubing, four inches in diameter.

"Sure wouldn't stop any jumpers," Hank said, tapping at the aluminum with a fingernail. He'd always wondered why so many suicide cases chose the Brooklyn Bridge for that final plunge, when it would be so much easier and more effective to dive headfirst into the Gowanus. If you were serious about what you were doing and not just some drama fag, you'd come out here. They'd never find the body.

Given what the chemical fumes off the canal were likely doing to his brain and lungs, it might have been wise to run across the bridge as quickly as possible. Instead, he peered over the side and down. A rickety metal ladder led to a concrete ledge below him. The water was black and still, the surface undisturbed by even the slightest ripple. Cancerous wooden pilings sprouted from it like clusters of mushrooms unevenly lopped off at the top. Everywhere and inescapable was the stink of death and industry.

More dark, nondescript warehouses lined the far side of the canal. Beneath them along the stained concrete bank was another ledge, holding three or four small, malformed trees and gray bushes. Unnatural weeds were crawling up through the cracks. Beneath the ledge lay the silent dark canal.

Taking it in all at once, Hank Kalabander thought it was indescribably beautiful. Yet beautiful or not, it was time he got moving again.

Halfway across the bridge he heard a voice.

"Hey, buddy!"

Hank slowly turned his head but tried to keep his feet moving. Leaning against the opposite guardrail, a man in a fishing cap was waving at him.

Shit. If he'd known this bridge was already occupied, he would've looked for another.

"Hey, buddy. *C'mere*, you gotta see this."

Hank knew better. Hank always knew better. But ever since he was a kid, he'd been a hopeless sucker for the phrase, "C'mere, you gotta see this." Especially when it came from strangers. You never knew what you might be missing, he reasoned. It might really be something.

Struggling against every bit of good judgment and sense left him at that moment, Hank released his grip on the guardrail, altered his course, and trotted a weaving path across the empty bridge, hoping to reach the other side before landing on his face.

What the hell am I doing? But before he could reconsider he was holding on to the guardrail again, standing next to the man in the fishing cap. They were both looking over the side.

"Hm?" Hank asked.

He was an old man, Hank could see now, and he was pointing down toward the ledge on the far bank. He was thin, the old man, and his chin was covered with uneven white stubble. He was wearing a light, garish shirt covered with blackbirds and triangles. "Down there," he said. "Look."

Hank looked, but all he could see were the dead bushes and weeds.

"What, the bushes?" He took pains to avoid slurring too much.

"*No*," the old man insisted. "*There*."

Hank tried to follow where the old man was pointing, but it was no easy task with everything wavering the way it was. Finally he caught sight of the blue plastic tarp beneath one of the dry and twisted trees. It was held down by three cinder blocks.

"Yeah," Hank said. "The tarp."

The old man nodded grimly, then turned to Hank. His eyes were serious and bloodshot. "Do you think there could be a little boy's dead body under there?"

Crime reporter or not, Hank was no longer certain he wanted to be standing out here alone in the middle of the night at the edge of a dangerous bridge overlooking a more dangerous canal with this man. But he couldn't help himself, and his eyes swung back to the tarp. He tried to focus.

To be honest, trying to guess from the outline pressing through the wrinkled blue plastic wasn't easy. It could've been almost anything under there. It might have been some kid's body, but it might've been a pile of dirt someone was saving, or a dismantled snowmobile, or a couple of large cakes. Hank didn't feel like guessing one way or the other. The fumes were getting to him.

"I . . . ," he said. "I honestly don't know. Maybe? Maybe not." His tongue was thick and dry, and he wondered if the old man noticed.

"Ah, that's okay," the old man said, crossing his arms and leaning on the aluminum handrail. "Just wonderin' what you thought. I think it's a body but I been wrong before."

Hank straightened himself. "Okay then, so . . . you have a good night."

As he began to walk away, the man turned and grabbed his arm, nearly throwing Hank off balance. "Hey!"

Hank regained his footing, trying to prepare for the worst. "What?"

"You like organ grinders?"

"Do . . . huh?"

"You know," the old man said, miming a hand turning a crank. "Italian guys with the monkeys?"

Hank blinked at him. "Always have," he said. "And now, ah, I really gotta go. Nice meeting you, though." He turned again, and this time the old man didn't grab him. Tapping a hand along the aluminum rail for support, he kept his ear open for footsteps and, as much as it was possible, kept his eyes focused on the far side of the bridge. His legs were growing weary. This was turning into much more of a walk than he had anticipated. Maybe he should've waited for the train. Could've avoided creepy old men that way.

The far shore of the Gowanus was much the same as the one he'd left behind. Bleak, deserted streets, abandoned cars, empty warehouses smeared with peeling graffiti, chain-link fences.

He flinched when he heard something snap and rustle above him. Looking up, he saw it was only a plastic bag snared in the razor wire. He shook his head and continued on his uncertain way. Occasional houses were squeezed in between the truck repair garages, the marble cutters, and the iron restoration outfits. Sawhorses lay on their sides across the sidewalk near orange plastic barrels, ruptured and spilling sand. In the deep shadows between two streetlights his shin found another fire hydrant, and he bit his lip before stepping back and limping carefully around it. That was gonna leave a bruise.

More dogs were barking. He looked around. The streets were narrow, and the sound could've come from anywhere. He wanted to walk faster but didn't dare.

He passed a shuttered diner and some more empty lots.

At Fourth Avenue and Union Street, he began to see more row houses and live trees began reappearing on the sidewalk, several of which tried to trip him as he passed. For the first time since he'd stepped off the subway a car sped past him. He heard a siren to the north. Or maybe it was the west. The echoes there were crazy.

When he reached the next corner he stopped and looked up at the street sign. Fifth Avenue. Hank turned left. The street was lined with storefronts and restaurants. The gates were still down on most, but the windows glowed in a few diners. He looked in as he passed. They all seemed as empty as the sidewalks. The morning rush was still a few hours away. It was comfort enough. He knew where he was now and how to get where he was going. He'd left that stench far behind.

Really not looking forward to work.

Then he remembered it was Sunday. He nearly laughed but coughed instead.

In the trees above him, the ragged birds were beginning to croak the approach of morning.

Four

Insult and Injury

Cops are looking for two men who assaulted a 25-year-old man on a Bed-Stuy street early Wednesday and stole his trusty bicycle. Johnny Marquez was confronted by the two men around 1:30 a.m. as he left work at Phil's B-B-Q Wonderland. A dispute erupted between Marquez and the strangers, one of whom, Marquez told police, "kept his hand in his pocket, like he had a gun." There were no gunshots, however, as the two thugs merely pulled Marquez from the bike, pushed him to the ground, kicked him once in the leg, then pedaled away into the night with one of the assailants balanced on the bike's handlebars.

They Are an Inscrutable People

Police in Brownsville are looking for the man who walked into an exotic pet store on Tuesday afternoon and walked out again with two ferrets he never quite bothered paying for. According to customers at Maxine's Mammals, the suspect—a pervy-looking Asian man between 32 and 47—waited until no one was looking before shoving the two squealing weasels down his pants. He then quickly left the store, according to one witness, "walking like John Wayne." Police are asking that the public be on the lookout for a hard-to-please gentleman with an unusually lively bulge in his trousers.

Whoopsies!

An overeager police officer pursuing a young nogoodnik through Flatbush on Monday afternoon accidentally shot a 12-year-old boy in a wheelchair instead. The bullet probably ricocheted into the youngster, but still, that's gotta be bad for the karma. Fortunately, the kid, being paralyzed, didn't feel a thing, realizing he'd been shot only after someone pointed out how much he was bleeding all of a sudden. He should be fine, though he may never walk again.

The original 16-year-old suspect, who'd robbed a Sav-Mor Shoe Store with a toy gun (so as not to injure any crippled children), was arrested at the scene.

Weenie Thugs

A 24-year-old soccer enthusiast from Boerum Hill with the unlikely name of Wedgy Wazonî was arrested together with a friend Tuesday night after they attacked a referee following a game in Prospect Park. It seems the ref made a call Wedgy didn't much care for, so he and his friend went after the guy with a baseball bat and a screwdriver. Despite all that hardware at their disposal, the ref was not seriously injured, proving that Wedgy, along with being a big crybaby, is also a big pantywaist. He and his pal, Gabe Aguirre, face multiple sissy charges.

Weenie Thugs 2: This Time It's Pathetic

When it comes to weenies, it seems 21-year-old Roger Tynbull knows his share. Tynbull, a Williamsburg resident, was sitting in a park with some friends Wednesday night when two dopey goth kids—apparently acquaintances of Tynbull's—approached and began ragging on him. Then one of the goth kids (they worship Satan, you know) started beating Tynbull over the head with a handy skateboard. They proceeded to kick and slap at him before stabbing him twice with a penknife and flitting away like naughty schoolgirls. The cause of the dispute is unknown. Tynbull was treated at the scene, and the cops, while attempting to stifle their giggling, apprehended the black-clad ninnies shortly thereafter.

Hank knew that telling people he was a crime reporter was stretching things a bit. He also knew that saying he worked for a New York newspaper was stretching it even further. The *Brooklyn Hornet* was more commonly known as a pennysaver, or a weekly neighborhood shopper, or a coupon circular, but it was the third most popular shopper in Brooklyn, with a staff of nine and a circulation of just under five thousand.

He wasn't exactly out there on the street interviewing victims and tracking down leads. He spent his days poring over the daily crime reports faxed to him by various Brooklyn police precincts—a parade of mostly minor infractions, from burglaries and assaults to shoplifting, bar fights, vandalism, and noise complaints. If he was lucky, maybe there'd be the occasional murder. From these he selected the most potentially entertaining and crafted them into the *Hornet*'s weekly crime blotter.

To Hank, it was a far better calling than being a mere crime reporter. There was an art and philosophy behind the blotter that you simply didn't find in straight journalism. It was more about creative storytelling than simple, lifeless facts.

He thought so anyway.

To Hank, the crime blotter was not simply a sadly neglected literary genre but a profoundly and uniquely American one as well. In every one-hundred-fifty-word entry, no matter how extravagant or seemingly irrelevant the crime in question, you had the makings of a miniature novel, with a clear narrative arc, heroes, villains, drama, conflict, and a resolution. Each entry was an encapsulated moment—a photograph—of physical or emotional violence in which someone's life was changed forever. If approached with the proper attitude, the crime blotter was a reflection of the entire culture at that particular moment in history. It said all that needed to be said about who we were and how we lived.

Not too many of the *Hornet*'s readers looked at the blotter the same way Hank did. In fact most didn't look at the blotter at all. They didn't need to be reminded that bad things were happening all around them. If they wanted to read about crime, they'd go to a real newspaper (or at least a real news website) and not the local pennysaver. To most, Hank's blotter was nothing more than some print there on the page between the "fifty cents off" coupons for paper towels and ads for the two-for-one sale on canned tuna.

"Kalabander?"

Hank had heard the footsteps approaching his cubicle and ignored them as long as he could. "Yeah, Shed." He slowly spun in his chair to face his editor. Hank suspected he knew what was on the piece of paper the tall man in the plaid, short-sleeved shirt was holding.

Sherwood ("Shed") Nutskin had edited the *Hornet* for five years now. It might not have been the biggest paper in New York, but it was his, and he knew what it was supposed to be.

Editor or not, Hank found it impossible to look him in the eye. If he looked him in the eye, there was a decidedly strong chance his own eyes would drift down those scant inches to Nutskin's mouth, and that's where Hank ran into trouble. Nutskin's mouth was a horrible thing. He had thick, deeply cracked, fishy lips, and hiding behind them was that one dead gray tooth right there in the front. The cracks would wriggle around as those dark wet lips flapped away, and with each flap, there it was, that awful dead gray tooth staring out at him. Once his eyes locked on to it, all Hank could do was stare, fixated with horror and disgust. He hated that hideous, repulsive mouth like he hated few other things in the world.

When he explained this to Annie one night, she'd said he sounded like a Poe character and suggested he might want to do something about it before Nutskin ended up under the floorboards. Even if he thought the world would be better off with that mouth buried under some floorboards, he figured she was probably right.

So to avoid losing control and smashing that sickening mouth with a brick one day, he went to some lengths to avoid looking at it. Whenever Nutskin wanted to talk to him in person, he tried to focus his eyes just over his editor's left shoulder, or at his hairline. If Nutskin ever noticed this, he hadn't said anything about it. This time, the fact that he had something in his hand was a relief. It gave Hank an object on which to focus, avoiding Nutskin completely.

"Where did you get this picture?" Nutskin asked, holding out the piece of paper. Hank snatched it from him and spun around to study it more carefully under his desk lamp.

The photo had been taken with a cell phone in a crowded bar. A young woman in a short black leather skirt was holding a drink aloft, smiling broadly and leaning forward in such a manner that her outlandish breasts seemed poised on the verge of spilling out of her low-cut, cherry red blouse.

"Needed a victim photo, so I grabbed it off her MeFirst dot-com page," Hank answered, still staring at the photo.

"Well, don't you think you could've looked a little harder? Found one that didn't make her look like a . . ." Nutskin's eyes darted around the room to make sure there were no ladies present. He dropped his voice. ". . . *whore*? It's not very, I dunno, *nice*."

"But maybe she *was* a whore," Hank reasoned. "You didn't see her MeFirst page. Chick was a skank. Or at least wanted people to think she was. You ask me, showing her any other way wouldn't be one hundred percent honest."

There was something pained in Nutskin's face. "But the girl was tied up, raped, and murdered. Her mother found her."

Hank scowled slightly, fearing he knew where this was going. "Everything I found was a hell of a lot worse, believe me. Given the resources we're working with here, it's the best you're gonna do. Wanna crop it, then crop it. I don't care. Think it's kinda funny this way, though." He handed the picture back. "I could change the headline to something like, 'No, She Wasn't Really Asking for It.'"

"That's not funny." Nutskin took the paper and looked at it again. "I'm still not completely comfortable with running a murder story in a family paper. I mean, we have the advertisers to keep in mind."

"Ah," Hank said, raising a hand to brush the worry away. "It'll be good for 'em. Remind 'em they live in Brooklyn and not, y'know, Cape Cod."

"I think that's just it, Kalabander. They can get stuff like this online or in the *Eagle* if they want. We're different."

Yeah, I saw this coming, Hank thought.

On one of the walls of his cubicle hung a framed reproduction of the front page of the *New York Tribune* from January 5, 1903. Beside a grainy photo of an elephant in chains was the headline:

TOPSY HARD TO KILL:
ELECTRICITY PUTS VICIOUS ELEPHANT TO DEATH—POISON USED TOO
KEEPER WOULDN'T HELP HANG HER.

Hank's eyes quietly wandered to the photo of Topsy as Nutskin's tired spiel got under way.

"Don't take any of this the wrong way," Nutskin said. "I think your crime blotters have a lot of personality."

"Yeah, that's my racket there, Shed," Hank said, barely paying attention. "Giving these gorillas personality."

"But that's just it." Nutskin emitted a small squeak of preliminary apology. "Do you have to be so *mean* about it? To the victims, even."

It was like a script they got together and rehearsed every week. "Sometimes stupid people get hurt on account of that stupidity."

"But why do you have to point it out so bluntly? And with so much name-calling?" Nutskin was beginning to sound exasperated, just as it was called for in the script. "Remember, this is a *family* paper. Families read us. I'm getting too many calls. Just got another one yesterday from someone whose daughter has mysteriously picked up the word 'lunkhead.' Now she calls everybody a lunkhead. Even her parents and teachers. And where do you suppose she got it?"

Hank shrugged and looked out the window behind Nutskin. "Dunno, Shed," he said. "Could be anywhere. Cartoons. Playground." He wanted to spin his chair around and get back to work.

"Kalabander, you've known from the beginning what this paper was about. People get enough bad news, enough insults. We try to focus on the good things about raising a family in Brooklyn."

"But you have a crime blotter," Hank pointed out. "You want me to report only the, I dunno, *happy* crimes? The nice crimes? You know I do what I can. Try to focus on the failed robberies, shit like that. There are very few serious injuries. It's the *comédie humaine*." He was tired. The words were coming out mechanically, and his French was just awful.

Nutskin looked again at the photo. "Which is why I'm wondering about this murder story."

"Woman gets tied up, gagged, raped, and has her throat slit in Windsor Terrace, of all places? Story's gonna get three lines in the *Eagle*, maybe five in the *Post*, and nothing in the *Times*. It'd look pretty weird if we didn't say anything about it, don't you think?"

In his heart, Hank thought it was kind of cute that Nutskin still seemed to be working under the impression that the *Hornet* was some kind of *real* newspaper, that people picked it up for the stories, and that he himself was some kind of real editor. So Hank played along as he could.

"Maybe you're right," Nutskin said, still looking at the picture. "I think I will have to crop this, though."

"Maybe you could crop it to just show the boobs and not the face."

Nutskin looked up. He didn't think that was funny either.

"Or whatever you think's best, Shed."

Nutskin looked as if he was about to leave, but stopped, and Hank nearly groaned aloud.

"Oh, and while we're at it, I'm supposed to remind you that you need to start using the word 'allegedly' more often. These people aren't guilty until the courts say they are."

"Mm-hm," Hank replied, then spun in his chair to face his computer again. At the top of the screen was the headline he had typed moments before Nutskin showed up: "Mugger's Bumbling Antics Amuse All."

Five

Hank paused as he was about to head up the stairs to his apartment. Tromping down the stairs were three men in heavy, filthy work boots hauling toolboxes, a thick roll of plastic sheeting, and two five-gallon plastic buckets.

The last man coming down the stairs shouted, "How do, Mr. Caliban!"

"Hello," Hank replied, confused as to how these men could recognize him, let alone almost know his name. After they let themselves out the front door, he went upstairs and saw the door was open. "Annie?" he called, as he noticed the plaster dust and muddy boot prints on the floor.

"Hey there, sweets," he heard her call from the bathroom. "I'm glad it's you."

"Were those our new Congolese friends I saw on the stairs?"

She entered the front room with a damp rag in her hand. "Dominican. Yes indeed," she said, as he headed for the refrigerator.

"What," he said, pulling out a beer, "they didn't do enough damage last week, so they decided to come back and break something else?"

"Something like that."

He set the beer next to the sink and was about to wash the sweat off his face and neck when he saw the basin was filled with clots of plaster mud. "Jesus," he whispered.

"I was coming there next," Annie said, stepping up behind him and squeezing his sides.

"Nah, I'll get it. Looks like you've done enough." Her face was streaked with sweat and dust. "But grab a drink, siddown, and tell me about the ensuing mayhem." He took the rag from her.

She opened the fridge and grabbed the iced tea, moving to the kitchen table. Hank turned on the tap and started wiping up the goop. "Not that much to tell," she said. "It seems while they were fixing the faucet in the tub, they cracked a pipe behind the wall."

He paused in his scrubbing and looked over his shoulder. "While fixing a dripping faucet?"

"Uh-huh. The water started leaking into the Hernandez place, so they had to shut the water off, knock some holes in the bathroom wall, find the leaky pipe, fix that, then replaster the holes."

Hank took a long swallow from the beer. "And they did all that in one day?"

"Some of it, anyway. More than I would've expected. They come back tomorrow, or maybe the next day, to sand and repaint. Or just put on another coat of plaster. But given how humid it is, it may take the plaster a few more days to dry, so everything will have to wait."

"I see." He scanned the basin, decided it was clean enough, and headed to the table with his beer. "So long as they show up after I leave and leave before I get home." Through the ceiling above them came a piercing howl, followed by the stamping of tiny feet, followed by some guttural shouting. Hank and Annie glanced up briefly but said nothing.

"And your day?" she asked.

"Hot." He tugged the front of his soaked shirt away from his slick chest.

"You feeling any better?"

"What, after that night with Rock?" He frowned. "Hangover cleared up. A few nicks and bruises. Nothing sleeping all day can't cure."

"I cleaned up those scratches on your arms when you got home, I don't know if you remember. You must've really scraped yourself along a fence or something."

Hank glanced at his arms and shrugged. "No big deal."

Annie looked worried. "I'm still amazed you made it home alive. You don't know what might've happened, walking through there at that hour."

"I don't know what *did* happen. But here I am." He raised his bottle. "Here's to that." He took a drink, then wiped his mouth. "Anyway, at the paper, I was firmly reminded again that I work for a family-friendly publication."

"So they want us to have kids," Annie guessed.

He grimaced and shifted in his seat. "God help us all." He stood, unbuckled his belt, and dropped his pants. "There. That's better." He draped the pants over the back of his chair and sat again.

"They want you to stop being mean to the kids."

"Kids, parents, criminals, everyone." He took another drink and shook his head. "Same old shit. No big deal. Won't bore you." He drained the bottle and set it on the table. "Lunkheads."

"Mr. Kalabander?"

Hank cringed when he heard the voice behind him. "What is it, Steve?" He did not turn around or stop typing.

There was no place to hide in that office. The "editorial wing," as they liked to call it, was nothing more than a short hallway with three chalk-white cubicles for the staff writers. On the other side of the "advertising wing" (the cubicles where the three ad salespeople sat) was the office Nutskin shared with Stephen Brand. A year earlier, Brand had been promoted to entertainment editor. All it really meant, Hank noted, was that Brand compiled the listings of upcoming local events. And he did a bang-up job of it, too.

"Stephen," the voice behind him corrected. "Here, I have something for you."

These people are so goddamn predictable, Hank thought. He made a wager with himself, and sure enough when he turned around he saw Brand was wearing a heavy, brightly patterned wool sweater. Ninety-two degrees outside (and ninety-nine in the office) and Brand was wearing a fucking sweater. *Tightass*.

He let himself smile, which he knew Brand would read the wrong way.

"Hi," Brand said, smiling back as expected. "How are you doing today?"

"Super." He saw the mess of curled faxes in Brand's hand. The faxes looked like they'd all been taped together by a drunken gibbon.

"Rusty's out covering the ground breaking for that new day care center, so I was wondering . . ." There was nervous hesitation in his voice. "I thought it might be fun for you to write up a little something about some of these events."

Hank reached out both hands and collected the Gordian knot of press releases and tape. "You might want to consider learning how to use e-mail one of these days," Hank suggested for the seventh time. "But yeah. Soon as I wrap up the blotter."

Brand pointed at the faxes. "There's one on top there in particular. They're having a big coat sale at the armory."

Hank looked at him. "A coat sale."

"I think our readers would be quite interested."

Scratching his temple, Hank said evenly, "It's the middle of July. We're in the middle of the worst fucking heat wave since before you were born. And you want me to plug a coat sale."

"I think our readers would be interested." The saddest thing of all was that he was utterly sincere.

"No, they wouldn't."

"I happen to think they would."

Hank was about to say something else, but he remembered that Brand was the one wearing the sweater. "Fine," he said, giving up. "Right after the blotter." He dumped the gnarl of paper on his desk.

"Oh, and speaking of the blotter?"

Hank looked back at him. "What."

Brand's ever present anxiety ticked up a few notches. You could tell with him because from shoulder to elbow his arms stayed tight to his sides, perfectly still, while his hands and forearms (especially the right hand) became a circus of completely meaningless gestures. "I just wanted to say that it's been very . . . interesting."

"Mm-hm," Hank said, knowing Brand didn't mean it as a compliment.

"But that's not how I taught you to do it."

"Interesting, you mean? No, I guess it's not," Hank said. He'd expected Brand to say something long before this.

"Sherwood's said something to me about it too. In some of our meetings."

Oh, "meetings," my ass. "Yeah, well . . ." Hank was both bored and amused by the idea of being chastised (of a sort) by a nimrod thirty years his junior. "I guess I thought it would be kind of fun and different to try doing them well."

"But there are certain rules that you need—" Brand began to say when Hank held up a hand.

"Sorry to interrupt here, but I'm just wondering. Are you wearing a colostomy bag under that sweater? Nice pattern by the way."

Brand's eyes roved quickly about the office as he struggled to grab hold of some meaning in this. "No?" he said uncertainly after a few seconds.

"Okay, no big deal," Hank said with a false smile. "Just wondering. I better get back to work now, so . . . you can go."

Not knowing what else to do, Brand turned and left.

Once the entertainment editor was safely away, Hank could breathe easy again. That should be it for the day. He picked up the mess of press releases and began peeling them apart, removing the short strips of tape and sticking them to his desktop. He glanced at each release as it was extracted. There was the big coat sale at the armory, yes, but there was also a used-shoe sale, weeknight samba lessons, a tulip exhibition, and a free seminar at a hotel in downtown Brooklyn entitled "Know Your Milk."

"Maybe he does know what the people want," Hank admitted quietly to himself. A young woman's voice arose from the other side of the cubicle wall.

"Mr. Kalabander?"

"Yes, Becky? I didn't know you were over there."

"Yes?"

"Well, I'm sorry if all our yammering was a bother."

"Nuh-uh? In fact? I just wanted to say?"

As she spoke, Hank could hear the unmistakable sound of her thin thumbs punching away at a tiny keyboard. Over the months he'd learned that she compulsively texted everything she said and thought, though he had no idea to whom. "Um, what he said? About the blotter? I think your blotter is really good? His was so, y'know, *boring*?"

The thumbs kept tapping and she never left her seat.

"Well, thank you, Becky," Hank said without leaving his seat either. "That's very nice."

Becky was nineteen, and she had started at the *Hornet* a year earlier as an intern. Upon graduating high school, she'd been hired as the third staff writer, and since then she had apparently found her own little journalistic niche.

"So are we gonna see another gem from you this week?" Hank asked through the cubicle wall.

"Uh-huh? A nice lady in Sheepshead Bay? I'm heading down there in a few minutes?"

"Has she turned a hundred already, or is this just a preliminary?"

"Just today? I'm going to the party?"

"Well, that should be fun, then." Hank found Becky as predictable as the rest of them, but for some reason he didn't feel compelled to insult her. Not intentionally, anyway. One reason might have been that she sat in the cubicle next to his. The other was that she would probably cry. He didn't need that on top of everything else.

That voice of hers, though. It could rankle. He didn't know what it was or how it happened, but at some point, for some reason, every woman in the country between the ages of eight and thirty-five started speaking in exactly the same way. A nasal, raspy creak, and all those goddamn question marks. Hank didn't know why this happened. All he knew was that it drove him nuts.

He turned back to the screen and typed another headline: "Machete Season in Full Swing."

A few minutes later he picked up the phone and dialed a number. After the third ring a coarse, laconic voice answered.

"Seventy-fourth Precinct press desk. Lieutenant Crosslin."

"Hey, you rotten, yellow-bellied son of a bitch, how them kids treatin' you?"

"'Bout the same as you, you worthless commie pigfucker."

On his end, Hank frowned and wished he had a cigarette. For some reason, every time he talked to a disgraced cop, he wanted to smoke. "Why is it that everyone's calling me a pigfucker these days?"

"Don't you read the papers?"

"Try to avoid it."

"Good man. Now what the fuck do *you* want? If it's about that Williams cat, he's out of our hands until the boys at Bellevue are done with him. All I can tell you."

Lieutenant Grover "Bud" Crosslin had been a decorated member of the NYPD until a drinking problem and a minor addiction to opiates took their toll, and five misdirected bullets happened to find their way into four unarmed bystanders one day. Now he worked the press desk at the Seventy-fourth, doling out bits of unclassified information to those few reporters he liked and patching those he didn't through to detectives who never existed.

Hank was happy to settle for faxes from the other Brooklyn precincts—it made things easier—but he preferred talking to Crosslin personally.

"Nah, I'm all set with Williams if my pansy of an editor here'll let me run with it."

"Goddamn kids today," Crosslin interjected. "They're all queers, you ask me. Got no guts."

"Don't get me started," Hank told him. "So. Deadline's in two hours. Any last-minute additions to the menagerie?"

Six

The sun was climbing high over Blossom Cutie, Maryland, and the temperature was already pushing the mid-eighties. Rocky Roccoco, meanwhile, was still sleeping soundly in the dirt alongside the tent housing his Monstrous Wonders Museum. He had wrapped himself in a thin pink blanket.

"*Roccoco!*"

Startled, Rocky pushed himself upright with some painful effort, letting the blanket fall from his shoulders to his lap.

"*Heeey,*" he groaned, eyes still closed. "Not so *loud*, you crazy you." He forced his eyes open just enough to see the unmistakably Paleolithic silhouette of Fielding Blount, owner and manager of Blount Amusements, standing before him, cane in hand.

"What's all that?" Blount demanded, pointing with the cane.

Rocky made a show of trying to understand what Blount was pointing at, but he figured he already knew. Not too far from where he sat lay a jumbled pile of empty bottles. Whiskey, mostly, with a few gin, vodka, and beer bottles in the mix for variety.

"Hm," Rocky grunted, trying not to taste the inside of his mouth or let too much sun into his skull. "Buncha the boys were whoopin' it up."

"And where did all those dead chickens come from?" Blount asked in a tone no less gruff, as he pointed at another pile not far away.

"Like I says," Rocky huffed as he climbed to his feet. "Buncha the boys were whoopin' it up."

"Gate opens in three hours," the bear-shaped Blount reminded him. "It's Saturday." His voice was suddenly restrained, and that was much more terrifying in its way than his bellow. "So you better get yourself and your crew together and get that shit cleaned up."

"Yassah, bawz," Rocky drawled, head down, as he began shuffling back toward the tent entrance.

"Don't walk away yet, Roccoco, that's not why I came out to find you."

Rocky stopped and turned as Blount stepped toward him, looking up at the banner line over the entrance.

"I like you, Rock. You know that. You think anyone else on this lot would get away with half the shit I let you get away with?"

Rocky decided to hold his tongue. Didn't want to go ratting out any neighbors. Especially not Vexina the Gypsy or Big Pete at the Shooting Gallery.

"But this season's show's a real stinker. You know the take's way down from last season. It's because the show's tired. The townies just don't want to see your mannequins. Not when they got the Internet and all that shit."

Around them, the rest of the fair was starting to wake up. Buckets of fry oil were heating, the small repairs and grease jobs were under way on the rides, cotton candy was being spun, the fronts were being raised on the flat stores. Paper cups, plastic wrappers, and unloved prizes were being swept away. Large women in T-shirts and sandals were spray-painting cheap white hats they would later sell for ten bucks a pop, and the hard-bitten souls at the rigged games were making sure there was no way in hell the plastic rings could fit over the middle peg. The lot was starting to sound and smell like the carnival again.

"Show ain't that bad, ya take the time to look at it."

"No, Rock," Blount cut him off. "It is. It's pretty bad." He looked up again. "Nice banner line, but no payoff. I'm not asking you to live up to the banner. Just try a little harder."

"Nobody laughs when they leave," the short man said, patting himself down in search of his cigar.

"Yes they do, Rock. I've seen them. And that's the problem." Blount moved in closer and tried to put a friendly arm around Rocky's shoulder, but the height difference made it impossible. "Look, Rock, you and I, we've both been in this business a long time. Look at all these kids here." He swept an arc with his cane toward the lot in front of them. "It's one of the reasons I like having you around. We speak the same language."

"All right," Rocky said. "Swell. So what's the rumpus?"

"I can't have you getting lazy on me. That wouldn't look good. You need to show these kids how it's done. So here's the deal."

"But—"

"*Butbutbut*," Blount sputtered theatrically, twirling his cane. "But me no buts. Here's the deal. We make the jump to Rhode Island in two weeks. By that time you need to get yourself a new star attraction. A live act. I don't care if it's a gaffe, a geek. I don't care. Something more than what you got in here now. Just so long as it brings in the townies."

Rocky's eyes opened fully for the first time that day. "A new show in two weeks? That's fucking insane. You forget where we are? Blossom-fuckin'-Cutie." Where was that cigar? If ever there was a time he needed to gesture with a cigar, this was it.

Blount raised an eyebrow and tapped his chin with the cane. "Okay, maybe you're right. Make it end of the season. That gives you eight weeks. If by the end of the season you don't present me with something, I might need to move you out and move the Johnny Macabro show in."

"*Macabro*? That *hack*? It's nothin' but a spook show, and not a very good one. Last I heard he was pullin' the old popcorn spider gag, and that ain't scared anyone in ten years."

"Maybe, but you got some valuable real estate here, Roccoco. Macabro's show draws. The rubes go for it, which is more than I can say about your stuffed bear."

"Yeah, but if you're gonna threaten me, at least threaten me with somethin' better than fuckin' Macabro, *Jesus*. That's just an insult."

"Take it as you will, Rock, just liven up the show. Unless you wanna be an A and S man again, or run an Add-up joint." He turned to walk away. "You got eight weeks, Roccoco, because I'm a reasonable man."

Rocky stared after Blount's broad back. "Oughta give you a reasonable boot in the ass, Rochester," he whispered under his breath. He turned and saw the pile of dead chickens waiting for him.

The barbershop had first opened on Washington Street near the Manhattan Bridge in 1932, and though the neighborhood around it had changed considerably in the eighty-plus years since then, most everything about the barbershop itself remained steadfast and unsullied. Even the barber himself. *Especially* the barber, which was the primary reason Hank had been stopping there once a month like clockwork for nearly a quarter century.

Hanging from the ceiling were four incandescent bulbs that glowed yellow from inside translucent, tulip-shaped glass shades. The red leatherette covering the heavy chrome chairs had been worn stiff and nearly brown by a million wide asses. The narrow shelf beneath the long mirror was a clutter of coffee mugs filled with combs and scissors, squeeze bottles of light hair oil from defunct Italian companies, open and crusting jars of pomade, discarded white towels, and boxes of tissues. The radio was always playing though it played nothing but Sinatra. Against the back wall a small bar had been set up, with a stack of plastic cups and a dozen half-full liquor bottles, mostly things Hank had never heard of and was reluctant to ingest.

He was sitting in the first chair near the front door as usual and, as usual, Angelo Orsini (still pissed at ninety-two) was lifting small clumps of Hank's gray hair with a black comb while playing a pair of thin scissors like castanets an inch away from his ear.

"These young guys come in here," Angelo was saying into the mirror so he could look Hank in the eye as he spoke. "Theys don't know what theys want." He snipped a tiny bit of hair away, then returned the chinging scissors to their spot beside Hank's right ear. Hank knew it was better to keep his mouth shut when Angelo was on a roll. "They say theys wants it short, but they don't know *how* short, see? So's I asks 'em when was your last haircut? And this guy, he says a month an' a half. But I been cuttin' hair for seventy-three fuckin' years. I know how hair grows an' mister, I tells ya, that weren't no *month* an' a *half.*" He stopped suddenly and pulled the comb and scissors away from Hank's head. "So what do youse want?" He had already been at it for about ten minutes without asking. But given the number of haircuts Hank had received there over the years, the regularity of his appearances in that particular chair, he figured it was nothing but reflex and muscle memory for Angelo at this point.

"Well," Hank said, craning his neck to look up at Angelo, who was still looking at him in the mirror. "I think I'd like it a little longer and a little thicker, if you don't mind."

Angelo's arms didn't move but there was something deadly in his eyes. "You wants it longer," he said.

"I'm joking."

Angelo's expression didn't change. "Yeah, you say youse jokin'. You say youse want it longer. But I can do that."

"It's okay," Hank said, making a mental note to never again try joking around with Angelo. It could be dangerous. "What you were doing was fine—the regular."

Angelo sighed deeply, lifting his arms, and the scissors began flashing again. "So I watched this movie on the tube last night," he said. "One of the cable channels."

Hank had learned over the years that Angelo had no patience for movies or television. Moving pictures of any kind seemed to bother him. The only exceptions were films and television shows with barbershop scenes. Those he liked. Whenever he started talking about a movie, which wasn't often, Hank could count the seconds until a barbershop was mentioned.

"Anyways, I forget what it was called, but it had Carole Lombard in it. What an *ass* on that broad."

Ew, Hank thought as he continued counting and Angelo continued occasionally snipping away bits of his hair.

"So anyways, she plays this manicurist, right? And thinks she can snag herself a rich guy if she starts workin' in a barbershop . . ."

Afterward, Hank walked the four blocks to the office. The Gemora Building was a massive beehive that hid the *Brooklyn Hornet* safely away in a forgotten corner of the sixth floor. It was also home to dozens of other outmoded businesses. The Gemora was where typewriter repairmen, chair caners, and the painters of window signs went to die.

Hank entered the office and picked a copy of that morning's issue out of a cardboard box on the floor. "Hello there, Blanche," he said to the receptionist, a woman in her fifties who was everything a Blanche was supposed to be. If she hadn't been hired as the *Hornet*'s receptionist, she would have spent her mornings yelling things like "whiskey down" and "adam an' eve on a log, sink 'em," at a burly, hirsute cook named Petros in some Bay Ridge coffee shop.

"Heya, Mr. K. Nice day outside, why don'cha?"

"Little warm out there for me, gotta say," Hank replied, wiping the sweat from his forehead. "Still."

"Need to get yourself a fan," Blanche said, pointing at her own.

"Maybe someday, I ever get a raise."

On his way to his cubicle, he ran into Rusty Wescoat, the third of the *Hornet*'s staff writers, on his way out to snag another big scoop.

"Hello there, Rusty," Hank said, though there was no camaraderie in his voice. He stepped out of the eager twenty-two-year-old's way, but Rusty stopped.

"Hi, Mr. Kalabander," he said, blocking Hank's path. "I was hoping I'd run into you."

"Yeah?" Hank asked, casually looking down at the cover of that week's *Hornet*. EverBrite Dentistry Services of Greenpoint was offering a midsummer deal on cleanings. Two for one.

"I was wondering if I could ask your advice on something I was working on?"

Hank looked up. "You want *my* advice?"

"I really do, yeah."

Hank spotted the ironic curl beginning to tug at Rusty's mouth as the smug little bastard tried to repress a chortle. Hank's guts chilled. He stood up straight and stared Rusty in the eye, resisting the urge to grab him by his permanent press collar.

"Okay," Hank said, deciding to take a different tack. "Sure. You want my advice? Here's some words to live by, kid. My mother taught me these things and she's never steered me wrong."

The self-satisfaction left Rusty's face as Hank took a step closer.

"Number one, never accept acid from a stranger. Number *two*." Hank's tone was sharp, and he was spitting out the numbers. "Never—and I mean *never*—trust a man named BeBe. And number *three*, never marry a woman obsessed with Sylvia Plath. But I guess you won't need to worry about that last one." He snapped his paper, stepped around Rusty, and turned the corner into his cubicle.

"Your *mother* taught you those things?" he heard Rusty ask behind him.

And number four, Hank thought. *Don't fuck with the old man, peewee.* He took a seat and shook his head. Then he picked up the phone and dialed the Seventy-fourth Precinct.

"Hey, Poindexter," he barked when Lieutenant Crosslin picked up. "So what've them lowlifes done for me lately?"

It was only later in the afternoon that he opened the paper to see how the blotter looked.

First thing he noticed was that the picture of the drunken whore with the big boobs was nowhere to be found. It seemed the entire entry was missing. But it was what he'd pretty much come to expect from that sniveling nosepicker Nutskin. He frowned and started reading what was left.

Spider-Man He Ain't

Dieter Jeffries imagined he would be the cleverest burglar ever by (allegedly) crawling across the rooftops of the 8th St. brownstones in Park Slope last Monday afternoon and entering his intended victim's home through the skylight. Unfortunately the 21-year-old Jeffries forgot to take one thing into consideration.

When Andrew Braddock and his wife, Josephine, returned home that evening, they (allegedly) found Jeffries still unconscious on the kitchen floor, surrounded by the shattered glass of the skylight. Nothing, obviously, had been taken, and officers soon arrived on the scene. While in jail, Jeffries might want to consider a new diet.

Unchained Malady

Little Orson Blake, 11, called 911 all by himself last Saturday afternoon to report that his favorite bike (one of five he owns) was allegedly missing and presumed stolen. During the interview with officers, the chubby-faced Cobble Hill lad admitted he had left the bike in front of the house without a lock or a chain or anything. He also admitted that he wasn't exactly sure how long it had been allegedly missing. Police are now allegedly searching for the bike, but not that hard.

Time for Rehab

Carroll Gardens resident Charles ("Chuck") Pierce, 34, admits that he had been at a local watering hole into the wee hours of July 8, where he allegedly imbibed more than his share. He insists, however, that it wasn't pink elephants or singing mice that allegedly jumped him on his way home—it was a "hairy, hulking beast" that "smelled really bad." Pierce claims the monster allegedly grabbed him and growled an "otherworldly" roar, but that he was able to rip himself away before it inflicted any harm. Pierce eventually made it home just fine suffering only minor scrapes and bruises. Police are currently looking for Bigfoot about as hard as they're looking for that spoiled brat's bike.

Prison Grays Are Nice and Soft

Sunset Park resident Subra Parrish, 41, was arrested at 10 a.m. Wednesday at the Stop & Buy bodega after he allegedly attempted to walk out of the store with five bottles of Snuggle fabric softener. When confronted by the store manager, Parrish allegedly explained that he had very sensitive skin, and that without Snuggle his clothes would chafe. He is being charged with attempted petit larceny.

Forty-five seconds later, Hank knocked on Nutskin's open door, relieved to see he was alone.

Nutskin looked up from his computer. "Yes, Kalabander?" In the upper right-hand corner of the window behind the editor, Hank could see part of the bridge. It gave him something to look at other than Nutskin's mouth.

"Yeah, Shed," he gestured with the paper he was holding, his thumb marking the blotter page. "Okay, the dead skank I can understand, but what happened to my machete story?"

"I cut it."

"Well, obviously you cut it," Hank said, trying to sound less snotty than he was tempted. "I'm just wondering why. I thought it was funny."

Nutskin exhaled through his nostrils and turned slightly in his chair to face Hank directly. After a pause he said, "A man killed his mother, his grandmother, his aunt, his little sister, and a fifteen-month-old cousin with a machete—"

"Allegedly," Hank inserted.

"*Yes*, allegedly, and you made a joke out of it."

"Well, *someone* had to."

"That wasn't even the worst of it," Nutskin said, his voice tightening as he grew visibly agitated. "You made a *racist* joke out of it."

That didn't even make sense. For just a flash, Hank's eyes jumped from the bridge to Nutskin's face, then back again. "*What* racist? That's insane. All I did was suggest that maybe Day'vawhn Williams was a little ticked that his mother had named him *Day'vawhn*. I mean, wouldn't you be? What the hell kinda name is that?"

"I will not have racist sentiments of any kind in the pages of the *Hornet*, and I won't tolerate them in the *Hornet*'s office either."

"Oh, c'mon there, Shed," Hank said, thinking Annie would in all likelihood tell him to stop right there. "Take a look around the office. It's not like anyone's gonna sue. We're a little light on the affirmative action front."

Nutskin stared at Hank. Hank stared at the bridge, wondering how long it would take Shed to get the joke. Both men were silent.

Nutskin forced himself to take a step back. If there was one thing he hated more than racism it was conflict, which was why dealing with Kalabander always made him nervous.

Although there was still strain in his voice, he forced a smile and spread his arms. Hank prayed he didn't want a hug. "Henry. Look. Sorry I had to cut the story, but I'm your editor, and this is my paper, so it's my prerogative." His throat was loosening as he spoke, the tension being replaced with condescending tones designed to be interpreted as "reasonable" and "understanding." Those well-rehearsed tones had never—not once—fooled Hank. "You know you've been pushing things a little lately, and sometimes, well, someone just has to clip your wings a bit before you get yourself in trouble."

"Mm-hm." Hank wanted to slap Nutskin out of his chair, but that meant potentially touching his mouth in the process.

"Oh, come on there, Henry, buck up," Nutskin said, his smile broadening. "You know, it takes more muscles to frown than it does to smile."

"I'm well aware of that," Hank told him, his expression unchanging. "I'm exercising."

When Hank returned from lunch (even the turkey sandwich was sour) he found a fax waiting for him on his desk. Taped to it was a note from Brand. He read the fax carefully, then spent the afternoon trying to come up with something interesting to say about a needlepoint workshop.

An hour before he was set to leave, the phone rang. It was Annie calling from the bookstore.

"Hey there, sweet thing," she said. "How's the day been?"

"Been a day," he said. "You like needlepoint?"

"Nnnope."

"Thank god. What goes on?" It was rare for her to call him from the store.

"Looks like I'm gonna be here for a bit," she said. "Collector's driving in from Jersey. Wants to take a look at the Hardy set. It'd be a real boon if I could unload it on him."

"Okay. Good. So long as he doesn't show up with a trunk full of his wife's Harlequins, thinking he's gonna make an even trade."

"Exactly," she said, then paused. "Wow. You really *do* listen every once in a while."

"Yeah, well."

"Thank you for that. Now, since I'm not sure how long this guy's gonna keep me waiting, you might want to pick up something on the way home."

"I can do that."

"The other thing," she said. Hank sensed something almost apologetic on the way. "The workmen—"

"Aw, Christ," Hank said. "What now?"

"They're ripping out the ceiling in the building's entryway."

"But they still haven't fixed the bathroom."

"I guess they need to do this first, before they can do that. Something about the pipes. Anyway, short of it is that you have to go in through the ground-floor apartment and up the back stairs."

Hank rubbed his forehead. "Through old man Zabor's apartment?"

"He's younger than you."

"That's beside the point. He's goddamn Peter Lorre."

"Don't worry," Annie assured him. "It's okay, I told him to expect you to come tromping through there."

"*What?*" His voice shot up. "That makes it even *worse*. Now he knows I'm coming. He'll be lying in wait."

"There's nothing wrong with Mr. Zabor."

"No, of course not. He's a fuckin' peach. But you get home and I'm not there, look for me in a jar in the basement."

* * *

Hank was standing in line at the grocery store checkout. The red plastic shopping basket he was holding contained a six-pack, a TV dinner (Salisbury steak, which he knew would upset his stomach later), a bag of sandwich buns, and a box of cookies. He was relieved more than anything else that the store's air-conditioning was still functioning. He hated grocery stores, they usually confounded him, but he'd taken his time that evening.

The elderly man in front of him in line was wearing one of those furry hats with ear flaps. Hank had always liked those hats, and he admired the people who wore them. Except maybe those who wore them when it was ninety-six degrees outside. Nothing else about the man seemed odd or inappropriate—just the fur hat with the flaps.

The old man turned suddenly as Hank was scanning the tabloid headlines. The names of all the misbehaving celebrities were completely alien to him. "Are you a magician?" the man in the hat inquired.

Hank belched deeply in surprise at the question, keeping his mouth closed in an effort to silence it.

"Pardon," he said, when it was gone. "Now, pardon?"

"You a magician?" the man repeated. He seemed honestly curious.

A hundred snappy responses to this query flashed through Hank's mind, most involving some variation on "making this beer disappear." Instead of using any of them, he replied, "I should think not."

"You look like one."

Hank glanced down at himself: the belly, the half-untucked shirt, the stained pants. His gaze returned to the old man in the fur hat. "Y'know, sir," he said. "No one's ever told me that before."

The old man smiled and turned his attention back to the cashier to pay for his mustard, mayo, anchovies, and quart of half-and-half. Before he left, he turned to Hank one last time. "I think you'd make a great magician."

"Thank you." Hank tried to force a smile around his bewilderment.

Seven

There was a light knock on the other side of Hank's cubicle wall.

"Yes?"

"Looks like someone's been reading your blotter?" Becky said.

"Hm?" Hank reached up with both hands and grabbed the top of the cubicle wall. With a heave and a groan, he pulled himself to his feet and peered down into Becky's side. She was looking at one of those handheld devices of hers.

"What's this now?"

She looked up at him from beneath her dark, severe bangs. "Look," she said, holding the device up to him. He squinted at it.

On the bright three-by-four-inch screen was a web page. At the top it read "Stone's Throw, by Lou Stone Jr."

"It's a blog?" Becky explained.

"I see." He glanced past the machine and down toward Becky. "Now what?"

"Read it?"

He took the machine from her and sat down. He wondered how long it would be before he started hearing Becky's withdrawal whimpers. It took him a moment to get his bearings around the small screen, but then he saw what she was talking about.

BIGFOOT IN BROOKLYN!

carrol gardens resident chuck pierce, 34, admits that he had more than a few at his local bar before being assaulted on his way home early on the morning of july 8. but it wasn't a pink elephant that attacked him. according to pierce, it was a "hairy, hulking creature" that "smelled really bad" and emitted an unearthly scream. in short, it was bigfoot!!! pierce was able to tear himself away from the creature before it did too much harm, but who knows if the next victim will be so lucky?

Hank read the entry a second and third time before stepping around the corner to hand the device back to Becky. "Apparently the young people of today have forgotten how to use a shift key," he said. "They don't plagiarize very well either."

"I know?" she said snatching the machine from him like it was a lost teddy bear, immediately going to work with her thumbs. "It happens to me all the time?"

Her eyes were fixed on the screen, and Hank knew he likely wouldn't get any further explanation out of her. He was curious to find out what sort of fiend was plagiarizing stories about Brooklynites celebrating their hundredth birthdays.

"Have a good night, I imagine," Blanche called after Hank as he left the *Hornet*'s office that evening. Every night she offered up something like that, and every night it stopped him, even after accepting that under the circumstances whatever she said made perfect sense.

Stepping out onto the sidewalk he winced. It was going to be a long five blocks to the subway.

For years city officials as well as the people who lived and worked there had been talking about the coming rebirth and revitalization (always those same two words) of the neighborhood surrounding the *Hornet*'s office. To date, though, it hadn't quite happened. A few new restaurants, a cell phone store, and a chain pharmacy had opened, but there it stopped. All those hundreds of upper-income young families supposedly poised to swarm into the neighborhood never made it. The residential buildings under renovation in anticipation of the influx had been abandoned by the contractors, left empty brown hulks without plumbing, electricity, roofs, floors, or windows. Torn plastic sheeting still rattled occasionally in the hot breeze, and broken sawhorses blocked what were once front doors. Thick weeds sprouted from the sidewalks and grew unchecked in the empty lots. In a summer like this one, everything just seemed that much uglier.

Hank couldn't say as he minded much. It was a desolate walk to and from work, but he'd never minded a little desolation if it meant the affluent young couples stayed the hell away.

Half a block in front of him, a black dog appeared from between two abandoned buildings and bounded into the middle of the empty street. It stopped suddenly and stared at him. Hank stared back, not relishing the idea of running for his life in this heat.

The dog's beige muzzle was thick and square, and even from this distance Hank could see the knotted muscles in its legs and upper body. It was clear this was no simple stray. It was also clear that some of these buildings weren't quite as abandoned as they appeared.

The sweat sliding down Hank's neck and back had started to itch, but he didn't dare scratch at it. He struggled to keep his arms at his sides. He didn't want to make any sudden moves.

The black dog snuffled, shook its head, and yawned at him before turning and trotting back the way it had come, disappearing again between the same two buildings.

Half an hour later, after a miserable and crowded train ride, he carefully picked his way through the loosely bundled tarps, filthy aluminum ladders, paint rollers, and shattered plaster in the building's entryway and was nearly forced to hopscotch up the staircase in order to reach his apartment.

He was breathing heavily when he unlocked the front door and stepped inside.

"Jesus," he greeted Annie, who was at the kitchen table with her laptop open, going over some paperwork from the bookstore.

"You came up the front way again," she scolded him without looking up. "Why not use the back stairs? It's easier."

"And take my chances in the evil lair of Zabor, King of Saturn? Yeah, I'm fine." He headed for the refrigerator. "He always looks at me like he's gonna suck out my brain and transplant it into a . . . I dunno, a dachshund or something."

"Oh, he's not that bad. In fact he probably thinks the same about you."

"Yeah?" Hank said, opening a beer. "Good."

In the apartment above them, a set of small feet began pounding, as if the child was running in place or stomping grapes. It stopped abruptly and was followed by an extended shriek.

"Which one was that?" Annie asked.

"Rodrigo Junior," Hank said. "The seven-year-old." Over the years he'd come to identify the four upstairs neighbor children by their screams and foot pounding techniques. They said nothing more about it as the stomping resumed.

He took a seat across from her. "So'd our Bolivian friends—"

"Dominican."

"Whatever. Have they given you any idea how long downstairs is gonna be like that? Or are they just trying to make it look like home?"

She shook her head, closing the laptop. It was clear she wasn't going to be getting any more work done for a while. "Not sure. Depends on when they decide to come back."

"So they haven't done anything with the bathroom yet."

"They were up here for a minute today. Go take a peek."

Hank said nothing, a growing, quiet trepidation on his face. He turned and looked down the hall toward the bathroom, then back at Annie. He didn't move. She nodded at him with a contained smile.

At last he stood and left the room, and Annie once again began sorting through the bookstore receipts.

Two minutes later he returned. He was carrying something close to his chest. She couldn't see what it was until he tossed it on the kitchen table, where it landed with a sharp clang and a clatter. Annie began to reach for it, then realized it was the faucet from the sink.

Hank took his seat again and nested his fingers across his belly. "So," he asked, "how's things at the store? We gonna cover the rent this month?"

Two days later on his way to the office, as he did two or three times a week, he stopped at one of the last corner newsstands left in Brooklyn to pick up a newspaper. The stand—a ramshackle wooden shed that had once been painted blue—was run by a rheumy-eyed ex-

Port Authority redcap named Harry Winer. He'd been in that same spot selling papers, porn, and cigarettes for over forty years. Every day, rain or shine, he was out there. Very few people knew his name anymore.

"Hey, Harry," Hank said as he stepped up to the window.

"Hiya, Hank," Harry replied, looking up from his copy of the *Daily News*. Against the wall behind him, above the cigarette case and the hand-scrawled sign reading "No Open Packs / No Singles," was a display of some four dozen overlapping skin magazines, each dangling by a corner from an alligator clip. Most of the titles were impossible to read but maybe that was for the best.

Hank bent with an *oof* and began flipping through the miasma of newspapers piled on the low shelf below Harry's window. There were Spanish-language papers and Irish papers and Armenian papers, all of which he pushed aside. He never, ever looked at the *Times* and only barely bothered with the *Daily News*. These days the *Sentinel* was hardly worth anyone's time. Just a shadow of its former glory. Mostly he went for the *New York Eagle*, a tabloid that in recent years had been giving the *Post* a run for its money. He found the *Eagle* beneath an unwrapped bundle of the *Wall Street Journal* and clawed in his pocket for change.

"So ya hear about this latest city council bullshit?" Harry asked from above.

Hank offered him a grunt, still sorting through his change and trying to make sense of the *Eagle*'s cover story. Apparently some actress he'd never heard of had announced her engagement to a basketball player he'd never heard of. The *Eagle*'s copywriters had condensed this news into a pun Hank didn't even want to understand. He folded the paper and stuck it under his arm.

"What bullshit's that, now?"

"Now—get this—*now* they're tryin' to ban the outdoor sales of things. Like what? Like *newspapers*, that could turn into *litter*." He gave the final word a sour, cynical twist. "Do you fuckin' believe this?" He slapped his paper shut and tossed it out the window to the sidewalk, the pages fluttering and separating as it fell.

"That is pretty nuts," Hank had to agree.

"Damn straight it is. An' ya know *why* they're doin' it, right?"

Having chatted with Harry for as many years as he had, Hank did know why. "To force you outa business?"

"You got *that* right, my friend. Been tryin' to shut me down an' shut me up for twenty years now. Porn laws, cigarette laws, public furniture laws, zoning laws . . . an' now since they can't ban newspapers, they can do the next best thing. They drove all the other newsies outa town, all of 'em but me, an' it drives 'em nuts. An' you know why?"

"Because you tell the truth?"

Harry snapped his fingers and pointed at Hank. "You got it, my friend. Ole Harry Winer." He jabbed a thumb at his own chest. "He tells the truth an' he *sells* the truth. An' it scares the shit out of 'em."

"Well," Hank said, dropping seventy-five cents on the counter. "You know we're in this together, Harry. I'm rootin' for both of us."

At his desk ten minutes later, Hank was flipping through the *Eagle*, reading the headlines with only minimal interest.

"So this lesbian girlfriend of yours," he called over the wall. "You said she was a musician?"

"Yolanda?" Becky called back. "Uh-huh? She plays flute in a jazz quartet?"

Yolanda? Hank rolled his eyes. *Jesus*. "So do they play, y'know, real jazz or is it one of those deals where nobody knows how to play their instruments so they just do that twinky-twonky crap and call it free jazz?"

Becky was quiet for a minute. "People say she's real good?"

"Uh-huh," Hank said. "Thanks. Just curious." He focused on the paper again.

He knew what he was looking for. The primary reason he chose the *Eagle* over all the others was not its international coverage or its hard-hitting investigative reports. Not even the comics. No, he picked up the *Eagle* because it had the best crime blotter in town. Not as funny as Hank's, maybe, but it was thorough. When Crosslin and the other precincts came up short, Hank could sometimes pinch a little something from the *Eagle*.

The top entry that day—all three lines of it—concerned an eight-year-old boy from Washington Heights who'd been shot execution-style, apparently while playing in Madison Square Park. No suspects, no motive, no leads, no witnesses willing to talk. The end. As literature goes, Hank thought, it was a bit lacking.

The rest of the blotter was the usual assortment of convenience store robberies, rooftop rapes, and nightclub shoot-outs.

He began flipping back through the pages toward the front when suddenly he stopped on page 5. A small item in the lower left-hand corner caught his eye.

"'Sasquatch' Smacks B'klyn Souse Silly," read the headline.

Brooklyn resident Charles "Chuck" Pierce, 34, told police he was assaulted on the morning of July 8 as he stumbled to his Carroll Gardens home after several hours in a local tavern. It wasn't your ordinary mugger who attacked Pierce, however, or even a pink elephant. According to Pierce, it was a "hulking, hairy beast," who "smelled really bad."

Pierce, who escaped unharmed, could not confirm that he was attacked by Bigfoot, but the description seems to match. The legendary man-ape is generally rumored to wander the forests of the Pacific Northwest, and his reasons for visiting Brooklyn are unknown.

Attempts to contact Bigfoot for comment have thus far been unsuccessful.

Hank then noticed the byline at the bottom: Lou Stone Jr.

At least the little fucker found the shift key, he thought. He folded the paper back on itself and stepped around to Becky's cubicle, where he found her sitting in front of the blank computer screen staring down at her lap and punching away at her electronic thing.

"Looks like your Mr. Stone has friends in high places," he said, holding out the paper. She swiveled in her chair and looked.

"Hey!" she said with what appeared to be genuine delight. "That's great? Congratulations?"

Hank stared for a moment, saying nothing, the tip of his tongue creeping out from between his teeth and touching his upper lip before retreating. "I guess, ah, that's not really the point. Here's what confuses me." He attempted clumsily to fold the paper back to its original state. "In the blotter, see, they have a bit about an eight-year-old kid who was shot execution-style on a playground, and that got three lines. But this stupid thing here—this drunk who mistakes a homeless guy for a gorilla—gets a half column." He noticed the front page again. "And this shit's on the front page." He held it up. "What's wrong with this picture?"

"That's easy," she said, returning to the machine as she spoke. "Consider the source? Little kids here are, like, killed every day?

And it's a bummer? And it's not every day that people get attacked by Bigfoot? It's like one of those only in New York things?"

"I guess I keep forgetting what I'm dealing with here," Hank said, rapping the paper.

"And another thing? The police had to, like, shift all that manpower away from looking for that little kid's killer so they could look for the gorilla?"

Hank blinked at her as she tapped away. "Yeah . . . that's a valid point." Then before turning away he added, "Sometimes, Becky, you surprise me."

Back at his desk, Hank heard Rusty Wescoat and Nutskin coming down the carpeted hallway, loudly discussing Rusty's next big scoop. Hank wedged the telephone receiver between his shoulder and ear and poised his fingers above the keyboard so he had an excuse to ignore them.

After they passed, he figured what the hell and dialed the number for the Seventy-fourth.

"Brooklyn Seventy-fourth Precinct press desk, Lieutenant Crosslin."

"Hey, yellabelly," Hank said. "Just curious. You talk to anyone else about that Chuck Pierce case?"

"That who-what now?"

"Chuck Pierce, that drunk who ran into the gorilla in Carroll Gardens." There was silence on the other end of the phone. Hank sighed. "Thirty-four-year-old, got drunk, says he was assaulted by a hairy, smelly beast?"

"Gonna need more'n that," Crosslin said. "What am I, fuckin' Kreskin over here? You got a date?"

"July eighth," Hank said. "Early."

"And you expect me to remember? Oh, wait," Crosslin said. "Yeah, okay. The guy in Carroll Gardens."

Hank rolled his eyes. "That's the one."

"So what's the question again?"

"Do you remember if you passed that one on to anybody else?"

As expected, Hank could almost hear Crosslin shaking his head before he spoke. "Nah. The real papers—that is, everybody but you—just wants the hard stuff. Why?"

"You see this morning's *Eagle*?"

There was another long pause before Crosslin said, "No. But I see where you're goin' with this, you ladder-climbin' glory whore. They give you a credit?"

"Of course not. Why would they? They don't know what the word means. Besides, everything's free for the taking now, ain't you heard?" Hank was getting angrier than he would have expected about all this. He wished he had a cigarette he could grind out bitterly in an overfull ashtray.

"Goddamn kids," Crosslin said. It sounded like he was getting angry too. Then Hank remembered that he was pretty much always angry. Especially about the kids. "Always stealin'. See 'em in here every day. Don't even think it's wrong."

Sometimes Hank had to wonder what kind of treatment he would've received from Crosslin when he was sixteen. "Face it, Lieutenant, as a culture we're fucked."

"You tellin' me?" Crosslin said, his voice more resigned than anything. "I'm the cop, here."

Eight

Those Darn Subliminal Messages

You'd think going to a dance party would make for a fun, lighthearted evening. All those happy people dancing about and all. That's certainly what 22-year-old Fernando Diaz thought when he went to a dance at a Prospect Heights community center on the sixteenth.

It apparently turned out to be one of those weird voodoo trance parties, because it was only after he took a cab home and started getting ready for bed that Diaz noticed, much to his surprise, he'd been stabbed three times—twice in the chest and once in the arm. Imagine!

Crazy Heart

Also in Prospect Heights that very same night, a 35-year-old emotionally disturbed man suffered some ominous chest pains of his own. Jesse Freed, who allegedly suffered from a number of medical problems along with that nasty touch of schizophrenia, allegedly started swinging on his father (lord knows why) in the family kitchen. Police were called, slapped the cuffs on an uncooperative Freed, and removed him from the house on a stretcher.

The cuffs came off once he calmed down and the cops delivered him to a nearby hospital, where he had a seizure and allegedly died.

Pet Shop Boy

Somehow nobody noticed when an uptight Asian man in his 30s allegedly wandered into the Palace of Exotic Pets in Crown Heights around noon on Thursday, opened a glass cage, removed a three-foot iguana named Sparky, shoved it down the front of his pants, and walked out again looking much less uptight.

Nobody noticed, that is, until a staffer discovered that Sparky was missing and the manager reviewed the security tapes. Maybe everyone was at lunch. Or maybe everyone had been huffing the flea powder again.

That

Hank's fingers paused on the keyboard. He sensed something. Becky was off covering another hundredth birthday party at another nursing home, and Rusty was over on Fourth Avenue covering the grand opening of the Megamini Mart, the world's largest convenience store. He could feel Brand standing behind him, hear him breathing. He could even somehow sense his sweater. He continued typing and did not turn around.

"Excuse me, Henry?"

The moment Brand's voice reached his ears, Hank's fingers began missing all the keys they were aiming for. He still refused to stop or turn around. It was one-thirty on a Tuesday afternoon, and being one-thirty on a Tuesday afternoon Hank knew what was coming.

"Steve," he said by way of a greeting.

"Stephen," Brand corrected. "I was, um . . ." He began to stammer. Hank knew he would. Being an overly civilized sort, he never knew exactly how to behave around others who did not behave in an equally civilized manner, such as turning to face a speaker when spoken to. "Ah . . . I . . ."

"Just put them there on the pile," Hank said, gesturing with an elbow toward an incoherent stack of curled faxes and strips of tape. "I'll get to them."

As he continued typing gibberish, he heard Brand take a step forward and press the new faxes down upon the old ones before walking away. Once Brand was gone, Hank deleted everything he had typed (hoping Brand had read it while standing over his shoulder) and turned to the fax pile. As usual, mixed in with the smeared press releases for a "pet psychic jamboree" and a "bandages for the homeless giveaway" were the weekly police reports from the Sixty-fifth and Eighty-ninth Precincts. He crumpled the press releases and dumped them in the trash, looking forward to the trip home. At least the police reports would give him a chuckle. They always did.

A brief but wicked thunderstorm ripped across the city shortly after eleven that night but it did nothing to alleviate the temperature. What it did was leave the air even thicker and damper than it had been. The streetlights glittered on the wet pavement and in the puddles on the sidewalks. Apart from that, everything was dark.

There weren't many cars parked along that block, and no lights glowed from the empty windows in any of the buildings Donny Sullivan passed.

His mom thought he was at work at the office supply store. She never asked what kind of office supply store would need to stay open until two a.m., or why her sixteen-year-old son was always borrowing money from her even though he told her he was at work an average of fifty—sometimes even sixty—hours a week. He knew she wouldn't ask.

His dealer normally operated out of Coney Island, but two days earlier Donny was given an address in Red Hook, and if he wanted to score he'd have to pay a visit.

After taking the train and two buses to get there, Donny found that only one in every three or four of the abandoned warehouses had any sort of number painted on the front, and none of them matched the one on the slip of paper in his pocket.

"Shit," he said quietly but he kept walking. It was hard to tell how much of the sweat that slicked his face, neck, and arms was the result of the heat and the humid air and how much was the result of his growing need.

He jumped when he heard a heavy thump and rumble a few yards behind him. It sounded as if someone had kicked and upended a plastic trash can and sent it rolling. He turned, but at first he could see nothing but the darkness between two hollow warehouses and the flicker of the streetlights off a long-abandoned pickup missing three tires.

Then he heard the thump again from the opposite side of the street.

"Carlton?" he called.

* * *

The reports from most of the precincts had been spotty and generic that week. The usual unremarkable grab bag of stabbings and robberies. Nothing so flamboyant or stupid that even the coldest and sketchiest of details gave him a boost. It was looking like it might take some fancy footwork to transform any of these things into a work of art to fill out the rest of that week's blotter. If only he had an indecent exposure case, or a bloody beating involving two or more family members wrangling over a banjo.

Then something in the printout from the Seventy-fourth caught his eye. Hank picked up the phone.

A moment later he heard Crosslin's chipper voice on the other end. Hank had never seen Crosslin's office and so had never seen his phone, but he worked with the assumption that the lieutenant had one of those dense, black, eight-pound desk jobs with a spring-operated dial, circa 1947, all the numbers smeared away through years of use and a row of square red and white buttons across the bottom.

"Heya, cutie pie, there someone there I can talk to who *ain't* Puerto Rican?"

"My grandmother was Puerto Rican." Crosslin didn't sound amused.

"So I make my point. Listen, I have to ask you—"

Crosslin stopped him there. "Hold it, don't tell me. Let me guess. This concerns a certain sixteen-year-old junkie named Donny Sullivan and a twenty-nine-year-old hooker named Barbara Payton, though her wha'cha call *professional* name is Monique."

It took a few seconds before Hank spoke again. "You're shittin' me. Who's the hooker?"

"It seems you haven't read the whole sheet yet. Unlike every other fuckin' hack in this town."

Finding the three-page fax on top of the pile where he'd left it, Hank started scanning quickly for the name.

"You're late, Kalabander, an' now you're tyin' me up here. Been on the phone all fuckin' day with the *Post*, the *News*, the *Eagle*—" There was a sharp buzz on Crosslin's end. "Hold on," he said. "Here's someone who's even later'n you." He put Hank on hold, which gave him time to read the report more carefully. He found the Barbara Payton notes on the last sheet and had just finished it when Crosslin returned.

"Christ," the lieutenant spat. "Normally I only have the dubious pleasure of *your* company."

"Wait a second," Hank said, scanning the condensed Sullivan report. "You say the kid was a junkie?"

"He's been in here before. Possession, mostly. Off the record, of course. But as you know, only about a quarter of the real story is ever official."

Officially, Donny Sullivan's statement read, in part: "It was just like that other guy said. It was a big, hairy, smelly thing. Like an ape. With red eyes. And he attacked me."

Ms. Payton, by her own account, had been strolling around Prospect Park just south of the zoo at two-thirty in the morning, simply minding her own business, when she was assaulted by "a big, hairy monster," who jumped out from behind some trees and grabbed her. "I know it was the same thing that attacked that guy in the paper," she told police. "Some kind of Bigfoot thing." Both victims were examined by physicians after filing their complaints, but neither had suffered anything more serious than scrapes and bruises.

"Jesus, people are stupid," Hank said.

"You callin' me to confirm that?"

Truth be told, that was pretty much exactly why Hank was calling.

"I just can't believe the other papers are going for it."

"Like flies on shit."

"Why aren't they doing something about that kid who was shot in the park? Not that I really care all that much, but still."

"Who?"

"Yeah."

Even before picking up the phone he knew he wasn't going to use the Sullivan story to round out that week's blotter. He'd already done his part, apparently—he just wanted to commiserate.

A drunk, a junkie, and a hooker, he thought after hanging up. *Next it's gonna be a homeless crackhead and a pre-op trannie.*

Learning that the other papers were on to it merely capped the deal. No way he was going to go with something that would be run into the dirt days before it saw print in the *Hornet.*

He grabbed another of the faxes, scanned it, and chose one report at random so he could just be done with it.

Gee, Your Hair Feels Terrific

It's been a rough semester for city college students. If they aren't jumping off balconies, getting gunned down outside the library, or dying of mysterious unknown diseases, someone's sneaking into their dorm rooms at night to fondle them. That's what happened to a Brooklyn College freshman last weekend. The summer school student was in her room at 3:30 a.m. when three men—at least one of them a student—allegedly strolled through her unlocked door. As one of the creeps grabbed her butt, another, allegedly identified as 18-year-old Simon Bergmann, "fondled her head and hair" before fleeing.

Although the whereabouts of the other two is unknown, Bergmann was evicted from his dorm and is now facing burglary and sexual abuse charges. That job at the wig factory is just gonna have to wait.

Becky was right about one thing. When the story appeared in the *Daily News* and the *Post* the next day, both short inside pieces were lighthearted but smug, and both used the phrase "only in New York." The term always grated on Hank for some reason. More so now, as it didn't seem to make any sense in this case. Both papers also used lines that were coincidentally similar to lines that had appeared in Hank's original blotter piece, but of course neither cited him. Hank didn't notice any of that, though, which was probably for the best. What caught his attention, as usual, was the *Eagle*, whose front page banner screamed "B'klyn Bigfoot Attacks Two More!" Sharing the cover was an artist's sketch of the creature, which closely resembled sketches of Bigfoot he'd seen in the past, but meaner. This one looked more like something you'd see on *America's Most Wanted.* Hank wasn't at all surprised to see the byline belonged to that damn Stone kid.

"You believe in monsters, Harry?" Hank asked as he folded the paper and dropped the coins on the newsstand counter.

"We vote for 'em, don't we?" Harry grumbled. "An' I see *you* every day. So in answer to your question, I'd hafta say yeah. Why d'you ask?"

A few minutes later, after saying hello to Blanche and heading for his cubicle, Hank was stopped by Nutskin, who was carrying the *Eagle* as well.

"You see this?" he asked.

Hank tapped his own paper.

"And you knew about this?"

"That I did, yeah. It's no big deal." Hank, just for fun, tried to see how close he could let his eyes drift toward Nutskin's mouth without actually registering it.

"But it wasn't in this week's blotter. That last one was pretty funny, even if it was a little hard on that man's drinking problem."

"Did it once. Didn't want to be redundant," Hank explained. "Besides, I also knew that every other paper in town had it and that we wouldn't hit the street until two days later."

That almost seemed to make sense to Nutskin. Then he caught himself. "But you've run with that pet store guy, what, five times now?"

"Three. And the difference, Shed—and this is important—the difference is that the pet store guy is actually doing something. Those are crimes, not just addicts makin' shit up. I'm not in the business of running crackpot yarns."

Having made his point, he took another step toward his desk, then stopped. "Besides, don't you think if we ran all these monster stories in the blotter, we might scare the children? They're the ones who're reading it, remember."

Nine

I'm dry. Where's that Injun waitress?"

"Shhhh," Annie said, staring down at the table. "She's over at the chippie roost, talking to a friend of hers. She'll be here. Please don't call her an *Injun* when she shows up."

With a small wheeze, Hank shifted around in his chair and saw the young woman standing at the podium near the front door, straightening a few menus and chatting with another waitress. He'd hoped he'd made enough of a show of turning to look that they'd notice and react but their conversation rolled on.

It was the third night that week they'd been forced to go out for dinner, so it was Annie's choice.

After work on the water pipes in the building's entry hall had resulted in a flooded basement apartment and a puncture in the gas line to Hank and Annie's stove, the contractors had to move into their kitchen, where they were in the process of tearing out part of the floor. They had to fix the gas line before they could get back to the entry hall and the leak that caused the flood. Once all those things were taken care of, they could finally finish work in the bathroom. And once that was complete, maybe they could fix the kitchen floor and move the stove back where it belonged. As things stood, they had no gas and no hot water (and, during the day, no water at all).

"Dammit," Hank whispered as he swiveled back around. "I may just go up to the bar to get the next round myself."

"Don't do that. Think of it this way. At least you won't have to walk across the canal to get home."

"Wouldn't matter if I did—I'm *sober.* Fancy-ass place and I can't get a drink. I thought these people were supposed to have a work ethic. She's just standing over there gabbing about boys and . . . and *Vishnu.*"

"Just *hush,*" Annie snapped. "There are a lot of people in here."

"Wha'd I say now?" Hank asked, perplexed.

Malkhit's Hideaway had opened six months earlier and was four blocks from their apartment. Indian pop music played from a single speaker in the back, pristine white tablecloths covered the tables, and the primary lighting source came from the hundreds of strings of Christmas lights stapled to the walls and around the windows. It was crowded that night. With only ten tables in the dining room, it was almost always crowded, and crowded with people Hank couldn't tolerate.

He stared at the woman seated at the table eight inches away from theirs, the one who'd been on her cell phone from the moment she walked in.

Hank turned to Annie, and without bothering to lower his voice he said, "You know I'm gonna have to kill her before the evening's over. Just beat her to death with my empty glass here." He lifted the glass an inch for emphasis. The woman's two children, probably ten and eight years old, looked at him with a mix of fear and hope in their eyes.

"Yeah, your mother's an asshole," Hank told them.

Annie finished her own drink and gestured to the waitress as she passed. “This thing is really bothering you, isn’t it?”

“What thing’s that? This cow here?” He tipped his head toward the next table.

“The business with the *Eagle.*”

He shook his head as he shrugged off the suggestion. “Not particularly. The average American attention span currently rests somewhere between twelve and fourteen seconds. Story’ll be gone by tomorrow or the next day. It’s not even a story to begin with. Waste of energy.” He scratched at his ear. “You ever hear of the Winsted Wild Man?”

She shook her head.

“Remind me to tell you some time. Now *that* was a good story.”

The waitress showed up with their drinks and took their order (finally). Before she left, she collected their empty glasses and took them away.

“I’m not talking about the story,” Annie said once the waitress was gone. “I’m talking about this Stone person stealing it from you.”

Hank, who seemed more interested in his drink at that point, grunted but said nothing else.

“I can tell—you’re ornerier than usual tonight.”

“Well,” he said, offering an exaggerated frown. “There’s also the fact that our home is in ruins thanks to the illegal alien version of the Three Stooges, and there’s this charmer here telling us all about her trouble with the clerk at the drugstore.” He jerked his thumb none too subtly at the woman next to him, who didn’t seem to notice.

“I still think you should call this Stone kid on it. If you don’t, these kids will just steal and steal and not think anything about it.”

“It’s the way journalism’s always worked.” He was looking around the restaurant, but for what she couldn’t tell.

"I still think you should call him."

He squeezed his eyes shut. "Let's talk about something else. Any interesting creeps come in the store today?"

There was some truth behind the question. Facing online competition from a seemingly infinite selection of rare book dealers from around the world, Annie's shop had to depend on customers from the city's steadily aging and shrinking population of literate eccentrics and Luddites. Yet somehow they had remained loyal enough that she still managed to do reasonably well.

"Abernathy stopped by this afternoon," she said. "Today he was looking for *House of Dolls* and Apollinaire's *Memoirs of a Young Rakehell.*"

"Ew," Hank said, making a face. "Don't even want to think about it. What is it with old fat black *queers* and their Nazi porn? I mean—"

"*Marv!*" she hissed, aiming a vicious kick at his right ankle under the table.

"Ow! *Fuck!*" he erupted, leaning down to massage the future bruise. The woman at the next table finally stopped talking briefly enough to glare at him. "The name's Hank, and I don't see what the problem is."

"You've got to watch what you say . . . Hank. You're gonna get yourself killed one of these days."

"By *what*, one of those—?" He saw the look on Annie's face and stopped himself.

"I just never know where you're going to go from there," she said.

"The lawyer, one of these days, you keep kickin' me. I don't even see what the big deal is. I mean, it's *true*, ain't it? About Abernathy? It's an apt summation."

"I don't think you could seriously call *House of Dolls* Nazi porn."

"Oh my god, of course you can," Hank said with a dismissive smile. "I don't care if it *was* written by a Jew. It's about a Nazi whorehouse, and these days it's read by people who're after Nazi porn. Therefore, it's *fucking* Nazi porn, QED. And I don't see why so many old fat black queers are into it."

They both stopped suddenly and looked up to find the waitress standing beside their table holding their plates.

"Do *you* know the answer?" Hank asked her.

As he wiped the sweat from his face during the walk from the subway the next morning, Hank realized Annie was right. As usual. It was getting to him—or at least more than he had been admitting to himself, and more than he should allow.

Once at his desk it took more doing than he would've expected, but with Becky's help he finally tracked down a phone number for Lou Stone Jr.

A woman picked up the receiver.

"Uh, yeah," Hank said. "Hello. I'm trying to reach Lou Stone, please."

"That's me," the woman responded. She seemed very happy with herself for that.

Hank rolled his eyes. He didn't have time for wacky hijinks. "Okay, fine. Is Lou there, please?"

"Speaking."

Hank closed his eyes and tried to keep his voice even. "Lou Stone from the *Eagle*."

"Uh-huh?" There was a pause, and then the woman started to giggle.

Goddamn kids and their pot.

"Forgive me," the woman said, "but I can never resist that. This is Louise Stone Jr. from the *Eagle*, yes . . . I'm actually Lou Stone the Fourth, but since I turned out to be a girl they named me Louise."

Hank didn't know whether or not to believe any of this, and he didn't know what to say. "Are you sure?"

He heard her take a deep breath, apparently having been through this before, even if it was her own damn fault. "My great-grandfather was a bit of a practical joker and put it in his will that every firstborn for the next ten generations be named after him. I call myself *junior* because it seems to make things easier. On several levels. He was a journalist too. Up in Connecticut."

Christ, he shoulda left it in his will that you learn how to shut the hell up.

"That's swell," Hank said. "Listen, the reason I'm calling . . ." For a moment he forgot why he was calling. Learning that Lou was in fact Louise had thrown him. So had her prattling. "Uh, my name's Henry Kalabander, and I'm—"

"Henry *Kalabander*?" she interrupted. "From the *Hornet*? The crime blotter guy?"

That also threw him. "Uh, yeah."

"*Wow*, this is such an honor. You put out the best blotter in the city. I never miss it."

He was suddenly convinced she was making fun of him. But it was still the first time anyone outside the office or his apartment had commented on the blotter at all, let alone recognized his name.

"Yeah, um, thanks," he said.

"Oh, you're great. I write a blog, too, and you've been a real inspiration for that. I can't believe you're calling me."

He was hesitant to tear Stone a new one after all that, but seeing his opening he stepped in anyway. So he loses his one fan, so what? "Yeah, that's kind of why I'm calling, see? It seems I've been a bit more than a simple inspiration. You took my story."

There was a brief silence. He could hear tinny music playing behind her. It sounded like jazz from the twenties or thirties. "The Brooklyn monster," she said.

"Got you on the cover of the *Eagle*, I see." He was getting his focus back.

"Mr. Kalabander . . . wow, that's how you pronounce it? Like salamander?"

"Yeah."

"Neat. I thought it was Egyptian or something. But Mr. Kalabander, your piece ran, and you weren't going to do anything more with it."

Hank could feel the anger kindling at the back of his head. "You don't know me, Ms. Stone, and so you don't know that. But that's not the point. Anybody could've gotten that story if they'd looked at the reports out of the Seventy-fourth. But you didn't, see? You lifted my story. There are actual *lines* from my blotter that have appeared more than once in your stories. And as far as you've run with it, you haven't given me a fucking credit. That's some serious business. Legally and, ah . . . morally." He couldn't believe he'd just said that.

He heard her exhale heavily but couldn't tell if it was out of shame or annoyance.

"I know it's a nothing story. Gonna be gone in a day or two. But that don't make what you did right, see?" He could feel his old Cagney impression slipping in around his tongue and tried to curtail it.

"Try looking at it from my perspective," Stone said. She didn't sound terribly penitent. "You're a staff writer over there at the *Hornet*, I'm guessing."

Hank cut his eyes to the left. "Yeah?"

"So you get a check every week, no matter what. I'm freelance." He could hear the anger growing in her voice. "You get paid whether the blotter runs or not. I only get paid if I produce."

"So you just *steal* things other people have written? This is your argument?"

"I didn't think you'd care. I have to pay the rent. You must have been there at some point."

"Sure, but that didn't give me the right to start robbing people. What the hell's wrong with you?"

Hank had never hit a woman in his life, but he was considering the idea.

Ten

It was almost 11:30 p.m. before fifty-six-year-old Juanita Lopez at last had the time to bag up all the trash and drag it down in the service elevator.

The Denham was a four-building, fourteen-hundred-unit housing complex in Bushwick, and the dumpsters were kept in the courtyard out back. That meant two or three times a week Ms. Lopez, who lived alone, had to set aside at least half an hour to take the garbage out.

She didn't like going out there at all, let alone at this hour. All the guns and the drugs. The neighbors told her they'd even heard there'd been dog fights back there earlier in the week. And now with people talking about a monster? But the garbage was starting to smell in this heat. It had to go out. She just wanted to get it over with and back to the safety of her apartment so she could get some rest.

Before pushing the emergency exit open, she peered out the small, square bulletproofed window. From what she could see under the security lights, the courtyard seemed empty, and the dumpsters were only fifty feet away.

She propped the door open a few inches with a wooden wedge

and stepped out onto the gravel pathway. Dragging the two bags of garbage behind her, she looked around again. Apart from the distant expressway traffic and her own footsteps crunching on the gravel she heard nothing. No one else was moving or talking, and there were no bodies on the ground.

With small, careful steps she moved toward the three massive green dumpsters, already overflowing with plastic trash bags. That meant she would have to throw her own bags up top. But they were so heavy tonight, and she was so tired. Maybe no one would notice if she left them on the ground.

With only twenty feet to go and concentrating on the dumpsters in front of her, it took Ms. Lopez a moment to realize that she had seen something move. A shadow sliding out from the other shadows ahead of her.

She refocused her eyes. It wasn't something she imagined—it was there, low to the ground, but growing. She stopped walking and heard another sound, a snort and a quiet growl. At the edges of the bright pool cast by the security lights she saw a glint of white teeth.

Leaving her bags behind her, she spun and ran for the door, her feet slipping in the gravel.

"*Monstruo,*" she whimpered as she ran, blinded by frightened tears. "*El monstruo está comiendo mi basura!*"

"*. . . but officials say the church group was actually selling the children orphaned by the tsunami into prostitution.*"

Hank nearly screamed with laughter, splashing beer on his lap and the couch in the process.

"Oh, that is *so* inappropriate," Annie said, elbowing him. "That's terrible." He barely heard her as his laughter devolved into a series of dry coughs. He lowered his beer to the ground to avoid spilling any more.

They were sitting on the couch watching the ten o'clock news. The kitchen was definitely off-limits and the bathroom, while still functional in spots, was a potential death trap. At least they still had the living room, the bedroom, and the area around the kitchen table. For now, anyway.

Hank found that evening's broadcast more uproarious than usual. The elevator mishap on Wall Street would have been enough, but that child prostitution story was the kicker. Watching him carefully during the broadcasts some nights, Annie worried quite seriously about his mental stability.

He was still wiping the tears away when footage of terrified Indonesian toddlers clustered outside a ruined building was replaced with the nearly plastinated face of the anchorman.

"Coming up next," he promised in a voice far too chipper for that evening's stories. "Is there a *monste*r roaming Brooklyn? Some residents say yes, and we'll tell you why."

"Oh, Jesus Christ." Hank's laughter left him as his right hand began slapping the couch and Annie's legs in search of the remote.

"Don't," Annie said, grabbing his arm. "Let's see what they have to say."

"I don't *care* what they have to say. It's just idiotic." His hand was still searching. Annie didn't tell him she had the remote next to her. She knew he'd never get to his feet to change the station manually. "I just don't care."

By the third commercial he had given up the search, folded his arms, and stared coldly at the screen, his mouth tight. The day after he talked to Ms. Stone, he had been relieved to discover that there was no mention of the stupid thing in the pages of the *Eagle* or—he presumed—any of the other dailies, and he figured that was it, it was over.

"Is Bigfoot, or a monster of some kind, on the loose in Brooklyn?" the anchor began with an incredulous, toothy grin after the commercial break ended. "According to the NYPD, over the past two weeks there have been three reported sightings of what witnesses describe as a 'hairy, hulking beast' around the Gowanus and Carroll Gardens sections of Brooklyn, as well as in Prospect Park." Projected above the anchor's left shoulder was a round yellow logo featuring the silhouette of a gorilla, its arms raised. For some reason, the artist had also given the gorilla devil horns and red eyes. Beneath it were the words "Monster Alert."

"They gave it a fucking logo," Hank muttered. He reached for his beer.

"As first reported in the *New York Eagle* . . ." Hank's fist smacked against the side of his head, spilling more beer. ". . . the alleged monster is large, hairy, and *smells* bad. Police do say that at least one of the victims was extremely intoxicated at the time of the sighting, but to date all three victims have refused to speak to the press."

"Because they sobered up and felt like half-wits," Hank called to the screen. He turned to Annie. "Speaking of which, I need another drink. You want one?" He started to push himself to his feet, but she stopped him. On the television, the anchor was saying, ". . . and while none of the alleged victims have suffered anything more than bumps and bruises, the police are encouraging residents to . . ."

"C'mon, at least watch the end of this before you wash it all away."

Reluctantly, he leaned back again.

"What do *you* think?" the pasteboard face on the screen asked. "To find out, we sent our very own Paul Langtry to a tavern near where the first monster sighting occurred to find out. We now go *live* to P. D. Sharkey's in Carroll Gardens." The anchor put his hand to his ear for no apparent reason. "Are you there, Paul?"

When they cut to the live feed, the first thing that appeared was an arm waving a sheet of paper. Behind the arm was a raucous bar filled with heavyset white men mostly in their twenties and thirties, almost all of them wearing baseball caps.

"*No!*" the man Hank and Annie presumed was Langtry shouted off-camera. "I don't *know*! It's in the shit in my file folder! The one labeled *ape*! Look in there! Where in the *fuck* are you looking? Look for *ape*!"

The voice went silent and the anchor's face abruptly reappeared. "We seem to be having some technical difficulties with our feed from Paul Langtry. We'll return to him when—*oh*!"

"Broadcast news proves itself again," Hank said, as the anchor put that pointless hand to his ear.

A moment later they were back at the bar and Langtry was standing next to a clean-shaven, round-faced man in a Mets cap and a corporate T-shirt. He seemed unsteady on his feet.

"We're here at P. D. Sharkey's in Carroll Gardens, just a few blocks from where the monster, whatever it was, was first spotted." He turned to the unsteady man in the cap. "So," the reporter asked, "do you know anyone who's seen the monster yet?"

The man smiled and raised a full pint glass to the camera. "I get enougha these in me, buddy, I'll see whatever the hell you want me to see."

Realizing he didn't dare take the interview much further, the reporter gestured to the cameraman, who followed him through the rambunctious, hooting crowd and across the bar, where he stopped next to an overweight, dark-haired man sitting alone at a table with a beer in front of him. The obviously preoccupied man slowly turned to notice the camera and the microphone.

"Let's see what kind of response we get over here," the reporter said, nodding at the seated man. "Let me ask you, sir, have you heard the stories about a monster supposedly lurking around Brooklyn?" He tipped the microphone to the man's mouth.

"Yes," the man said earnestly, staring into the camera. "Yes I have."

"And do you believe these stories are true?" As he asked, a group of five drunks gathered behind the seated man and made faces at the camera.

"Oh, I most certainly do, yes. Yes, indeed." He seemed deadly serious and spoke in the stilted tones of the overeducated.

"Well in that case," Langtry pressed, "who or what do you think the creature might be?"

The man nodded sagely and paused a beat as he formed his answer. Turning back to the camera he said, "I think it's a *Mexican*, Peter."

Langtry yanked the microphone back and faced the camera himself, clearly pissed, as eight or nine well-soused hooligans crowded in behind him, waving, howling, and giving the finger to the viewers at home.

"Well, there you have it. The residents of Brooklyn do believe that there is something strange in their midst. Just who or what this thing is, however, remains uncertain. To date, no one has been killed by the beast, but how long will it be before someone . . ." He paused dramatically. "Is? I'm Paul Langtry, reporting live from P. D. Sharkey's in Carroll Gardens."

Before the cut to commercial, Hank saw one of the drunks snatch the microphone out of Langtry's hand. That made him feel a little better.

"So what's this you were saying about the story disappearing in a day or two?" Annie asked.

"Just shut up," he answered. "I'm getting a drink. And now I'm not so sure I'm gonna bring you one."

Eleven

Three days later the story had not gone away as predicted. At some point during that seventy-two-hour period someone, somewhere, had also forgotten that the whole thing was a joke.

Shortly after nine-thirty, Hank sat calmly at his desk, tearing a copy of that morning's *Eagle* into thin vertical strips, each of which he dropped neatly into the wastebasket beside him.

Before he began tearing, the headline had read: "Could It Be REAL?" It was another Pulitzer contender from Louise Stone.

There were similar screaming headlines across the front pages of all three tabloids. Among the broadsheets, the *Sentinel* hit pay dirt, coining the moniker "Gowanus Devil" for whatever it was the drunks and junkies imagined they were seeing. The *Eagle* had been toying with "Brooklyn Beast," the *Daily News* with "Brooklyn Gorilla," and the *Post* with the inexplicable "New York Ripper," but when the *Sentinel* came out that morning everyone seemed to know instinctively that "Gowanus Devil" would stick. If not as mellifluous as "Brooklyn Beast," it did have geographical specificity, so as not to besmirch the respectable and affluent residents of nearby Brooklyn Heights and Park Slope. Even the *Times*, no longer able to dodge it, finally ran a brief, sober Gowanus Devil story on page 3 of the metro section. And every one of the papers had its own artist's rendering of what the creature might look like. All of them were nearly identical—merely slight modifications on the original NYPD sketch. To Hank, they all looked like something you might see in one of those Johnson Smith novelty catalogs.

Might as well be a unicorn or Porky Pig, he thought.

Not only had everyone forgotten the whole thing was a joke—they'd even started speculating about what the creature might be. The *Daily News* claimed, with no proof of any kind, it was an escaped gorilla, while the *Sentinel* guessed it might've been the result of a Plum Island research experiment gone terribly wrong. The *Eagle*, meanwhile, was steadfastly sticking by the Bigfoot theory.

Hank had no interest in finding out what might be awaiting him on the Internet.

Three and a half weeks earlier, the NYPD was receiving, on average, zero "hairy monster on the loose" reports a day. Then it was one. Then two. Hank was not surprised to learn that after the insistent media coverage and the viral spread of the stories electronically, as of a day earlier (Tuesday), an enormous apelike creature of some sort had been spotted in all five boroughs. Yet even with the millions of video phones and surveillance cameras at the ready throughout the metropolitan area, no one had been able to snap a picture of the thing.

After listening to five minutes of slow paper shredding in the next cubicle, Becky set her device down and cautiously peeked around the wall to see what Mr. Kalabander was doing. He was weird sometimes.

Upon seeing the trash can overflowing with thin strips of newsprint she asked, "This whole thing is really bugging you, isn't it?"

There was a pause in the tearing (he was up to page 27). He

looked over his shoulder. What threw him this time was the fact that it had been an actual question and not just something that sounded like one.

"I'm sorry? Like, you should really be getting the credit?"

That was more like it. He shook his head. "No, Becky, that's not it. It's not the credit. I wouldn't want the credit for this. It's not the story either." He hoped he could make it clear to her. "It's that it's *not* a story, see? There is no monster. Or whatever the fuck they're calling it this week. Gowanus Devil." He saw the shock on her face when he said a naughty word. Poor child. "There's no proof, no physical evidence. A sloppy drunk sees a homeless guy and makes up a story. The papers start repeating it, and the TV faggots get in on the game, and it's passed around on that fucking *Internet*—all without the tiniest goddamn *shard* of anything. And before you know it, eight million jackaninnies believe the sloppy drunk's story and make it their own." He stopped, out of breath, glaring at Becky as if he wished he could blame her for something. "See?" His breath was wheezing out hot and he was sweating. "*Emperor's new clothes.* That's what's getting to me."

Becky stared at him, shocked. "You really shouldn't call people that?" she said. "Because it's wrong?" She ducked back into her cubicle, snatched up her device, but then didn't seem to know what to do with it.

"What, jackaninnies?" Hank asked.

Later that afternoon, shortly after finishing small bits about a quilting bee and a walking tour of "historic Gravesend" for the entertainment page, Hank saw Nutskin leaving the bathroom. Not yet willing to start looking at that week's precinct reports (knowing what he'd find), he needed a distraction. "Hey, Shed."

Nutskin paused, still wiping his hands on the front of his shirt.

"Just wanted to tell you how relieved I am to see you haven't bought in to all this bullshit."

"In this office we don't curse," Nutskin reminded him.

Hank's eyes wavered for a moment. "Okay, um, but I was saying you aren't buying in to this shit about the monster. Putting Rusty on the trail. It's a relief." Nutskin wasn't accustomed to receiving compliments from Kalabander, let alone regarding the *Hornet*'s editorial policies. He adjusted his weight and turned to face Hank more directly. Hank, in response, dropped his eyes to Nutskin's collar. Then down two buttons, just to be safe.

"You know, I thought about it over the weekend," Nutskin said. "We did break the story, after all. But like I told you last week, when you wanted to run that second monster attack in your blotter, it's not our style."

"Ah, huh," Hank said, drumming his fingers on the wall he was leaning against.

"It's a little too dark for *Hornet* readers, I think. Remember, we're trying to be upbeat about the neighborhood. This is a great place to live and raise a family. We don't need to go reminding people that there's a monster out there threatening their children."

My god, he's been rehearsing that, Hank thought. *Probably waiting for CNN to call.*

"Yeah, well," Hank said, when it was clear Nutskin had finished his sound bite. "I'm just glad you're not joining in." He excused himself and headed for his cubicle, thinking those precinct reports might not be so bad after all.

At first he thought it was Becky who'd taken the seat next to him on the train that night. Same artificial soft creak in the voice, same inability to speak a declarative sentence. A quick glance had proven he was mistaken. That was a relief. Becky had adamantly refused to speak to him for the rest of the day. He had no idea why. Whoever this woman was, though, she was the only one on the train who wasn't talking about some godforsaken monster. That was the only thing he was willing to grant her.

"My grandmother still lives there?" the woman was saying. "So we all went over there for the holidays?"

"Really?" the kid who was with her asked. "So you speak fluent French, then?"

"No? I mean, like, when I was growing up I spent all my summers there? But I never, like, really learned the language?"

"Wow. Do you—" the young man began.

"People hear that I spent all my summers in France?" the woman went on. A quick look out of the corner of his eye told Hank she was probably in her mid-twenties. "And so they think I must have had, like, a lot of money? But not really? I mean, it was just what we did?"

It was clear they were on a first date and the kid was trying to play Mr. Interested by asking a lot of insipid questions. The operative word here is *trying*.

"Is the subway really complicated?" she asked, but before her hapless suitor could answer she rolled on. "I was in Boston once? I mean, I love Boston? But I was there once? And I got on a train going the wrong way? And I was trying to get to the airport? So I was late? And I got lost, so I started crying in front of all these people? And . . . ?"

Poor sap, Hank thought. *All he wants is to get himself laid, but she's gonna suck his soul dry long before she touches anything else.*

Blessedly, Hank's stop was next. He wasn't sure how much

more of her chirping he'd be able to take without some sort of hostage situation developing.

"I really love Boston?" the girl was repeating. "And I really want to go to Harvard Medical School?"

Oh, god help us all. As the train squealed into the station, Hank pulled himself to his feet with a groan and stepped around the couple to face the doors. Then a thought occurred to him, and he leaned back toward them. The woman was still rambling on about some pointless crap.

"'S'cuse me?" Hank asked with an artificial smile. She stopped talking though her mouth remained open and they both looked up at him. The doors opened. "Wherever you're headed right now," he said, "I sincerely hope you die there."

With an exaggerated wink, and before either of them could respond, he slipped off the train as the doors closed between them.

Annie had called earlier in the day and asked Hank to stop by the grocery store on his way home. He was happy to take advantage of the store's air-conditioning for a few minutes, and this time no one accused him of being a magician.

As he stepped out of the sliding doors back onto the warm sidewalk gripping a heavy plastic bag containing at least an approximation of the things his wife had requested, he saw a man sitting on a milk crate on the curb. He was a bearded, raggedy character in a dirty, ill-fitting Yankees T-shirt, holding a bent paper cup in his hand.

Hank watched as a prim and severe woman pushing a stroller veered violently as she approached the man, apparently out of fear he might snatch and eat her baby as she passed. Hank always got a kick out of that. He waited until she jogged past with the stroller, the muscles in her face and neck twitching, then stepped across the hot concrete and stood over the man.

"Well, my god, Khalid, where the hell you been?"

The man raised his large, dreadlocked head and watery eyes and slowly allowed the image to register. Once it did, he leaped from his crate.

"Hanky!" he cried, and he held out a fist in Hank's direction. Hank stared at the fist for a moment before grabbing it with his free hand and shaking it.

Khalid clapped him on the shoulder. "Hanky! I been waitin'!"

"Been by every day but ain't seen you out here."

"Ah," Khalid said. "Doc says I got th' walkin' pneumonia or some shit." He still had a tight grip on Hank's shoulder. "How you been, man?"

"Oh, been fine, yeah," Hank replied, trying to take a quiet step out of the range of Khalid's pneumonia. "World's drivin' me nuts, but there's nothin' new in that."

Khalid began coughing and doubled over, casting a fine mist of spittle and mucus down the front of Hank's already damp shirt. For a moment the coughs turned to gags, and Hank was afraid Khalid would puke on his shoes, too. The pedestrians stepping carefully around them gave them even wider berth.

When Khalid could stand upright again he apologized. "Man, it's this pneumonia the doc says I got."

"You . . . you wanna sit down? Take a load off?"

Khalid smiled. "What, when my friend Hanky's here? No way, man."

"You gotta take care of yourself."

"I do man, I do. You don't worry 'bout Khalid here, he take care o' hisself." He clapped Hank on the shoulder again.

"You better," Hank said, clapping Khalid awkwardly on the shoulder in response. "You may be the only sane man left in this stinking town. Speaking of which, lemme ask you something."

"Sure thing, man," he said, leaning in close, turning his head to aim his ear toward Hank's mouth. "Ass' me anything. You know I tells the truth."

"You heard any of those monster stories goin' around?"

"*Ooooohh*, man." Khalid tilted his head back, grinning, his eyes half closed. "Yeah I heard them stories, man. *Crazy* shit . . . You wanna know what I think it is?"

"I would love to know what you think it is." The grocery bag was starting to dig into Hank's fingers. He remembered, too, there were a few things in there that would go bad if he didn't get them home soon.

"I think iss this *heat*, you follow? Drivin' people crazy. Makin' 'em *see* shit."

Hank nodded slowly. "I think you're dead on with that . . . So you're not afraid of any monster?"

Khalid cackled loudly. "Scared? *Maaan*, there's a monster out there, that muthafucka gota be ascairda *me*."

Hank smiled himself and looked away at the people passing around them. All those uninteresting faces. "Yeah, like I said, Khalid, you may be the last sane man in New York."

"Damn straight. Di'n I always say so?"

"Well," Hank said, hoisting the bag a few inches, "I better get this shit home before it starts to rot. But you take care, and I hope that pneumonia clears up."

"Khalid grabbed his arm. "Good to see you, Hanky. You be by again soon?"

"You know me."

"Good, uh . . . say Hanky, Ise wonderin' . . ." He gestured slightly with the bent cup and fixed his eyes on Hank's hand.

Hooking the dripping grocery bag onto his wrist, Hank reached for his wallet.

Khalid coughed violently again, still holding on to Hank's arm.

"Y'know . . . Hanky," he said. There was a cold seriousness to his voice. "I *seen* heads, man . . . Lottaf 'em."

"I know you have, Khalid." Hank slipped out a few bills. "Why do you think I give you money?"

Twelve

"*. . . The real question facing all of us now is, where did this beast come from and what can we do to stop it? For a few possible answers we have with us this morning Doctor . . .*"

"Stop it from *what*?" Hank shouted. "It hasn't *done* anything!"

He gave the button a savage punch and the radio went dead. "I can't listen to this crap anymore," he spat with disgust. "There's no escaping it."

"Even the NPR now?" Annie asked. "That's disheartening."

Hank brushed the plaster dust off the chair and took a seat at the kitchen table, examining his coffee for debris of any kind. "Don't see why you're surprised," he said. "For all their socialist audio filters and their sanctimoniousness . . . sanctimony . . . their hoity-toity shit, they're just as superstitious and gullible as everyone else. Think they're so goddamn sophisticated. If this was happening in India somewhere, they'd be sniggering in their Sugar Pops at those poor backward savages, but put it in New York, they start flappin' their arms and cluckin' like chickens. Idiots."

"Sniggering in their Sugar Pops?" Annie asked.

"Whatever. You know what I mean."

She looked over at the silent radio. "Hank, what have you created?" She tried to muster a laugh as she pulled the tea bag from her cup and laid it on the dusty table. He wasn't amused.

"I didn't do anything." He seemed much more upset than she felt was necessary over all this. "I ran a *stupid* hundred-word piece about a drunk and that's it. I also ran a bunch of other stupid stories about people who actually *did* things, but nobody cares there's some serial animal rapist on the loose."

She stared at him hard across table. He wasn't looking back. "Why is this bothering you so much?"

He shook his head. "Sorry. Just sick of hearing about it. I know it'll go away soon. Some slattern on a reality show'll give birth to Siamese twins or some shit and everyone'll forget about it. They'll all be able to get back to their pathetic empty lives again and talk about, I dunno, the stock market."

"You're probably right," she said. "It's just a distraction."

He looked out the kitchen window. It was cloudy but there was no promise of rain.

"But remember that ninja burglar case on Staten Island a couple years ago?" she asked. "Suddenly everyone who was robbed was robbed by the ninja. That went on for how long? Year, year and a half, until—"

"Yeah," Hank snapped. "Okay. There's no need to remind me." He looked at the clock, then his watch. "Speaking of apemen, when are the—"

"Hank."

He pursed his lips. "What time are they coming?"

"They said about ten."

He nodded, drained his coffee cup, stepped around the stove, and headed toward the sink to wash it out before remembering there was no water in the kitchen for at least another week.

Annie watched him quietly, having seen the same routine play out for the past five mornings. "On the bright side to all this," she said. "Have you noticed that nobody in the neighborhood's letting their kids play outside anymore?"

"Well, thank god for that at least," he replied, heading toward the bathroom, coffee cup in hand. "Means the kids upstairs'll get to stay in and stomp around all day. Just wish it would scare a few Dominicans into finishing a goddamn job so they could run back to Dominica to hide."

When the front door of the Kaplan home opened and nine-year-old Terra bounded in with the Kaplans' nanny, Miss Shumya, Terra's mother was mortified to see a grass stain on one of the boy's knees.

"What . . . is *that*?" Ms. Kaplan shrieked, pointing a thin, quivering finger at the boy's knee.

A further examination revealed Terra had scrapes on his hands and dirt on his elbows as well.

"De boy he done be playin' debbil at de park wit' 'iz frients," Miss Shumya explained.

But when the infuriated Ms. Kaplan turned on the boy, he offered a different explanation.

"A big monster did it," he said, rubbing his nose with a dirty hand.

Ms. Kaplan's eyes flew open as her rage shifted into distraught terror, and all the Valium in her system evaporated. She whirled on Miss Shumya. "*How* could you let something like this happen to my little boy? How *could* you? You're *useless*! Stupid black *trash*!"

With tears running down her face, she grabbed Terra roughly by the arm and dragged him stumbling into the kitchen. She snatched her cell phone off the polished marble countertop and, fingers and lips trembling, dialed three digits.

"*Yes!*" she screamed into the phone. "*Yes*, it's an emergency! . . . *Shut up!* I will *not* calm down! My son was just *mauled* by the Gowanus Devil!"

Thirteen

Hank knocked once on the half open door to the office Nutskin shared with Brand. "You wanted to see me?"

He'd been ignoring the note left on his desk as long as he could. He didn't want to know what this was all about.

"Ah, Kalabander," Nutskin said, looking up from the computer screen. "There you are. Finally. Come in. Take a seat."

Hank pushed the door open and stepped in, quickly realizing there were no empty chairs—just the two presently occupied by Nutskin and Brand, who was staring at him from the corner.

"That's okay," Hank said. "I'll stand." He looked to Brand, who showed no sign of leaving.

Nutskin swiveled in his chair to face him and Hank's eyes shifted to the window. "Blotter seemed a little . . . drab this week," he said.

Hank frowned. "Yeah, guess it did. I'll show you the reports. Most everything's a monster sighting. One woman saw it riding the Wonder Wheel at Coney." He shrugged. "Trying to avoid those, so I gotta work with what I got left."

"Parking violations?"

Hank nodded quickly. "It's what I got left. Pretty much the only thing people didn't try to pin on a monster. That and truancy, and even those damn kids are doin' their best to say an apeman did it."

"Mm-hm," Nutskin said. "That's sort of what I wanted to see you about."

Hank was afraid of that.

"Kalabander," Nutskin went on, adopting the pious tones he saved for speechifying. "The *Brooklyn Hornet* is a family newspaper, and our job is to . . ."

Our job, Hank thought, *is to deliver fucking grocery store coupons to the doorsteps of fat housewives and the elderly.*

". . . good things about living in Brooklyn," Nutskin was saying before Hank finally cut him off.

"Shed, Jesus. I know the spiel. What's the skinny? You wanted me to stay away from monster stories so we wouldn't scare our seven-year-old readers. So I didn't run any monster stories. Fine with me."

Nutskin nodded. "I know, and I appreciate that. But I'm wondering if it's not time we got on the bandwagon."

Hank looked over to Brand, who hadn't said a word. He turned back in Nutskin's general direction. "But what about it darkening up happy fun time?"

"It's a problem, yes I know. I can't say I'm thrilled with the idea . . ." He lifted a copy of that week's issue and held it up for Hank to see. The cover story's headline read, "Kentile Flooring to Extend Hours for Summer Madness Sale!"

"Have you seen the ads this week?" Nutskin laid the paper back on his desk and began flipping the pages. "Most of them make references to this Gowanus Beast . . . let's see . . . 'Monster savings,'" he read aloud. " 'Monster specials,' 'Beastly markdowns,' 'Save twenty percent if you've seen the Gowanus Beast.' Well, you get the idea."

"Wait," Hank said, confused. "I thought it was the Gowanus *Devil.* It's *Beast* now?"

Nutskin nodded. "Pine Barrens chamber of commerce sent out a C and D letter to every media outlet in town. Seems they hold copyright on 'devil' so now it's 'beast.' Get it?"

"Pretty much, yeah."

"This is clearly the biggest thing happening, and I don't think we can ignore it any longer."

Hank was quiet for a moment. He knew coming in here was a bad idea. Now his lower back felt like it was on the verge of buckling after standing still for so long. He turned to Brand, who seemed to flinch every time Hank looked in his direction. "I'm sorry, can I ask you a question?"

Brand's head twitched and Hank took it as a nod.

"How can you sit there normally like that with a colostomy bag? I mean, wouldn't everything get all blocked up? I've always been curious."

When it seemed obvious that Brand was too flummoxed to answer, Hank said, "That's okay. It's a private matter, I understand." He turned his eyes to Nutskin's shoulder. "And I still have no idea why you called me in here. You want me to put some stupid monster crap in the blotter? Fine. Consider it done. But you could've left that in the note too and skipped all this rigmarole."

"No, that's not exactly it," Nutskin said. "Stephen and I were talking . . ." He nodded to Brand. "And we thought you should be the one to start covering the story. After all, you're the one who broke it in the first place."

Hank looked from Nutskin, to Brand, then to the carpet.

"*God* no," he said.

* * *

"Hey, ya fat homo, fuck any goats lately?"

"Only your mother, dickhead. What makes you wanna waste my time today?"

It sounded like Crosslin was busy again. The office behind him was certainly livelier than usual, a clatter of voices and ringing phones.

"I'll keep it short. Miss Goody-Goody here just asked me to do a monster story."

"But you turned him down, of course, didn'cha, ya stupid son of a bitch?"

"Of course."

"Good man. No need to feed this thing. 'Less you think you can make it stop. But nah, don't even try. We got enough trouble over here."

"Yeah?" Hank asked. "Things getting stupid?"

Crosslin hacked directly into the receiver and Hank heard him spit, he hoped into a trash can or nearby spittoon. "Ah," Crosslin said when he was finished. "Nothin' we can't handle." (Hank had learned that by "handle" Crosslin meant "ignore.")

"We get a couple a day in here," the lieutenant continued. "Mostly fretful types, don'cha know? Neurotics seein' shadows. Ain't as bad as the papers make it sound. But it still takes paperwork, so it's a pain in the ass. Plus I gotta deal with assholes like yourself all day, an' I'll tell ya, they never fuckin' listen."

As Crosslin spoke, an idea started to mutate in Hank's brain. Once it had taken shape, he realized he hadn't been paying attention to what the lieutenant had been saying. "So . . . what was that again?" he asked.

Crosslin slammed the phone down. Hank frowned and replaced his own receiver in the cradle. He folded his arms and leaned back in his chair.

Maybe, he thought.

As one of the only sane and rational men apart from Khalid left in New York City (in spite of what his wife might think), and being the reporter behind the piece that started the whole frenzy (in spite of what everyone else might think), Hank Kalabander knew that it was now his responsibility to prove there was no such thing as the Gowanus Devil, or Beast, or whatever the hell they were calling it now. It was up to him to make people understand that what had driven perhaps thousands of supposedly cultured and sophisticated New Yorkers all koo-koo bananas was nothing more than a simple, old-fashioned case of mass hysteria.

He may not have spent any time in (or even near) journalism school. He might not know what "deep background" meant and he still had trouble with the word "allegedly," but he had no trouble at all telling people they were a bunch of superstitious boneheads.

He ignored the stabbing pain in his knees and pushed himself out of his chair. He took a deep breath and headed for Nutskin's office.

Allegedly, he reminded himself on the way.

Fourteen

The brown corduroy sport jacket was ragged around the cuffs and the elbows had been worn thin nearly to the point of transparency. Slipping into it, he realized why he hadn't worn it in ten years. But it was his only jacket, so it was his only choice. Hell, he rationalized, investigative reporters aren't supposed to dress all snappy anyway. They never did in the movies. The jacket had been covered in plaster dust when he first pulled it from the closet, but he'd been able to shake most of it off in the hallway.

"I still don't think this is the best idea you've ever had," Annie warned as he admired himself in the mirror.

"No?" he asked, concentrating on the cigarette burn over the right pocket. "And what would the best one be, suggesting we do something about that bathroom faucet?"

She slapped him on the shoulder from behind. "I'm just worried about you going out there in this nasty old jacket in this heat. Remember what the doctor said."

"Yes, yes, yes," Hank sighed, turning and giving her a kiss on the forehead to shut her up.

"I also worry about the people you're going to see. Why can't you just call them? They can't kill you if you're on the phone."

Hank shook his head. That kiss obviously hadn't taken. "Not as effective as talking to them face to face. Rule number one of journalism."

"You just made that up."

"You see any news lately? Seems most journalists are just making it up. So let's see if I can find out what's really going on." He kissed her again, harder this time. "Humor me. I know what I'm doing." He grabbed his empty briefcase (that was for effect) and made sure his notepad and pen were in his pocket. He reached for the door and opened it. "See you tonight," he told her. "Unless . . . you know."

He stepped into the hall and closed the apartment door firmly behind him.

The place to start was the beginning, he figured. To date, Chuck Pierce—the first person to claim he saw the beast—had refused to talk to the press. This perhaps made sense from Pierce's perspective, Hank thought. But he also thought it was simply because those other hacks were lazy and hadn't tried hard enough.

It didn't take him long to track down an address, and another twenty minutes to get from the office to the Carroll Street station, which Hank recognized all too well now.

Once upstairs he checked the street signs, took a right, and started walking. Three blocks later he closed in on the address he was looking for.

It was a nice block, one of the few left in Brooklyn where most of the houses actually had something resembling a front lawn. Most of the lawns, he noted, sported bathtub Marys, but that was no surprise, considering. Carroll Gardens was generally accepted as an upper-middle-class mob neighborhood. It was quiet there, and the neighbors took care of their own. Private social clubs dotted the commercial strips, as did nameless storefront operations that didn't sell any of the dusty, incongruous merchandise displayed in their front windows. Most important of all, there were no bars on the doors and windows of any of the houses, because there was virtually no crime to worry about. Nothing perpetrated randomly, anyway. That was something nobody ever pointed out about this first alleged assault—unless there were certain elements of the story that simply hadn't come to light yet.

Hank stood in front of a narrow, three-story, white paneled house and checked the address again. This was it. There was no Mary in the yard, which left Hank wondering if it made the Pierces pariahs among the neighbors.

He pushed open the wrought-iron gate, walked up to the front door, and rang the bell.

He had no idea what he was doing. He set the briefcase down and reached for the notepad.

From the other side of the door came the sound of locks turning and deadbolts sliding. Six, if he heard correctly. Finally the door opened a crack. The tired eye of an old woman stared out at him from just above the chain.

"Yeah?" she demanded in a hoarse croak.

"Hello, ah," Hank said, trying to be charming. He could feel the sweat running down the side of his face. "I was wondering if Chuck was home, please?"

"He ain't here," the old woman said. That eye was cold and hard.

"And might I take a guess that you're his mother?"

"I'm his manager."

"I . . . see," Hank said.

"Why?"

He expected this. She'd probably be just as suspicious if it was a cop on her doorstep, or Jesus, or the plumber she'd called ten minutes earlier. Hank tried to smile. "I'm sure you've probably had more than your share of this in recent days, ma'am, but I'm, ah, a reporter, and I was looking for—"

The door slammed shut. He was expecting that, too. At least the locks weren't snapping back into place yet. He rang the bell again.

Much to his surprise, the door opened a crack.

"Hello again," Hank addressed the suspicious eye. "Look, I know this must be annoying—I tried to call earlier—"

"Had to take the damn phone off the hook."

"I can understand that," said Hank, who had never actually tried to call. "It must be crazy."

"What's your offer?"

"Pardon?"

"Your *offer*. How much?"

"How much . . . what?"

"We ain't givin' no free interviews. You're just gonna make fun of my boy, and if you're gonna do that, we might as well get something out of it. He saw what he saw."

"I don't doubt that, Mrs. Pierce." Hank quickly swabbed his sweaty face with a sweaty hand. "And I can understand wanting to get something out of it and make your life worthwhile. You still have a thirty-four-year-old kid living at home, after all. I'm just trying to figure out what it was your son saw." *Greasy, money-grubbing old hag*, he thought but knew he had to play along.

Mrs. Pierce seemed to consider this. "Where you from?" she asked.

"Originally? Trenton, I guess."

"What *show*?"

"Oh." Somehow he knew this wasn't going to go well, even before he left the apartment that morning. "I'm, uh, I'm from the *Brooklyn Hornet*, ma'am."

"Never saw it, and I watch 'em all. That on cable?"

"No, it's . . . it's not a *show*, Mrs. Pierce. It's a newspaper. It comes out every week."

She considered this. The eye staring through the door narrowed. "That the thing gets dumped on my steps every week? The pennysaver?"

"I would guess it is, yes." Hank knew confessing he was from the *Hornet* would cause problems. He kicked himself for not telling her he was with the *Times* or *USA Today*.

"Piece a *crap*," she snapped. "Come 'round here and mess the neighborhood all up, make more work for me. Gotta pick it up and throw it away every week."

Hank was starting to lose the charm. He was tempted to stick his fingers in the door to keep it open, but he knew if he did he'd likely lose them. Maybe if he got a shoe in the door instead. He was suddenly tempted to poke a finger into that wet old eye staring at him.

"I'm very sorry about that, Mrs. Pierce, but believe me, I have nothing to do with distribution. I'll say something to the people in charge when I get back to the office."

She was still squinting with disgust. "An' your shitty rag *alread*y made fun of my boy. Before all them others got started."

He had been trying to formulate a suave new attack, but then stopped. "What did you just say?" He couldn't believe someone else knew. He almost wanted to thank the old crone, but the saner part of his psyche could tell from her tone this probably wasn't the time or place to go taking any credit for anything.

"*You started it!*" she yelled through the door. Hank heard her hand slap against the wood. "My boy got hurt, an' you called him *names*. And now look at how many people been hurt because of it!"

Hank took a step back, raising his hands. She seemed the type who kept the shotgun propped in an umbrella stand next to the door. Standing there, he also decided that now seemed like a good time to try that different approach.

"Ma'am, Mrs. Pierce," he said, hands still raised. "I'm sorry. I had no idea. And again, I assure you I had nothing to do with it . . . I had no idea we'd ever done anything like that to your boy. We're a nice paper. About nice things. Families an' such."

The door was still open, and she didn't seem to be reaching for the gun, so he went on. The sweat was flowing freely down his face now. The damn jacket was killing him.

"Tell you what, let's forget about it. No questions, no Chuck. I'll just grab my briefcase and leave." He replaced the notepad in his pocket. "But before I go, do you think there's any way I could step inside and get a drink of water, maybe wash my face off in the bathroom? It's pretty brutal out here, and my doctor tells me it's no good for my heart."

If there was one thing Mrs. Pierce understood, it was doctors. How she hated doctors. She hated doctors even more than she hated newspapers.

After stepping back to let Hank inside, her personality changed completely. They shared a bond when it came to evil doctors, and now Hank was her guest.

He saw why there was no bathtub Mary in the front yard. It was the centerpiece of the shrine that dominated much of the Pierce living room. The statue of the Virgin Mary was surrounded by candles, rosaries, crucifixes of various detail, religious trading cards, and paintings of saints. In what space was left the living room was filled with overstuffed furniture upholstered in black leather and trimmed in brass tubing. On the wall was a three-by-four-foot oil painting of Jesus, sword held aloft, riding a white stallion through the clouds.

Mrs. Pierce was telling him about her endocrinologist when he took a step forward to examine a family portrait. Chuck was easy to pick out, the only boy among the five children. Standing uncomfortably off to the left beside his father, Chuck was a rotund kid in his twenties, dressed in a T-shirt whose orange and white stripes stretched tight across his belly like lines of latitude. The unhappy face looked vaguely familiar, but Hank thought everyone nowadays looked the same.

In the ten or so years since the photo was taken, to gauge from the woman in the picture, Mrs. Pierce had been through hell.

"So what does Mr. Pierce do?" he asked, pointing at the broad-shouldered man with the slick black hair.

"Oh, he was a contractor," Mrs. Pierce said. "But he died shortly after that picture was taken."

"I'm sorry to hear that." Hank was studying Chuck's dull face, looking for some hint of anything. "Was he sick?"

"It was an accident at the construction site. Some bricks fell."

"Yeah, that's awful," he said, giving up on the picture.

"Since then my Chucky's taken care of me."

"Uh-huh. Great. Now, where's your bathroom?"

"Up these steps," she pointed. "To your right,"

Lining the wall up the staircase was a series of framed eight-by-ten reproductions of Emmett Kelly clown paintings. *Five minutes ago she would've shot me if she'd had a gun. Now she's sending me upstairs alone.*

After washing up and getting a drink in the bathroom (the fluffy pink toilet seat cover matched the bath mat, the curtains, and the

Dixie cups stacked beside the sink), he took his time heading back to the staircase.

As he neared the first door next to the bathroom, he stopped. It was open.

There was no question that this was Chuck's bedroom. Pennants hung on the walls touting local high schools that had closed a decade earlier. The beer can collection lined the shelves above the bed. And the bed itself—much to Hank's delight—was made of fiberglass and shaped like a race car. Socks and underwear were scattered on the floor and dangling over the back of a chair. He knew if he had only five minutes, he'd be able to find the secret stash of battered skin magazines.

This was all too perfect—so much so it almost felt like a setup.

Something caught his eye. A small bookshelf not filled with beer cans. Checking over his shoulder, Hank tiptoed into the room. He prayed the thick shag carpeting would cover the noise. He knew he had to move fast.

There were five books on the shelf: a paperback horror novel with a textured cover, an illustrated book about monster movies, a well-worn video game guide from 1987, something called *The Devil's Triangle Two*, and—bingo—*The Hunt for Bigfoot.*

The real jackpot was on the next shelf down, where Chuck stored his small DVD collection. He had *National Lampoon's Animal House* and *The Norseman*, as Hank would have expected. But the remaining six movies on the shelf were *The Capture of Bigfoot*, *The Abominable Snowman*, *The Creature from Black Lake*, *The Legend of Boggy Creek*, *Snowbeast*, and *They Call Him Sasquatch.*

Well, I think we have all we need here, folks, Hank thought. *Move along.*

He pocketed the Bigfoot paperback and headed for the stairs.

* * *

Annie was right. Running around outside in this punishing heat wearing a corduroy jacket was simple foolishness. You didn't see anyone else out there in corduroy. No, he decided a block away from the Pierce house, he'd do the rest of his running around from his desk. It wasn't much cooler in the office, but at least he could sit and avoid moving. And he'd take off the damn jacket.

Determining how best to follow the investigation from there wasn't difficult. He already had the police reports from the hooker and the junkie, and they were both quoting from his story about Pierce anyway, so there was no pressing need to talk to them.

He'd seen Pierce's picture and his room, and these two alone should've been proof enough that the first witness had apemen on the brain long before any of this began. For all of it, he still needed something else to pad out his damning exposé.

More important than all the dotty softheads who claimed they had seen this thing were the few sober individuals left in town who hadn't seen anything yet, and didn't expect to see anything. Only problem was finding them. Hank figured he knew where to start looking.

A woman picked up the phone on the third ring. "Brooklyn Zoological Park," she announced.

After waiting on hold for five minutes—a stretch during which his eyes once more gravitated toward Topsy—Hank was put through to Dr. Satoshi Nakamura, one of the zoo's chief veterinarians.

"Mr. Kalabander," Dr. Nakamura said in those crisp tones, Hank noted, you so often heard in second-generation Japanese Americans. "I must admit I'm rather startled to hear from someone in the press."

"You mean nobody's contacted you about this apeman business yet?"

"Not a one. But why would they? They're looking for a monster, and all we have here are plain old real animals."

That made a lot of sense. "Yeah, can't say I'm all that surprised, Hank told him. "A mysterious creature of unknown origin makes for a hell of a lot better copy than a logical scientific explanation."

"I can't promise to give you an explanation, but—*oohh!*" Dr. Nakamura chirped inexplicably, then started laughing.

"You okay there, ah, doctor?"

"Oh, yes," Dr. Nakamura said, the laughter dissipating. "I've just never been interviewed before . . . it's very exciting."

Hank sighed. "Uh-huh." He waited while the doctor got himself back under control.

"Ah, so," Dr. Nakamura said. "You want to know what I think about this monster."

"Yes, I guess that's—"

"The Japanese know a great deal about monsters, you know, though ours, on the whole, tend to be much larger than this pip-squeak here. Is that the proper word? Pip-squeak?"

"Um," Hank replied. "Yeah . . . pip-squeak would do it."

"Ah, very good then!" Once more, Dr. Nakamura began to giggle. "Am I doing okay so far, pip-squeak?"

Hank wondered silently how it was he always seemed to find them. "You're doing fine, doctor," he said. "So why don't we get started? Now . . ." Hank looked down at the legal pad in front of him. He'd jotted down a few questions before calling the zoo. "I just need to check this. As you may have seen, a number of the reports in the press speculate that the creature in question, should it exist, is some kind of a large primate. I was just calling to see—given that the first sightings were closer to your zoo than any other—if you happened to be missing any, you know, gorillas."

"I'm very sorry, Mr. Kalabander," Dr. Nakamura said, sounding apologetic. "But we do not have gorillas here, though I wish we did. All we have here are baboons. Lots of pip-squeak baboons."

Hank closed his eyes. This whole thing was turning into much more work than he anticipated. "Okay, then, are you missing any *baboons*?"

"Oh, no," Dr. Nakamura assured him. "We have not lost any baboons. That would be a terrible thing. Nasty creatures, these baboons. And lusty! It's like a pornographic movie down there some days."

"I'm . . . ," Hank said, not sure how to respond to that. "Good."

"And all the sea lions are present and accounted for, sir. We also have a capybara and a red panda, but they're still here as well. I'm sorry. I could go count the kangaroos if you like."

"That really won't be necessary, no," Hank said. "I'm glad everything's in order at the zoo. But would you care at all to speculate, as a professional, as to what this thing might be, from the descriptions you've read?"

Dr. Nakamura pondered the question for a bit. "Well," he said at last, sounding almost serious, "as a professional, I can tell you that it's not a baboon. Not ours or anyone's. If it had been a baboon, the injuries these people sustained would have been much more extensive. More than simple scratches and scrapes . . . It might be a gorilla, but I think we would've heard of any escaped gorillas in the vicinity. No, he's much more mysterious than that. Nocturnal. Hmmm . . ."

Hank waited as Nakamura thought aloud.

"*Oooh!*" the doctor peeped excitedly. "Have you ever seen the movie *Ju jin yuki otoko*?"

"Um, no . . . I, ah, can't quite recall that one coming through, no."

"Well, from a professional standpoint, I think that's what you're dealing with."

Hank waited for some further explication but nothing seemed to be forthcoming.

"Oh," he said. At the bottom of the page of notes he'd scribbled, Hank wrote the word "Jew."

After spending the next few minutes assuring Dr. Nakamura that he had done an outstanding job as an interviewee, Hank thanked him for his time and hung up. He opened a new file and hurriedly typed up his notes of the conversation. Those that seemed to matter, anyway. If the escaped gorilla theory was correct, Brooklyn Zoo was the only local place that made any sense. He couldn't imagine anything escaping from the Bronx or Central Park zoos, getting on a train or walking across the bridge, making it down to the Gowanus, and yelling booga-booga at a drunk without once being noticed. And if there was nothing missing from Brooklyn, well, so much for that silly theory.

Of course there was always the possibility that the thing—if there was something out there (and he didn't believe there was)—was someone's pet. They'd caught that guy in Harlem a few years back with the lion and the alligator in his apartment, and that other guy with the tiger. If someone's illegal pet gorilla escaped he could understand why the owner wouldn't report it to the cops.

Hank shook a terrible joke from his head. That was a real long shot, so he decided to set it aside as he returned to typing up his Nakamura notes.

He didn't think it necessary to report Nakamura's own theory that the monster was really a Jew. That would only get people riled up more.

* * *

"Good afternoon, Plum Island Animal Research Center." The woman sounded pleasant and chipper.

"Ah, good," Hank said. "It took me a while to find a number. This is the Plum Island Research Center, right?"

"No, sir, I'm afraid you have the wrong number."

"But you just said—"

"No, I didn't say any such thing." She still sounded pleasant.

"Listen, this is very simple. There's a ridiculous story about some kind of wild monster roaming the streets of New York, and a number of fingers have been pointed at Plum Island, so I'm just trying to get a statement from someone there regarding—"

"I'm sorry sir, I wish I could help you, but you've obviously dialed the wrong number."

"No, it's really just . . . when I first called—"

"Wrong number. I've never heard of any such place. What was it you called it? Peach Grove?"

"Okay, tell you what. Let's make it a hypothetical. Just me talking to you, a regular citizen, and asking you what you think. Now, if there *did* happen to be a secret government research lab off the coast of Long Island, and if they *did* do secret animal experiments there, do you think it's at all possible that one of these animals—some sort of primate, just to use an example—could've escaped recently and might now be wandering the streets of New York, scaring people?"

He wasn't quite sure at what point during his hypothetical question she hung up.

Thank god Hank had another idea. A possibility nobody else had mentioned yet. Not in so many words, anyway. He looked up another number. Before he began dialing, however, he stood and checked around the corner to make certain the other cubicles were empty.

Becky, he knew, was off to another daylong event at some rest home, and that little puke Rusty was off celebrating Brooklyn commerce in some incredibly tedious fashion. Good. He returned to his seat and picked up the receiver.

A nervous young man answered the phone. "Parkfield Psychiatric."

"Hi, yeah," Hank said. "Could you tell me if Dr. Alvero Contreas is available, please?"

Again he was put on hold, surprised and relieved to learn that Alvero was still there. Better still, he was in his office.

As he waited, he patted his shirt pocket expecting to find a pack of cigarettes waiting there. Finding nothing, he idly began doodling pictures of bunnies on fire. He heard a click and then a voice on the other end.

"Henry!" the delighted voice chimed. "So good to hear from you."

"It's good to hear you, too, doctor," he said. "What goes on?"

"Oh, fine, fine. And yourself? That's the important question."

"Oh, fine, yeah. Gotta job, gotta wife."

"No problems?"

Hank thought for a moment, ticking through his assorted problems. "Nothing worth mentioning, no."

"Very good, then. I'm happy to hear that. Nothing like what had . . . ?"

"No, none of that. Not at all," Hank cut him off. No need to hear about it again. "I'm just fine. Really."

"Ah, very good. Then to what do I owe the pleasure?"

"Well, doctor," Hank said. This guy was always so goddamn chirpy.

"I'm calling on business, actually. See, I'm a reporter now, and—"

"A reporter!" Dr. Contreas exclaimed. "Well, look at you! That's simply delightful. Tell me, who are you reporting for? The *Wall Street Journal*? I would expect nothing less from you."

This was starting to scrape on Hank a bit. Wonderful man, the doc, but a little overbearing. "Something like that, yeah." He just wanted to get on with things. "See, I'm working on a story about this monster you may have heard about. In Brooklyn."

"Oh," Contreas said. His voice had shifted. He was much quieter. "Are you sure that's wise?"

Hank immediately realized how it must have sounded, especially to Dr. Contreas. "Oh . . . now . . . let me explain. See, I'm trying to find a logical explanation for what these people say they're seeing. If there is anything at all out there. Personally, I think we're dealing with a case of mass hysteria, but I'm checking on some plausible, non-monster explanations."

"Explanations that don't involve demons or ghosts or . . . ?"

"Right. No. I'm trying to tell people there's nothing out there."

"I must say you had me worried there for a moment."

"No worries. My wife's keeping a close eye on me."

"I'm glad. You'll have to tell me all about her sometime. But you're saying you've told her then? About your time here?"

"No," Hank admitted flatly. He didn't feel like dealing with this shit now, or ever again.

"Why not?" the doctor pressed.

"Saw no reason for it," Hank explained. "Now, why I'm calling. I'm just trying to see if you're aware of any patients at any of the area psychiatric facilities who happen to be missing at the present time. I'm especially interested in any who might be particularly, you know . . . *hairy*?"

Dr. Contreas thought about this. "As . . . ," he said, "for the latter,

I can't say. As for the former, though, no. No one has walked away recently. Nobody who wasn't supposed to, anyway."

"You sure? Everyone's present and accounted for? I mean, I haven't seen anything reported about nuts on the loose but . . . you know. Not everything gets reported."

"No, we haven't had anyone go missing in some time. No breaches in security. And certainly not anyone who could pose any kind of a threat. Although I shouldn't need to remind you of this anymore, Henry, we'd appreciate it if you wouldn't use that word."

Yeah, go talk to my wife, Hank thought. "All right, then," Hank said, ignoring the scolding. "That's all I wanted to know. Thanks, Doctor Contreas, and take good care."

"You, too, Henry. Please be careful. And feel free to stop by for a visit anytime. By the way, were you ever able to resolve that matter regarding the bill?"

"Um," Hank started to say, then quickly hung up. A sudden chill tore through his body and he trembled violently for an instant, arms wrapped tight around his chest. He wasn't expecting it to hit him that way. In a city full of shrinks, why in the hell had he called Contreas? Never even got to ask him the flip-side questions, about the copycats who claim they see monsters after hearing someone else had.

Well, fuck it. He didn't need to ask Contreas. He could figure that one out for himself.

He took a deep breath, wishing again he still smoked. He was glad he had one more call to make. It would help wash the acrid taste of that shrink out of his head.

He checked the clock. It was three forty-five. He picked up the receiver, dialed, and waited.

"Sorry to break your concentration, there, Rochester," he said when the familiar and gruff voice picked up. "Gotta question for you."

Fifteen

That was a weird goddamn phone call, Rocky thought, as he hit the disconnect button and returned the phone to the inside pocket of his vest. Hank had asked him only a single stupid question. And now Rocky had to get back to him later with the answer.

It could wait. Right now he had a paper to read. Hank was probably just drunk off his ass anyway, and wouldn't even remember calling.

"Hey, Rock, you gonna help out over here, or what?"

Rocky was sitting on an overturned barrel, chewing on a dead cigar and flipping through a Rhode Island paper one of the crew had dropped.

"Yeah, uh-huh," he said, without moving. His six-man crew was in the process of breaking down after a worthless five-day gig. Around him, the entire show was coming down. That afternoon they were loading the trucks and heading for Towshoe, West Virginia, just outside Wheeling.

Every crew on the lot was trying to claw its way through the morning stupor, but Rocky's crew seemed to take a certain pride in it, a bunch of skinny white boys with pencil mustaches, dirty bandannas, jailhouse tattoos, and track marks where there should be no track marks.

Thank god for crank, Rocky thought as he turned the page. With the next inevitable fistfight due to break out any minute now—you could gauge it by their voices—he figured it was wiser to supervise from at least thirty feet away. Blount had been on his ass for his management style, too, but screw it—his boys punched themselves out pretty quickly, and he didn't need to get his head busted while he was waiting.

As his eye neared the bottom of the page he stopped. The cold cigar between his teeth drooped. It was a small item on a page devoted to oddball stories from around the nation. Those stories were a showman's dream, and in this case a little more than that.

"Monster Stalks NYC," the headline read. It concerned an estimated three hundred and fifty sightings of a hairy, humanoid creature dubbed the "Gowanus Beast" by the local media. The moniker, the story explained, referred to the first sightings, which took place near the Gowanus Canal, an industrial waterway in western Brooklyn.

Suddenly Hank's stupid question made all the sense in the world.

Rocky sped through the wire story searching for any pertinent details, then checked the date on the front page. It was yesterday's. (He'd learned a long time ago that not checking the date could lead to a world of shit.)

He folded the paper, shoved it under his arm, and jumped off the barrel. "Whitey!" he barked around the cigar. "Git your ass over here."

"But *Rock*," the roustabout whined, "I gotta kick this guy's ass."

"Yeah, you'll do it later. Just get over here."

A shirtless, sickly-looking kid of twenty-five with a coil of rope over his sunburned shoulder gingerly stepped across the nylon carcass of the tent toward him.

"What is it, boss? You hear what Stan called me?"

Rocky ignored the question and took a few steps away from the tent. "C'mere, got a proposition for ya—and you crack wise you'll be shittin' that rope."

"Yeah?" Whitey looked down at Rocky with lifeless eyes and a burning cigarette dangling from the left corner of his mouth, next to what had become a suspicious and painful cold sore.

Rocky closed his eyes for just an instant. "Whitey, I'm in a hurry here, see? So let's make this quick. You been part of my crew longer'n any o' these other gazoonies, right?"

"Sure," he said. He never seemed to blink, this kid.

"'Bout six years now, right? *Right?* A lotta setups in a lotta towns."

"Sure, uh-huh." Whitey almost nodded.

"So in Towshoe I'm gonna give you a little test, see, an' let you run the setup all by your lonesome." Then Rocky squeezed his chin between thumb and forefinger. "No, more'n that. That whole stint, you get to run the show. Think of it as opportunity knockin' on your door. Howzat, huh? It's a carny's dream. All yours. An' to sweeten the deal, I'll throw in an extra fiver a week. So what more couldja ask? You got power and money, all right there. You'll be the fuckin' king o' Towshoe." He smiled, and the cigar pointed skyward.

Whitey shifted the rope from one shoulder to the other. "I don't get it. Why?"

Rocky pulled the cigar out of his mouth and spat. "Don't go lookin' a gift horse, kid. I could tell ya it's 'cause I think you got a bright future, that I respect you and have faith in you . . . but the truth is, I gotta run and I need a placeholder. An' you're it. Remember, an extra five a week."

Whitey shrugged. "I guess."

"Great, you start immediately," Rocky said, slapping him with the rolled-up newspaper before heading to his small trailer.

"But wait, Rock!" Whitey called after him. "Whaddo I tell Blount when he comes nosin' around?"

Rocky stopped and turned. "Tell him not to get all wormy. I'm comin' back sooner'n he'd like, an' when I do, I'm gonna have the best goddamn live act he's ever seen. I'm gonna clean the fuckin' midway." He thought a moment. "You can also tell him that he can shove that fuckin' Johnny Macabro up his ass!"

"Okay," Whitey answered, before heading off to tell the rest of the crew.

Fifteen minutes later, after packing a small bag and making sure there was nothing left in the trailer worth stealing, Rocky locked the flimsy door and headed down the midway, through the skeletons of the Zipper, the Slave Galley, the Hydrox Whoozee, the flat stores, the alibi stores, the wiener stands, and the duck ponds. He swung to his right to the Girl-to-Gorilla tent.

The banner was gone, but apart from that they hadn't started the teardown yet. Every jump, they were always the last to get out.

He stuck his head in the tent flaps and called, "Hey, *Fatty*! Where the hell are ya?"

He heard a noise from near the stage. "Hey, Rock, Fatty's not here."

He saw a woman of about forty-five in a red sequined bikini. She had a screwdriver in her hand and was in the process of dismantling the aluminum cage.

"Hey, Ms. Hammond," Rocky said, licking his palm and slicking down what little hair he had left. "Any idea where I can find him? Got a question."

"Call me Helga," she said in her thick Hungarian accent, hopping off the makeshift stage and approaching Rocky through the mildewed gloom of the tent. "Fatty's not here so it's okay."

"Hm," Rocky said. "I need to run, but I bet you can answer my question, can'tcha?"

"I can try." She slid the screwdriver into the waistband of her bikini bottom.

"Um." Rocky suddenly couldn't remember the question. When he redirected his eyes away from the screwdriver it came back to him. "Oh yeah. I'm wonderin' about the gorilla suit you guys use, see? The one for the act."

Helga stared at him. "We don't use a gorilla suit."

"Well whatever kind of costume it is, then. The thing you turn into for the trick."

She stared again. "There is no trick."

Rocky pursed his lips. He didn't need this crap, even from Helga. "C'mon Helga, I'm not a chump here, I just want to see the suit."

She removed the screwdriver again. "And I am telling you, Rocky. There *is* no costume. There *is* no trick."

As was the case most every evening, Hank and Annie were on the couch, watching the local news. Hank was finding the once comfortable routine more and more difficult.

"Oh, please god, no," Hank said after the anchor announced the network had conducted a series of man on the street interviews concerning the Gowanus Beast. Annie reached over and pulled his hands away from his eyes.

"Instead of just reading Stone's articles, you should listen to what people are really saying."

"They should never ask people what they think," he said. "It does nothing but illustrate why democracy doesn't work."

On the screen, a young, attractive woman wearing a black knit cap was seated in front of the fountains at Rockefeller Center. The subtitle identified her as a student named "Starshine."

"I'm gonna fuckin' puke," Hank said.

"Shhh."

"I think it must have magical powers, whatever it is?" Starshine told the reporter. Her voice was indistinguishable from Becky's. "Because? Otherwise? How could it appear and disappear that way without, like, anyone else seeing it?"

Hank held his tongue.

A grandmother visiting from Belgium, while never having seen the creature, somehow knew it was covered in shaggy black hair the exact consistency of flax, and that it weighed seven hundred and eighty pounds. No, countered a Hispanic man on his way home from work, it was actually three feet tall, gray, hairless, had glowing red eyes, and made people think it was big and hairy only through its mind-clouding abilities. And he knew this because his cousin saw it in her backyard.

Wrong again, insisted a sanitation worker from Queens. It actually looks like a green monkey but wears a copper helmet and it has long metal claws at least eight inches long. That's why people who see it always get scratched up that way.

Finally the voice of reason appeared: a Court Street lawyer who thought the only possible explanation for there being so many radically different descriptions of the Beast is that, in realty, it's a shape-shifting Indian demon.

Annie stared at Hank for a long time, waiting. When he did speak his voice was dead.

"We are so screwed."

Sixteen

It was shortly before seven and Mickey Jiminez was on his way to work at Paddy O'Hara's Bar and Grill off Union Street, a few blocks west of Grand Army Plaza. As he passed a narrow alleyway between two residential buildings he heard something move. Never being the sort who could mind his own damn business (a trait he'd acquired from his mother), Mickey stopped to investigate. Gustav, his supervisor, would understand if he was a few minutes late.

Deep in the shadows of the alleyway crouched a strange figure, broad at the shoulders and even broader at the belly. It had a beard and was gazing into some kind of machine Mickey had never seen before. It was oval shaped, and he could see a number of electronic dials glowing orange and white in the darkness. Clusters of wires sprang from the bottom of the disc and a long cord led to what appeared to be a wand or microphone of some kind. The man was slowly passing the electric wand (or whatever it was) over an overturned garbage can. What struck Mickey most about the scene was the man's long purple velvet cape.

He sure didn't look like one of the gangstas or dealers Mickey sometimes spotted around the neighborhood. Maybe one of the pimps. Mickey'd been hearing those monster stories everyone was talking about, but this guy sure didn't look like any monster. He was way too dorky.

"Hey man," Mickey called as he took a step forward. The man's head snapped up, a look of panic in his eyes.

"*Shhh!*" the man said.

Mickey took another step. "Hey man, wha'chu doin' in there?"

"*Shhh!*" the man repeated and turned his attention back to his dials.

"Hey man, I'm *talkin'* to you."

With a snort of frustration, the man in the cape hit a button on the alien device and the dials went dark.

The man stood upright, his expansive belly seeming to blossom as he did so. Only then could Mickey see that the front of the man's shirt was covered with ruffles. "I hope thou art *proud* of thyself, young sir," the bearded stranger groused portentously. "Thou hast *ruined* some very important readings. Now I must suggest thou depart from these regions forthwith." He offered a dramatic flourish of his cape.

Mickey was a bit dumbfounded by this. He was accustomed to dealing with shithouse crazies, but this guy was something special. "What's your problem, boss?"

"Ah, troubles may burden my hoary head indeed," the fat man said bowing his head briefly. "Yet whilst I am faced with numerous scourges human, divine, and otherwise in origin, at this moment of our brief passing, mine and thine, I am most afeared that none of them involve puny guttersnipes such as thyself. Now begone!"

That one had Mickey stymied. "What th' fuck are you talking about?"

The fat man looked annoyed.

"I beseech thee again, kind ox-headed youth," he said with another whip of his cape, "to depart me in peace. Whereupon I may continue my delicate investigations into the shadow world men dare not say is real."

This wasn't worth having his pay docked, Mickey decided. "Yeah, you're *nuts*, man," he said, before stepping back out to the sidewalk. He just prayed the crazy motherfucker didn't find his way over to Paddy's later.

The one thing Hank had to admit was true was that while New Yorkers were being criminally stupid about the Gowanus Beast, and while they wouldn't shut the hell up about it, they simply didn't seem terribly *frightened* of it. They weren't screaming through the streets with torches and pitchforks, trampling neighbors underfoot and setting fire to bodegas. Even those primitive souls who claimed it had attacked them seemed almost proud of the fact, like it had granted them some special status. They were never that badly hurt, after all—no one had been hospitalized for the contusions and scratches they'd received in their alleged encounter. To hear the victims tell it, the monster merely bumped into them and moved on. And to hear some of the examining doctors tell it, many of the scratch marks on the victims seemed to be self-inflicted. (The media people tended to ignore those doctors.)

The heat still hadn't broken by the second Monday in August, and as a result Hank was in a mood.

He had picked up that morning's *Eagle* and opened it to find something he had been waiting to see for some time. The tired artist's sketch of the Beast had been replaced, finally, with a two-page spread of alleged photographs of the creature snapped by the paper's readers.

As expected, the *Eagle*'s marketing people were all over this one, with an inundation campaign of teaser ads that began running a week in advance. And, also as expected, the end product—the first example of physical evidence to be offered—was less than mind-blowing. Most of the photos had been shot on the fly with cell phones, all of them were seriously out of focus, and not a one of them was of an imaginary man-beast.

Upon close examination, Hank was able to discern three obvious shrubs, one dead tree, one fire hydrant, and four large dogs. The rest were clearly human, unless the Beast had taken to wearing skirts, jogging shorts, and flip-flops. The photo collection immediately went viral on the Internet.

I really gotta get going on this story, he thought as he closed the newspaper. Over the weekend he'd been thinking he had everything he needed but now, in retrospect, all of that research he'd done was pretty useless, he concluded. No one on his expert panel had told him anything. So now what was he supposed to do?

When the phone rang the entire left side of his body twitched. His phone never rang.

"What?" he said after picking it up.

"You gotta get down to the Third Street bridge!" a breathless woman shouted on the other end. At first he didn't recognize the voice.

"Stone?" he asked.

"*Yes!* Yes, it's Stone. Now c'mon, you gotta hurry. Third Street bridge, west side of the canal. I'll meet you there."

Hank didn't move. "What in the hell are you talking about?"

He heard Stone's strangled gurgle of frustration. "They just found a kid's body under the bridge, all tore up. I think it's our guy. Heard it on the scanner. Come on! *Move!*"

Hank remained motionless. "Why are you calling me with this?"

Stone had no time to waste on explanations. "Because I *feel* bad, okay? Thought I'd do you a solid to make up. Let's *go*!"

"Fine, great," Hank said and hung up the phone. He turned back to the keyboard.

The phone rang again.

This time when he picked it up, Stone screamed, "*Now! Now! Now!*" then slammed down the phone.

He had no idea why, but Hank hung up the phone, left the office, and began trotting toward Third Street, praying he'd see a taxi somewhere along the way.

Hank was nearly delirious by the time he reached the dozen or so squad cars and emergency vehicles gathered on the west side of the Gowanus Canal. The Third Street bridge was another shabby, crumbling concrete structure that seemed unfit for pedestrians, let alone cars. Most of the officers were standing around at this point, drinking bottled water and chatting. No mobs of morbid curiosity seekers had gathered yet, leaving them little to do. There weren't even any other journalists around, no news helicopters thumping overhead. Hank was all alone. At least Stone hadn't sent him on a snark hunt.

He stopped for a moment outside the ring of official vehicles and put his hand to his burning chest. He was feeling a little faint. Best to compose himself before approaching the scene. He didn't want to go lumbering in there all knock-kneed and sweaty. He still wasn't sure why he was here. He also couldn't tell if the putrid stench hanging in the still air could be blamed on the canal alone or on the bloated, decaying corpse of the mangled child that supposedly lay beneath the bridge.

Something murky floated back to him. Just a line from somewhere. Part of one anyway, though he knew he'd never place it. Something about *a little boy's dead body under there.* It made him uneasy.

No matter. It faded back into the fog.

After his breathing had returned to normal, Hank began weaving through the cars toward the yellow police tape stretched across the foot of the bridge. He was three yards from the tape when he remembered something. He had no credentials whatsoever. He'd once asked Shed about getting an NYPD press pass for his blotter work but had been laughed at.

"Well, goddammit," he wheezed. Turning and leaving at this point probably wouldn't look so hot. Not with that cop watching him. They'd probably take him in for questioning. His only other option was to continue moving forward hopelessly. He'd give it the ole college try anyway, because he was an idiot.

The officer standing by the tape scrutinized the disheveled and sweating man approaching him with suspicious distaste. "Help you with something, buddy?"

Hank's brain was racing. "Yeah, uh," he said. "My name's Henry Kalabander, I'm with the *Brooklyn hmmmlet* . . ." He swallowed that last word. "I hear you found a body down there." He pointed past the officer. "Just wondering if I can get a few details for the paper."

The officer folded his arms, looked him up and down, and positioned himself in Hank's line of sight. Hank's shirt was soaked and sticking to his stomach. The tip of his nose and his cheeks were glowing pink, though the rest of his face was a sickly, almost greenish pale. There was a look of anguish and pain in his eyes.

"May I see your press pass, please, sir?" the officer asked.

Hank reached into his pocket and grabbed his wallet. "It's

uhh . . ." He let the wallet flop open and began flipping through his cards. "It's uh right here . . . someplace . . ."

Fully aware that he was about to be sent away like a lost, unwanted street urchin, he pulled out one of the business cards the *Hornet* had given him. The card was yellow and featured a cartoon of a smiling bee wearing a sweater.

"Okay, I must've left the pass in my office but here's my card." He handed it over, but he couldn't look the officer in the eye. The officer peered at it briefly and began to smirk.

"Fine, yes," Hank said. "Just tell me what the story is."

The officer looked up at him, that wicked smirk still on his face. "I'm very sorry, Mr. Kala . . . Kal-a-bander," he said. "But I'm afraid there's been some mistake. There's no flower show going on here, and no sale in the meat department. I mean, the kid may *look* like chopped liver but . . ." He laughed uproariously, then turned and began walking away from Hank, holding the business card aloft. "Hey Bucky!" he called to an officer under the bridge. "You catch that one? I says to this guy . . ."

Hank grabbed hold of the tape with both hands but didn't try to cross it. He'd made that mistake before.

"Could you just answer a couple simple questions?" he shouted at anyone who might listen. "Are there any strange footprints around the body?"

"Yeah," someone shouted back. "We'll make sure they find *yours*, you don't shut the fuck up!"

Hank still had no idea why he was there. Why had he listened to Stone in the first place? Woman was a thief, after all. If this was a real story, wouldn't there be press swarming all over the place? It was all nothing but a sick prank and he was playing the goat on parade again. He turned away from the scene, his shoulders slumping. All that running through all this goddamn heat for nothing. And now he had the walk back to the office in front of him. He was not going to smell good by the time he got back there, he could guarantee that.

He was about to cross the street into the narrow shade afforded by the warehouses when a small, dented red Toyota screeched to a stop just beyond the emergency vehicles. Covering one of the rear windows was a piece of cardboard held in place with several strips of silver duct tape. The door squeaked open and out hopped what could only have been Louise Stone Jr. She was wearing a loosely knotted necktie over an oversized striped shirt, sleeves rolled up to the elbow. Covering the frizzy red hair was a logo-free baseball cap worn backward. Hank would've placed her in her late twenties but, as he'd grown older, his judgments of such things had only gotten worse.

Without noticing him, she headed straight for the police line, tape recorder slung over her shoulder, a black notebook and pen stuffed into her breast pocket.

"Stone?" Hank inquired as she drew closer.

The woman in the tie with the determined look on her face stopped. "Yeah?"

After everything, Hank wasn't sure if he should offer her his hand or not, so he didn't. "I'm Kalabander."

Stone's face brightened. She grabbed his hand from his side and began shaking it vigorously. "Why, Mr. Henry Kalabander, it is an honor. Hey, you beat me down here."

"Years of training."

"You leaving already?" She spoke rapidly and was still shaking his hand, like a hard-bitten but ditzy professional woman from a thirties screwball comedy. Her eyes kept darting to the bridge, as if to make sure it wasn't going anywhere while she stood there flapping her gums.

"Yeah, I'm heading out." Hank extracted his sweaty hand. "I think I got all I needed."

"So wha'd you find out? Was it a messy death?"

"Ever seen a clean one?" he asked. "It's a little kid, all right. Looks like chopped liver."

"Yeah?" she asked with a much too eager smile. "Boy or girl?"

Hank made a face. "To be honest, it's kinda hard to tell."

Stone was getting excited. *All that energy in this heat*, Hank thought. *Must be speed.*

"Really. Do you think it was . . . I mean, are there any signs?"

"Ah," Hank snorted with disdain. "That's hard to tell too. You know how careful these guys are around a crime scene. If there were any footprints there, they're gone now. If I'm not mistaken, this is the same bunch who investigated the Lindbergh kidnapping."

"Shit," Stone breathed, looking back to the bridge. "Look, I'm gonna go down and take a look myself anyway. It's great to meet you, though, a real honor. We gotta get together sometime and compare notes."

"Yeah," Hank said. "That'd be swell."

"Great. Gotta run. Deadlines, right?"

"Yeah," Hank said. "Tell me about it." Just as he was going to say something about the crummy pictures in that morning's *Eagle*, he saw Stone unzip her tape recorder bag and slip out a laminated NYPD press pass. "Wait a second," he said. "How'd you get one a' those? You're a freelancer. I mean, you write a *blog*."

"Oh," she said, admiring the pass proudly. "*Eagle* brought me on staff last week. They're payin' the rent, at least as long as this story lasts. So let's pray it has legs." She waved the pass over her head and headed for the yellow tape.

He watched as she flashed the pass at the officer who'd mocked him, ducked under the tape, and disappeared down the cracked cement embankment toward the base of the bridge.

Goddamn thief, he thought as he began walking north.

As he walked he caught a whiff of his shirt and knew he was starting to smell rank. But he couldn't tell if it was just his deodorant giving up the ghost or something he'd absorbed from that wretched canal.

As for the kid under the bridge, it was a story, and a mighty big one to boot. It just wasn't the story he was working on—the one he was supposed to turn in to Shed in two days.

Seventeen

As he was trying to leave the house the following morning, Hank encountered a gauntlet of three men on ladders in the small entryway. The one in the middle was drilling holes in the ceiling around the light fixture, and the two flanking him were hammering away without any apparent reason or goal on the exposed pipes and wires behind the torn walls. Although there was plastic sheeting carpeting the floor, it no longer served any purpose, as it had been spread atop the paint chips and plaster dust and broken boards, as well as a number of power tools. Hank didn't want to know. He waited patiently at the bottom of the stairs for someone to notice him. Trying to pick his way around them to the front door would only end in bloodshed.

Sometimes the best and the wisest and the only thing to do is calm the hell down, he figured. It was the working thesis of his story, and it seemed equally appropriate there in the entryway.

"Ah, Mister Caliban! How do you do?" the workman on the ladder to the left shouted upon noticing him.

"Yes, well," Hank replied.

All three workmen stopped what they were doing, stepped off the ladders, and pulled them aside so he could pass.

"Have a very nice day, Mister Caliban!"

"Yeah, you too, Mandingo," Hank muttered under his breath, waving back as he stepped through the unholy mess and out the door.

Before he even reached the subway, the *Eagle* headline caught his eye: "Gowanus Beast Kills B'klyn Boy, 8."

"Oh, Jesus Christ." He scanned the other newspapers and it appeared that Louise had herself another big scoop. None of the other papers mentioned the killing on the front page. That meant they either didn't know about the kid under the bridge or weren't aware that the crime had already been solved and that an apeman of some kind was responsible. Or maybe, like Hank, they saw no justifiable reason to connect the two. He was sorry to do it, but for once he had to betray Harry and buy his paper before getting on the train. He had to know how Stone had pulled it off, and what she'd seen under the bridge.

Once on the platform, he flipped the paper open to page 3 and folded it back. In spite of what the headline implied, it wasn't a very large story, most of the space on the page dominated by a grainy photo of the Third Street bridge and an insert of the most recent school photo of the smiling victim. Scanning the story quickly, Hank could find no mention of any evidence at the scene or quotes from NYPD officials connecting the Gowanus Beast with the mutilated child. There wasn't even any mention of the Gowanus Beast until the final paragraph.

Although police officials deny evidence of any connection between the creature and the brutal slaying of little Garfield Jones, they also admit that they have no evidence proving the creature wasn't responsible, and are awaiting the medical examiner's report before drawing any conclusions. If the Gowanus Beast is indeed responsible for slaughtering a defenseless child, then we are all in danger.

Hank read the final paragraph again in disbelief, thinking once more that someone really had to put a stop to all this foofarilla. *And that last sentence is just plain awful.*

He refolded the paper and dropped it on a nearby bench as, from deep in the tunnel, he heard the sound of the approaching train.

At noon, and clearly in direct response to Stone's cover story, Mayor William "Wild Bill" Rebane called an emergency press conference at City Hall in order to confront the ominous threat to the city of New York posed by the apparently murderous Gowanus Beast.

Hank was not invited to the press conference, which was all the same to him. Listening to it in his cubicle allowed him to quietly bang his head on his desk without bothering anyone except possibly Becky.

In his trademark weary, slow whine—the kind of voice that told you immediately he was simply no fun at parties—Mayor Rebane announced an immediate increase in the police presence throughout the five boroughs, concentrating on those areas where the creature had most often been sighted.

"The Wonder Wheel," Hank whispered as he continued banging his head. Becky, alarmed by the repetitive thumping, was watching him silently over the top of the cubicle wall.

Mayor Rebane also announced that security officials would be conducting a thorough search along the length of the Gowanus, and he encouraged all citizens to remain vigilant, suggesting they take a much closer look at their neighbors, "because you never can tell. We're clearly dealing with a devious fiend here."

"Devious fiend," Hank repeated, eyes closed, head banging lightly against the pressboard.

If it came to it, the mayor said, he would not hesitate to contact the governor about mobilizing the National Guard. He closed by saying that even though they had no idea who or what the creature was, or in fact even what it looked like, working together they would "track it down and kill it, in order to keep our families safe." Afterward, he took no questions.

As soon as the press conference ended, Hank picked up the phone and called Nutskin's office to request a few days' extension on that story deadline.

Once that was set, he called Lieutenant Crosslin. "Hey," he asked the moment Crosslin picked up. "You got anyone claiming their neighbor's the monster yet?"

"No," Crosslin said. "Why?"

"Don't worry, you will," Hank assured him before hanging up.

It was going to be a rough night.

No one could say that the mayor's speech coupled with Stone's cover story (at least the headline) hadn't been effective. By eight o'clock that evening, ad hoc Neighborhood Monster Watch groups had sprouted in Carroll Gardens, Crown Heights, and Bed-Stuy. By morning one person had been hit by a stray bullet and two shop windows had been smashed—though it was unclear if these incidents were the work of an overzealous monster patrol or fourteen-year-old hooligans.

"Mencken was right," Annie said as she cast a worried eye out the window, listening for any approaching mobs.

"About what?" Hank asked behind her.

"About everything. Us." She turned to him. "I'm worried about the store. These aren't the sort of people who take kindly to books."

"It'll be okay tonight," Hank said, holding a fresh beer out to her. “Shop’s too far off the beaten track. Right now they’re too chickenshit to step foot off their own blocks. But keep an eye on things. It could get worse. Unless.” His eyes drifted off to a corner as he fell silent.

“Unless what?”

“Unless we take the crazy gamble that if these baboons read anything at all they read the *Hornet*.”

Eighteen

Sweating as he was, he marched to the office with an energy he hadn't felt in years. It was rage more than anything, he recognized. Along the sidewalks down the commercial strip outside the building, the street vendors were out early, hawking Gowanus Beast T-shirts, bobbleheads, postcards, and jewelry.

Hank stopped in front of a table where a short, elderly Korean woman was offering eight different "Gowanus Beast" T-shirt designs.

"How do you do it?" Hank asked her. "I mean, how do you get this shit out so fast?"

"Large, extra-large only," the woman said. "No extra-extra. Twenty dollar."

Following the mayor's speech, editorial writers and bloggers were beginning to expand and develop their theories not only concerning what the Gowanus Beast *was* but what it *meant*. Although it was clear to Hank that the monster was being used by the mass media and government officials as a distraction from more pressing but less exciting issues, suddenly it had become a symbol of those very issues. The pundits were out in force, pontificating over what it might represent in terms of the war, the economy, the national mood, the energy crisis, and the environment. Especially the environment, considering no matter whose jackass theory you accepted, the filthy, poisonous Gowanus Canal was connected with the Beast in some way. Either that or the government's (nonexistent) animal research center out on Plum Island. Pretty much the same difference. It all left Hank fuming.

He said hello to Becky (who had deigned to start speaking with him again, apparently), snapped on his computer, and set to work. First thing he did was get online and start looking for the most ridiculous cryptozoology site he could find.

By four o'clock, after checking and rechecking everything he could think to check, and after reading it through three times, Hank was finished. His first feature, and it was a damn good one, if he said so himself.

Then he decided to give it one more read before passing it along to Nutskin. Hell, he had until five.

Night of the Feebleminded

by Henry Kalabander

German philosopher Friedrich Nietzsche once wrote: "Madness is something rare in individuals but with groups, parties, peoples, and ages it's the rule." Over the past weeks, New York has certainly proven him right.

It started quietly in these pages, and if I had my way that's where it would have stayed. A tiny item in the weekly crime blotter about an admittedly drunken buffoon who claimed he was assaulted by a hulking, smelly, apelike creature in the early morning hours of July 8. It was no different from any of the other items in the blotter.

But then something happened. And what happened is that other media outlets gave the story much more attention and space than it probably deserved. When media outlets decide something is a big story, it becomes a big story, and the public begins to believe it, whether or not there's any evidence to support it. In this case, there wasn't.

The word of one drunk with a Bigfoot fixation, then two less than reliable sources claiming the same thing happened to them. No evidence, no proof. But that's all it took. Suddenly everything that happened in New York was blamed on a "hulking apelike beast." Now, still without any proof, the brutal murder of a little boy is being blamed on this "Gowanus Beast." It's reminiscent of that *Twilight Zone* episode with Claude Akins, "The Monsters Are Due on Maple Street." (If you've never seen it, now seems as good a time as any.)

What if it had been hinted that the "creature" was spreading a disease that turned everyone it encountered into an equally violent beast? That certainly seems to be what's happening. It's a spreading madness. It might also be argued that the number of concurrent sightings seems to imply that there is more than just one Gowanus Beast—that there are in fact hundreds if not thousands of them, that we have been invaded by monsters. What other explanation is there?

On his website You Bet Monsters Are Real, the esteemed cryptozoologist Ernst Prell speculated that the creature may in fact be a "Tulkin," which he describes as a "phantom of the mind," which has taken on tangible, physical form and has a life of its own. He claims it can vanish at will, and that's why there have been no good photographs (or any other solid evidence, for that matter).

Of course, those are ridiculous notions. The only explanation with any evidence to back it up is that we are in the grip of a kind of mass hysteria—as has been witnessed throughout history often with tragic results. Consider the Great Airship of 1897, Orson Welles's 1938 "War of the Worlds" radio broadcast, or the Mad Gasser of Mattoon in 1944. What we are experiencing is an uglier, even more insane and more brutal version of the 17th-century witch hunts in New England or the Red Scares of the 1920s and 1950s.

As I write this, the fear seems to be subsiding, if slightly. At least nobody was killed last night. Perhaps the residents of New York are pausing a moment to look at what they're doing and asking themselves, "Why?" Perhaps they're thinking back to the beginning, to where it all started, and realizing that there was nothing there to begin with.

Think about it, people. You've smashed windows and fired guns out of fear of BIGFOOT. You've been asked to accuse your neighbors of

```
being BIGFOOT. You've
formed mobs and wandered
around Brooklyn, guns at
the ready, looking for
BIGFOOT.
   How nuts is that?
   Sometimes the best and
wisest and only thing to
do is just calm the hell
down. Do I even need to
say it? I have seen the
enemy, and he is us.
```

Yes, that was it. He clasped his fingers behind his head and gave his chair a quick spin. That oughta put the little monkeys in their place.

He sent the piece on to Nutskin, considered looking through the growing pile of faxed press releases Brand had left on his desk, then thought better of it.

At ten to five, thinking he'd put in a good day's work and deserved to get out ten minutes early, he shut down his computer and headed for the door.

As he was entering the lobby he heard Nutskin jogging up behind him.

"Kalabander, wait up a sec."

Hank turned.

Nutskin seemed out of breath after the four-yard trot. "Hey, got the piece, thanks. But I was hoping maybe we could go over some minor editorial changes I had in mind? Only take ten, fifteen minutes."

Hank almost smiled, realizing Nutskin was trying to play the responsible editor here. He knew damn well there wasn't a word or a comma in that story that was wrong or out of place. It was tight as a drum. If Shed wanted to drop a semicolon in or expand a contraction to feel better about himself, fine. Hank clapped him on the shoulder and focused on his left ear. "Y'know, Shed, I trust you. You're a professional. If they're minor changes, you don't need me to go all prima donna on you. You just edit it the way you see fit."

"You're sure? It might be better if we went through things."

"Oh, you just do what needs doing," he said. "You're the editor here." He clapped him on the shoulder again and headed into the lobby to see what kind of baffling salutation Blanche had for him tonight.

Nineteen

At ten-thirty the next morning the phone rang in Hank's cubicle. With an irritated sigh, he kicked his chair back from the computer and picked up the receiver. On the street below the office windows things were quiet, but on his way in that morning he could feel the tension rising with the temperature.

"Hey, Hank, you busy?"

"Working on the blotter."

"Oh—it can wait. I could call back later."

"Nah, it's fine," he said, not paying much attention to the voice on the other end. "Damage is done. But I should probably take a break anyway. It's all monster stories and I think I'm overusing the terms 'gullible sap' and 'retard.' " The voice finally registered. "Wait, this is Stone?"

"*Duh.*" Hank couldn't tell if she was honestly annoyed he hadn't recognized her sooner or just being stupid. "I was wondering if I could bounce a theory off you?"

Hank let his eyes wander back to Topsy. He was sick of theories. "Is it about the brontosaurus? Because if it is, I know it already."

"It's not." She'd obviously taken the question seriously. "It's about G.B."

"*What?* Oh. Really." He didn't need to ask what "G.B." stood for. Goddamn kids couldn't even speak in words anymore.

"Yeah," she said, again not catching his tone. "Let me ask you, have you ever seen that old show *Kolchak*? It was from the seventies, I think."

Hank cut his eyes away from Topsy. "No," he said. He didn't know why he was still listening to this woman.

"Either had I, but someone posted them online, and this other guy who read my stories sent me a link. Said he thought I'd like them."

"This is what you called to tell me."

"No, not exactly . . . I mean there's more."

"That's super news."

Stone clearly had no skills whatsoever when it came to reading voices. "Um, without getting into the whole show, there's this episode called 'Primal Scream.'" She sounded very happy about all this. "These researchers in the Arctic brought back samples of organic cells. And when they thawed out they grew and turned into this apeman who started killing people in Chicago."

Hank said nothing for a moment. "And so you're saying you think that's what happened here. Some prehistoric cells thawed out and turned into an apeman."

"Or maybe fell in the Gowanus or something and that did it."

"I see," he said. "Yeah, tell you what there, Louise. I think you should put that one on the back burner for now. See if something a little more, uh, plausible comes along. Like, y'know, maybe it's an evil C.H.U.M.P. agent, sent here to sow the seeds of chaos. Or a guy in an ape suit trying to get fluid from the pineal glands of his victims."

"You think that's what's going on?"

"Yeah. Sure." He rubbed his forehead. "You should call the ME's office, see if there's a puncture wound at the base of that dead kid's skull." This had gone on long enough. "Let me ask you something, Louise," he said before she could respond to his pineal gland theory. "You run an irresponsible story that has absolutely no basis in anything. You drive the panic level in this town up about ten notches, and now you're calling me with cockamamie theories you stole off some old fucking TV show? What is *wrong* with you? Don't you realize what's going on out there?"

"Whoa there, Hank," she said defensively. "I had nothing to do with that headline."

"Maybe not," Hank countered. "But you're not sorry it came out that way, are you? You just accept it as the truth now, just like all the other monglos out there."

"No, I'm not sorry," she admitted. He could almost hear her puff out her chest. "But be realistic, Kalabander. We need to keep this story *alive*, dude, you should know that. This story's our bread and butter. I mean, come on, right?"

When she laughed, Hank was tempted to slam down the phone, stomp over to the *Eagle*'s offices, find Stone's desk, and choke her to death. More for calling him "dude" than anything else.

Later that night, Hank was still stewing.

"It's these goddamn kids. They lie, they steal, and they don't give a shit. I thought *I* was supposed to be the nihilist here. But these kids like Stone—" He stopped when he saw the muscles on Annie's face going slack. "I'm sorry. You've heard it before."

"No, it's fine, really," she said.

"I'm getting loud in public."

"Not yet, but you're headed in that direction."

Annie had no idea why she'd suggested a Chinese place when she knew full well Hank would undoubtedly say something crass and loud before the night was over. But they had to go someplace because the contractors had moved the stove and the refrigerator into the hallway so they could start tearing out a large part of the kitchen ceiling. The Green Dumpling Delight was nearby.

"Sorry," he said, and took another drink from the oversized beer bottle. He tried to keep his voice down. "At least with people like you and me, we know our history . . . I mean, we may not care but at least we know it."

"Speak for yourself," she chided.

"Santayana was right," he went on as if not having heard her. "And Alphonse Karr, for that matter, which I guess kinda makes Santayana irrelevant. Any case, here we go again." With a slurp and a gulp, he clumsily shoveled a pork dumpling into his mouth, nearly choked, and kept talking as he chewed. "I'm not talking about obscurities like the Mad Gasser here. Take the case of Jack the Ripper, right?"

Annie closed her eyes, and when she reopened them she concentrated on dinner. At least while he was talking about Jack the Ripper he wouldn't be calling their waiter a Chinaman or "Wing Wang."

He looked around the table and slid the bowl of rice closer to his plate. "Now, as I'm sure any Winky-Blinky here can tell you, a hundred and fifty years after the fact, people are still trying to figure out who he was. Am I right?"

"Mm-hm," Annie said through tightened lips.

"But the reason they're still talking about him, and the reason he was never caught is simple. He *didn't exist.*" He was starting to get loud again. "Some whore gets sliced up. Big deal, right? But the newspapers decided to blow it up and run with it. Then somebody else dies, and even though there's no evidence tying them together, the papers say they're connected. All for the same old reasons that're still in play right now. Then the cops get in on the game. Then some crank sends a letter to the editor and it just gets bigger. The papers start piling their own lies onto the half-truths the cops are feeding them and look out. Then lord help us the *people* get hold of it, right? And the fuckin' *people* start spreading their *own* rumors which are fed back to the papers and the cops—"

He stopped to catch his breath, and Annie stepped in.

"Hank, please. I know."

"It's simple chaos theory."

"I know."

"Hm?" He looked up from his plate, startled and curious.

"I know the Jack the Ripper theory. Then they tied a few more murders to those first two, and the newspaper artists messed things up further, and then later the historians came along and messed things up even more."

"Yeah," Hank said. He'd stopped eating. Annie could read the "how the hell did you know that?" look on his face.

"Hank," she said, laying her chopsticks across her plate. "I told you all that a couple years ago. Actually Abernathy told me at the store one day, then I told you."

"Really?" he said. "No."

"Yes," she nodded.

"Abernathy?"

"He was on a Jack the Ripper kick. We had a few things in stock. When he'd read everything, he'd reached this conclusion that there was no Jack the Ripper and decided to share it with me. I thought it was interesting, so I told you."

"I don't remember that at all. Was I drunk at the time?"

"Probably. I remember you were having a bad day and I thought it would cheer you up. Or at least distract you."

"Did it?"

"Apparently."

"Really. I just don't recall that at all."

"This sort of thing has been happening a lot, Hank," Annie said. "I tell you something, then a few weeks, sometimes a few minutes, later you repeat it back to me as if you'd just thought of it. It worries me. Maybe you should see a neurologist or something."

His expression darkened. "Yeah, maybe." He scooped more rice onto his plate. "Point being, it's the result of hysterical journalism, and because of it people will waste their lives looking for an answer that isn't there. A hundred and fifty years from now people will be convinced there was some kind of monster wandering the streets of New York, and they'll still be trying to figure out what the fuck it was because they'll be doing their research in old newspapers and web postings." He paused. "It was an apt analogy, is all." He picked up a bowl near Annie's plate and took a doubtful look inside. "So what's this slop?"

Although he had promised himself he would avoid it, the following morning he stopped by Harry's stand and bought a copy of the *Eagle*. Flipping through all the tedious monster coverage to Stone's piece, he saw that, perhaps merely out of spite, she had gone right ahead and run with that "thawed prehistoric cells" nonsense (without attributing the idea to a TV show, of course). Worse, at the end she'd even tossed in his pineal gland theory for good measure.

Oh, she's such an asshole, Hank thought. He didn't want to think about what kind of effect it was going to have on the proles.

At least he'd done his part—the *Hornet* feature would be hitting front doorsteps all over Brooklyn that afternoon.

When he opened the door to the office, three men were unloading cardboard boxes full of the new issue from their hand trucks and dropping them unceremoniously on the floor. Hank could always smell the distribution guys from a few yards away. He grunted as he bent, tore open the nearest box, grabbed a handful of *Hornets*, and headed for his cubicle, offering Blanche a small salute as he passed.

"Hot enough out there," she said.

Hank paused and waited to see what would follow but that seemed to be it. He raised an eyebrow and continued on to the back.

Neither Becky nor Rusty was in yet, which was a relief. He wanted to relish his first published feature in private.

He dropped the short stack of papers atop the faxes Brand had left the night before, grabbed the top one, unfolded it, snapped it straight, and leaned back in his chair. They'd finally put him on the cover, where he belonged.

"Monster Invasion," the headline read.

Hank frowned and sucked his teeth. All right, so the creepy little platypus changed his title. He'd half expected that. Nutskin was probably worried about offending their feebleminded readership. He'd let it slide. Then he read "by Henry Kalabandor."

Hank closed his eyes, trying to convince himself that it was only a minor misspelling. People would still know who it was. He opened his eyes and moved on to what mattered.

```
Yet a tiny item in the weekly blotter about an admittedly drunken man who claimed he was assaulted by a hulking, smelly, apelike creature in the early morning hours of July 8. It was
```

no different from any of the other items in the blotter.

But then something happened. Two more people saw the monster. That's all it took. Suddenly everything that happened in New York was caused by a "hulking apelike beast." The brutal murder of a little boy.

It's possible that the "creature" is spreading a disease that turned everyone it encountered into an equally violent beast. That certainly seems to be what's happening. It's a spreading madness. It might also be argued that the number of concurrent sightings seems to imply that there is more than just one Beast—that there are instead thousands of them, and that we have been invaded by monsters.

The esteemed cryptozoologist Ernst Prell speculated that the creature may in fact be a "Tulkin," which he describes as a "phantom of the mind," which has taken on tangible, physical form and has a life of its own. It can vanish at will, and that's why there have been no photographs. What other explanation is there? I have seen the enemy.

Upon finishing the story, the right side of Hank's face twitched. He blinked at the paper in front of him. A thin, sharp noise arose deep in his throat. Below his piece—or what had once been his piece—was a photograph of two drooling old men in wheelchairs. "A Hundred Years of Twindom," the headline read.

Twenty

Hank didn't bother knocking. He simply opened the door and walked into Nutskin's office.

"What the fuck is this?" he demanded, his voice a touch higher than he would've liked. He held the half-crushed edition of the *Hornet* aloft in his fist.

Nutskin looked up, surprised. "Careful," he said. "Language." His own voice was lilting, like a protective mother warning a drunken uncle. "We don't use that kind of language around here."

Hank stared at him. "That doesn't answer my fuckin' question. What did you do to this?"

Nutskin gestured at Brand's empty chair. "Why don't you sit down and we'll talk about what's bothering you. And we'll do so without yelling or cursing."

"I'll stand, thanks. What did you do?"

Nutskin leaned back. "So what's wrong? You've been edited before."

"*It opens with the word 'yet'!* The whole thing reads like an Irwin Corey routine!"

"Henry," Nutskin said patiently, "I'm sorry . . . ad sales were down this week, we lost a few pages. So in order to make the piece fit I had to do a little trimming. It was running long as it was."

"A little trimming? You misspelled my goddamn name!" His voice was too high again. He turned his head and cleared his throat.

"Well, now, to be fair," Nutskin said, "I did ask you to sit down with me so we could edit it together. If you had, you might've been a little happier with the way it turned out, though I am sorry about the name. You know, I never have been able to get that right. Is it *a-r* or—"

"It's not just the name," Hank said as he started to pace. "You flipped the whole idea on its head. Have you taken a look out the fuckin' window? This was supposed to knock some sense into people. Put an end to all this stupid monster shit. But instead you have me claiming it's some kinda alien disease." His doctor had warned him that if his heart began beating too fast he should lie down, but that wasn't going to happen for a while. His skull felt like it was squeezing his brain.

Nutskin remained much too infuriatingly calm. "I don't see why you're getting so excited. I thought it was a good story. I just tightened it up a little."

Hank, still pacing, had no idea how to respond.

"And as for stopping what's happening out there, you still might get your wish."

Hank's feet slowed. "How's that?" He noticed he could suddenly look Nutskin in the face, liver lips and all, without any unpleasant effects. Wanting to kill Nutskin before he stepped in the office seemed to be the key.

"Well, I thought it was a good and important piece you wrote, so after the papers showed up I had Blanche fax it to all the major news outlets in the city."

Hank froze. "What?" He felt something die and grow cold in

his chest. At the same time, something buried deep in the ancient folds of his brain told him he shouldn't launch himself across Nutskin's desk, but lord how he was tempted. There might have been a chance, given the *Hornet*'s circulation and readership, that the story would've gone unnoticed. Nutskin, however, had just incinerated that possibility. He turned to head back to his cubicle.

"Henry," Nutskin called. "Before you leave. I'd love to have you do a follow-up for next week. In fact I had an idea. And this time you should sit down with me when I edit it."

Hank paused. "What's the idea?"

"I thought it might be interesting," Nutskin said, "if you wrote a first-person account of your own encounter with the Gowanus Beast."

"What the fuck are you talking about? I never saw anything."

"That's not what you said in your story. At the end you wrote that you've seen the enemy."

That voice in Hank's brain was at it again.

"But . . . it didn't say that until you edited it that way."

"I still think it would be a great story—one that would really interest our readers."

"No . . . no . . . *no.* You're *wrong.* Again. Now *you* lissenda *me,* Falafel," Rocky said to the tired Egyptian in the tired, coffee-stained shirt who stared at him through the thick pane of bulletproof glass.

All the chairs and benches in the station behind him were filled with exhausted, hungry, and ornery single mothers, low-rent pimps, runaways, and the unemployed. The dense air smelled of sweat and bad breath. Some of those who'd arrived too late for the chairs and the benches were leaning against the walls. Others were sitting in corners, propping their heads on overstuffed backpacks and rolled-up sleeping bags. Outside the narrow dirty windows, eight or nine people were walking in circles, sitting on newspaper boxes, and smoking.

Over the middle of the floor hung a flat black sign, twenty feet across and ten feet tall. Although there was a list of destinations running down the right-hand side of the sign, there were no lights, nothing was changing, there was no indication at all when anyone might be allowed to leave.

"I been on your crummy buses for three goddamn days now, hear me?"

"Yes sir," the Egyptian clerk said crisply. "I have been hearing you for quite some time now."

"It has taken me three days to get from Rhode Island to this shithouse. Three days of sitting on buses with screaming kids and Jesus types and recovering alcoholics, got me?"

"Yes, I got you, sir." The Egyptian clerk reminded himself that taking abuse from people like this was written into the job description.

"Up until now, everything that could go wrong *has* gone wrong. You wanna hear?"

"Sir, I must ask you—"

Rocky began ticking off small disasters on his stubby fingers. "We got two flat tires. *Two!* Then we got lost. One of the Jesus types started screaming. The twelve-steppers started *singing.* The howling brat next to me puked everywhere. The rest stop was *closed.* Then I get here—I don't even know where the fuck I am anymore—"

"Allentown, sir. If you had made the effort to look at the sign above my window—"

"Allentown. Great. And I'm bein' told—now listen close, Mustafa—I'm bein' told that nothin's goin' any farther north than this. But nobody seems capable of telling me exactly *why.*"

"That is correct, sir."

The line of haggard and odiferous travelers waiting to tell the Egyptian clerk the same story stretched across the bus terminal to the far wall, then along the wall to the front doors. Even as those who were riding Rocky's back heard his questions and the clerk's replies, they clung to some futile, gray hope that they would be the one who could talk some sense into the foreigner and get the buses running again.

Rocky had chewed through his last cigar shortly after they left Pittsburgh and now found himself trapped in a bus station without a decent tobacco shop within fifty miles. He planted both palms on the glass, leaned his head in close, and lowered his voice.

"Wrong answer there, my camel-jockey friend," he hissed. "It . . . is . . . *imperative* that I get to New York immediately. Ya hear me? I'm already two days behind schedule. By the time I fuckin' get there, it could be too late." He turned his head away and thought. "So answer me this much. Are there any live monsters in Allentown?"

"Just one that I can think of at the present time, sir," the clerk informed him.

Rocky's glare turned murderous. "Don't crack wise with me, Sahib. This is serious business. I need to get to New York before that fucker Macabro beats me to it." He exhaled through his teeth. "If he does, it'll be on your head, an' believe you me, Rochester, you don't want that followin' you around."

He pulled his sticky palms away from the Plexiglas and spit at his feet. He took a breath. "So," he said, looking up again, "ya got any taxis in this popsicle stand?"

Very little had been accomplished in Hank's cubicle in the hours following his confrontation with Nutskin, except for fending off two of the ad reps who wanted to know what it was like to have actually seen the Beast.

He was tempted to ignore the phone when it rang, but before he could make that decision the receiver was at his ear.

"Welcome to the winning team, Kalabander." It was Stone. Hank didn't much feel like talking to Stone. "I thought you were going to trash the whole story, just stop it dead in its tracks."

"That was the plan," he mumbled.

"Hey, let the sunshine in there, Gloomy Gus!" she chirped. "This story's gonna make us both superstars. We could be like Woodstein and whatever the other guy's name was."

"Guildenstern." Hank offered with a roll of the eyes. "But with some kind of hairy ape monster instead of a president."

"You tell me the difference, I'll buy you a Coke."

Blanche stopped him on his way out that evening. When he was close enough to her desk, she grabbed his sleeve and pulled him closer. "Mister Kalabander, I gotta axe ya." Her perfume smelled of sulfur.

"Yes?" he said, head cocked, listening patiently.

"This thing you saw . . . this monster, y'know?" She looked around the room to make sure they were alone. "Wha'd it look like? Was it horrible?"

His back was starting to give way bent over like that, so he extracted himself and straightened. "Well, Blanche, I'll tell ya, it's really hard to describe. All I can tell you for sure is that—" He stopped himself and looked around before whispering. "You never, ever want to see it yourself."

Her eyes widened and a hand flew to her mouth. Hank nodded solemnly.

She took her hand away. "Frienda mine says it's one o' them Gowanus dogs . . . you know them wild dogs they got wanderin' around down there?"

He nodded.

"But that someone fed it with that human growth semen stuff, an' so now it walks around on two legs."

"Hm," Hank said. "That's sure one possibility. I'll be sure to keep you posted on whatever else I find out." He patted her arm and headed for the door.

"Be careful out there, Mr. Kalabander," she said after him. "In a manner of speakin'."

Still pondering the ominous implications of that one a few minutes later, he almost didn't see Harry waving at him from the newsstand. He was tempted to wave back and keep walking but there was an urgency to Harry's flapping.

Christ, I'm never gonna get home, he thought. He wasn't in the mood for the latest update on Harry's ongoing victimhood. He nevertheless stopped, then picked his way through the early evening pedestrian rush.

"Heya Harry, what goes on," he asked, trying to force a smile. Around him, a couple of people were ducking in to grab the late editions, tossing their coins on the counter before continuing on their way.

"Looks like you pissed off the mayor but good, Hank," Harry said. "That's bad news, I can tell ya that. You're gonna hafta watch your ass."

Hank blinked at him, letting the false smile fade. "What's this now?"

"Look at your feet."

Hank looked down but before his eyes found his shoes they passed across the headlines of the late editions.

"Is Alien Disease Spreading?" screamed the *Post*. "Gowanus Beast(s)!" dominated the *Eagle*'s front page. And on the cover of the *Times* was a photograph of an angry Mayor Rebane, a scowl on his face, a crushed copy of the *Hornet* in his upraised fist.

Looks like I did when I read it, Hank thought.

Opposite the photo was the most recent artist's rendering of the creature.

Beneath both was the headline "Mayor: Pennysaver Columnist's Theory Could Prompt Panic."

"Oh, shit," he whispered.

He snatched up the paper and began reading the first paragraph.

> According to Henry Kalabandor, columnist for weekly neighborhood circular the *Brooklyn Hornet*, the terror which has gripped New York this past week was not the work of a single apelike beast, but rather an invading force of thousands of creatures called "Tulkins" that have been spreading disease throughout . . .

He set the paper down, considered briefly returning to set fire to the *Hornet*'s offices, but instead turned and continued on the now very long journey home.

"Watch yourself, buddy!" Harry shouted after him. "This asshole don't joke around!"

Hank couldn't hear him over the taxi horns, the garbage trucks, and the people on cell phones. He also couldn't hear most of those things over the singular, overpowering thought in his head: *It's about damn time I got a credit.*

Twenty-one

The erstwhile leaders of the organically evolving Neighborhood Beast Watch movement decided it was time to stop limiting their patrols to the overnight hours. As the universal scope of what they were facing became more evident, they started hunting the creature—or perhaps creatures—that threatened their families through the daylit streets as well. Most of the groups roaming the sidewalks were both well intentioned and well armed, though inter-mob communication often left something to be desired.

In three separate incidents, teenage pranksters who thought it would be a hoot to hide in the bushes and jump out in front of antsy, unsuspecting citizens were shot or savagely beaten. All three survived but were placed under armed guard as they recuperated in local hospitals, and all three were facing serious hate crime charges upon their release.

Following the publication of Hank's story, the shrill newspaper, television, and online editorials expanded their speculations concerning the True Meaning of the Beast to analyze its significance in terms of hybrid cars, the vanishing bee population, the future of the space program, and the amount of sex in advertising. At the same time, Lou Stone Jr. became an in-demand guest on both local and national morning shows as the world's foremost authority on the Gowanus Beast.

Shortly before eight-thirty Sunday night, Michael Findlay, an Upper West Side dermatologist who had opened a private practice six months earlier, found that his medicine cabinet was devoid of antacids.

It was clear the oyster tostadas he'd had for dinner that evening weren't going away any time soon, so he told his wife, Evelyn, that he was just going to run to the drugstore down around the corner on Seventy-eighth.

"Just be careful out there," his wife called to him from the kitchen as he was putting on his shoes. "Remember, if you see that thing you're not supposed to make eye contact—it'll hypnotize you. Just turn around and come home."

"*Hyp-no-taahz*," he whispered as he turned the doorknob.

Findlay was less than half a block from his apartment on West Eighty-second Street when a member of the growing (and increasingly militant) Upper West Side Beast Guard fingered him as a likely candidate for beastdom.

It might have been his beard, or his height, or his dark T-shirt and Bermuda shorts. It didn't matter what it was that triggered the reaction. All anyone in the mob knew in that instant was that Dr. Michael Findlay, dermatologist, was in reality a disease-spreading alien apeman phantom out to destroy them, their families, and their way of life. Unfortunately, it took Dr. Findlay a moment to realize this.

"There it is!" someone in the mob screamed and pointed. "In the Bermuda shorts! Get it!"

At first he thought they were joking, but they were moving far too fast for that. He whirled in the hopes of running back to the safety of his wife and apartment, only to find his retreat had already been cut off.

"What do you *want*?" he shouted at them as he backpedaled down the sidewalk. He knew it was futile. Seeing his chance, he darted through the slow traffic and across the street to another small apartment building. His sister's ex-husband lived on the fifth floor. He didn't care much for his sister's ex-husband (or his sister, for that matter) but the doorman knew him and would let him pass.

Whimpering in fear, Findlay pushed through the double glass doors before the doorman could reach the handle to open it for him.

"Dr. Findlay, I—" the startled doorman began before he was forced to snap his attention back to the screaming mob spilling across the street toward the building. They crashed through the doors, knocking the sixty-eight-year-old doorman against the wall and to the ground.

"We got the thing cornered!" one of them yelped as he stomped on the prone doorman's ankle.

The elevator was no good, he knew. Findlay found the stairwell and bounded up the steps three at a time, past the second and third and fourth floors. He kept running, his chest burning and stomach heaving. His eyes were filled with tears. This sort of thing wasn't supposed to happen to him. There were shouts and pounding feet behind him. He couldn't feel his legs anymore when he burst through the emergency fire exit onto the roof.

He couldn't stop and rest. There was no place to rest. He had to keep running.

It sounded like a concussion grenade when the mob slammed through the fire exit.

"*There it is!*" one shouted.

"*I'm a dermatologist!*" Findlay shouted back, daring a quick look over his shoulder. As he turned back, he thought he saw something else up there—something large, with glowing eyes the color of blood—moving slowly from the shadows behind the air-conditioning unit.

Don't look in its eyes, his wife had told him. He dodged to his left and continued running, hoping he might jump to the next building. It couldn't be that far. A gunshot cracked behind him and he nearly stumbled. The bullet missed. He ran, sweating, his eyes wild and burning, until there was no roof left beneath his feet.

Several members of the patrol moved cautiously to the edge of the roof and ventured a look down at Findlay's twisted body on the pavement below. People were already beginning to gather, several taking pictures of the corpse with their cell phones. One or two people looked up toward the roof. One of those sets of upturned eyes belonged to a fat, bearded man in a purple cape. He seemed to be waving a wand over Findlay's body.

"Okay, men," the self-appointed leader of the Beast Guard group said to the rest of his crew. "I've heard the Beast can fly when it wants to, so that means this prob'ly wasn't the thing we're lookin' for." The others agreed. "That means it's still out there. So let's go get it!" They all cheered and whooped and headed back toward the fire door.

"Serves the stupid bastard right," Hank told Annie after the story was broadcast on the radio the next morning. They were in the bedroom, and he was buttoning the same shirt he'd worn for the previous three days. A quick sniff under each arm had convinced him it was probably good for another two. "Going to the drugstore at that hour when there's a *monster* loose. What the hell did he expect?" He coughed a dry cackle.

Above them, hard little feet were running from one end of the attic apartment to the other, stopping occasionally to send something crashing to the floor.

"Marv . . ." Annie said. She was getting dressed herself.

"Hank," he corrected without looking up. Suddenly the sound of a circular saw ripped through the air. It was coming from a few feet beyond the closed bedroom door. They stopped talking.

Annie waited a second after the saw was silent again before continuing. "What would you think about getting a hotel room for a few days? Maybe a week. This is insanity. And with these guys showing up at seven in the morning now? I don't know how much longer I can take this."

Hank was sitting on the bed, looking at the floor and shaking his head. "No. Let these guys just come in and take whatever they want? You know what they're like. Bullshit."

Outside the door the hammering began, soon followed by the light rain of plaster. Annie closed her eyes. He'd answered so automatically she could tell he'd only half-heard her. His moods had become harder and harder to track lately. Even when his spirits seemed to be up, she could sense something else going on. For the past few days his mind had been on something he wasn't sharing. She thought she knew what it was, too.

"Are you going to do a second story?" she asked.

He nodded slowly, his back to her. "Gonna try and do a first again," he said. "But how do you convince people who are carrying shotguns when even the goddamn *Times* and NPR are telling them the bogeyman's gonna get 'em?" He took a deep breath and bent to put on a sock. "As a civilization," he said, "we give ourselves way too much credit. Maybe I should just suggest they set everything on fire and be done with it."

Annie moved around the bed and stroked the back of his graying head. "Way it's always been," she told him. "We've always thought we were civilized, and we've always been scared of our own shadow."

He slipped an arm around her waist.

"So can we leave through the back way this morning?"

"And let that evil Dr. Zabor put a curse on us?" Hank said, looking up at her. "No fucking way."

When Hank arrived at his desk that morning, the red message light on his phone was blinking. That had never happened before.

"Um . . . Becky?" he called over the wall.

"Uh-huh?"

He felt foolish asking a child for help but there was no way around it. "You're comfortable with this technology business—could you possibly tell me how the hell I go about . . . uh . . . making this light stop blinking?"

Ten minutes later, after Becky asked several questions that weren't really questions at all, Hank had a very clear set of written instructions for retrieving voice-mail messages. Working carefully from that, he hit the proper buttons in the proper order and soon he heard an unfamiliar voice.

"Hello, Mister Kabel . . . bander." It sounded like a heavyset black woman in her fifties with a respiratory infection. She cleared her throat and he heard the rustle of paper. "In these wicked times . . . When the Lord is visitin' upon us with his . . . Wrath of a evil demon, now it is the time . . . To turn you life over to Jesus an' his love . . . For protection."

Hank was about to hit delete but then hesitated. He was just too damn curious.

"Remember the book of Luke, chapter . . . Fourteen, verse, uh, twelve . . . And the book of Isaiah, chapter, um . . . Nine, verse twenty. So . . . We invite you. To come. To a prayer meetin' this . . . Thursday evenin' at . . . At the Divine Inspiration Church of the . . . the Blessed Conga—congre-gation . . . With Jesus. If you do not have a Bible of you own, one . . . Will be pro-vided. For you. To use."

He hit the delete button. "Becky?"

He called again.

"Uh-huh?"

"Did, ah, you get a message from a semiliterate fat black church lady?"

There was a brief silence. "Nuh-uh?"

"Just wondering."

Twenty-two

Gowanus Beast Is Gay!" Tuesday morning's *Eagle* declared. "B'klyn Boy Molested Before Murder, M.E. Sez."

Hank felt oddly impressed by Stone's moxie on that one. Harry handed him his change and he turned away.

Only then did he notice that up and down the street people were setting up canopied tables and food stands, piecing together shaky and treacherous kiddie rides, heating vats of oil, and laying out ugly, handmade purses and sweaters. At nine-thirty in the morning the air already smelled of burned shish kebab and fried onions.

There was quiet unease in the air too. The people setting up the stands weren't smiling or laughing the way they normally did when preparing for another street fair.

Hank was no longer much of a fan of street fairs, which were such a staple of the New York summer. Not since the city banned beer sales. Time was he and his first wife could spend entire days at a street fair, weaving through block after block of noise, fried food, and cheap crap, plastic cups in hand, past cops who could do nothing but smile and wave. There was a time when they were almost like miniature carnivals, but no longer. Insurance companies, cell phone dealers, fast-food chains, and real estate brokers had started setting up their own stands, infiltrating and poisoning a once pure form. Now, instead of mini carnivals, they were condensed versions of the city itself. Commerce was all that mattered, and when commerce became the issue Hank stopped caring.

He slipped between a falafel stand and someone selling vinyl dog-shaped balloons on sticks and through the Gemora Building's front door.

At his desk, there were more press releases waiting. It occurred to him that he had no idea when or how Brand was leaving those things on his desk without him noticing. However it was done, he had to admit he was relieved. It was always a better day when he didn't have to deal with Brand.

Also waiting on his desk was a padded envelope. That was also something new. He checked, and yes indeed it was addressed to him. He tore open one end.

Inside was a hand-printed, hand-bound thirty-page booklet entitled *The War Between Lord Jesus and Vernon S. Isopod.*

According to the accompanying cover letter (written on yellow legal paper with a black marker), for years now Jesus had been sending Mr. Isopod nasty coded messages via the *Times* daily crossword puzzle. Mr. Isopod had finally had quite enough of this heavenly taunting, and so he wanted to share his story with the world. The letter also claimed that all this, somehow, had something to do with the Gowanus Beast.

Hank slipped the letter inside the booklet and set it to the side. It sounded like something worth exploring further but not at this particular moment.

He picked up the pile of Brand's faxes and began pulling them apart. The top press release had been sent by one of the more media savvy of the local fundamentalist churches, announcing its upcoming "Baptism-A-Thon," along with a "Communion Giveaway."

Hank watched as that one floated gently into the wastebasket.

When he stepped outside into the oppressive afternoon heat something seemed wrong. It was awfully quiet for a street fair in full swing. There was no tinny music, no unidentifiable meat sizzling, no murmuring of crowds. Granted, it was a Tuesday and so a lot of people were at work but, hell, in this neighborhood the place should've been packed with stroller moms, Jamaican nannies, and young Puerto Ricans in wifebeaters.

Hank peered up and down the street. It looked like two-thirds of the vendors were already gone.

He scanned what remained and crossed the street to a table displaying a variety of misshapen homemade scented candles. He could smell them a few yards away and they made his head hurt worse than usual.

Behind the table stood a thin, pale, bearded man wearing an embroidered vest and jogging shorts.

"Hey, lemme ask you," Hank said, looking him up and down with some uncertainty. "Uh, where'd everybody go? I was here a couple hours ago and the place was nutty with vendors."

"You seen the papers, man?" the candle maker asked. His voice was slow and dull.

"Yeah?"

"They say there's a *monster* around here someplace, man. Killed a *kid.* Most everybody split." As slow and dull as his speech was, he still sounded frightened. "Even the chicks who sell the *crystals* split."

"No foolin'." Hank didn't know where to begin with Cheech

here. "So you're saying that people packed up and left because they were afraid of . . . a monster."

The candle maker looked doubtful for a second. "Well . . . yeah? It killed a *kid*, man. Word spread real fast. Then they were all gone."

"And you're just hearing about this now? It's been all over the goddamn news for almost a month. You street fair people must smoke a lotta weed, reflexes like that."

"Hey, man, who knows *what's* out there." He waved both arms and glanced to the sky. "All the toxins we dump in the earth every day?"

Hank looked down the street. "Yeah, like I said." He'd heard another voice and cocked an ear to listen. It sure as hell didn't belong to a candle-hawking hippie. He started walking away.

"Hey, man," the candle vendor called from behind him. "You wanna buy some a my wax? Hand-dipped. Great for aromatherapy."

"Yeah, maybe later, there, Rainbow," Hank replied.

Half a block away, he came upon a dwarfish man in striped pants standing behind a large overturned cardboard box. Sitting atop the box were three playing cards folded lengthwise into small tents.

"*Ev*eryone's a winner," he was chanting. "Find the red queen and win yourself a little green. So simple a child could do it. Just find the red queen . . ."

With his stubby fingers he began dancing the cards over and around each other, pausing every four or five moves to flip over the red queen. Two men stood near the box, hypnotized by Rocky's manipulations.

"What in the *fuck* are you doing?" Hank asked him.

Rocky looked up. "Oh. Heya, Al-a-ga-zam. Just passin' the time, tossin' a few broads." He dropped his gaze back to the cards. "And givin' these fine gentlemen here the opportunity to walk away with some fresh cash money in their pockets, they find that red queen." He flipped the queen again. "All's they gotta do is take a step forward—"

"Oh, just stop it," Hank insisted. "And *you* two," he said, turning to the would-be customers. "Save your money. Go get a drink or something. Buy some crack. You don't have a chance in hell here."

The men quickly left and Rocky glared at Hank. "What's the idea a' skunkin' my game, Salamander? You're a one-digit, always doin' that. Had 'em in the palm of my hand."

"Sorta like the red queen? I'm amazed you ain't been busted—there are cops everywhere."

Rocky took a look around. "You see any law around here?"

Hank looked up and down the street. Not only had most of the vendors split, but it looked like all the cops had, too, along with the pedestrians and the cars and the bicyclists. He'd never seen Washington Street so quiet. He hated to say it under the circumstances, but yes it was much *too* quiet.

"So not only have I *not* been busted," Rocky said, reaching into his pocket and removing a thick wad of bills. "Half an hour's work right here," he said, proudly waving the money toward Hank's face. "Sophisticated my ass. Town fulla straight Johns with their pockets fulla dough, just *itchin'* to throw it at me. Who am I to tell 'em no?" He smiled, revealing his crooked, brown teeth. "Yeah, sometimes I think I'm in the wrong business."

Hank was still staring at the wad of cash when he asked, "Speaking of which, don't you have a sideshow to run? You're supposed to be in, where, Arkansas about now? Season ain't over yet."

Rocky folded the bills, replaced them in his pocket, and continued tossing the cards around as he spoke. "Crew broke down a few days back. Told 'em to make the jump without me. I saw the papers and figured you'd be lookin' for me."

"Wait," Hank said. "*Looking* for you? No, I wasn't. But how the hell did you find me?"

"I didn't. Just set up here for a bit, wanteda see how the action was, and you found me. Funny how things works sometimes."

This was turning into another one of those days. Sometimes Hank wished he could have a day somewhere along the line that didn't inevitably turn into one of those days.

"Well . . . ," he said, not sure where to go next. "Why assume I'd be looking for you in the first place?"

Rocky continued to watch his own hands as he flipped the cards around, pausing to show the red queen to no one. "You got monster troubles. We got a history. You sure as hell ain't gonna catch that thing alone. So you need me . . . An' I need a monster."

"I see. But I thought I told you the other night. I'm better now."

Rocky shook his head. "You're never better."

At the stroke of five, the buildings around them began to empty out, and Hank started getting nervous. He always tried to beat the rush by a few minutes. "So Rock, wanna get a drink?"

Rocky looked around. "With all these customers about to line up? Later, Jackson. Now dangle. Unless you wanna shill for me. You still know the head method, right?"

"Of course I know the head method—right for left, up for middle. But I can't do this now. Mayor's out to get me as it is."

Rocky scowled and waved his hand impatiently at Hank. "Ah, then go peddle yer papers. You're too educated anyway. Gimme an address, I'll meetcha when I meetcha, and we'll work out all the details."

Hank gave him the address of a bar near the remains of his apartment. He hoped Rocky would remember the number. The little man was concentrating on scamming a few quick bucks out of the sophisticates who had never seen a three-card monte game up close before.

Twenty-three

"To little folk, some poison oak." Hank tipped his glass.

It was quiet in the Trog Lounge for that hour on that night of the week. Seven or eight people were balanced on the stools along the bar, a few more were gathered around tables in the back. Nash the Slash was playing on the jukebox, and strings of colored lights encircled the windows and dangled down the walls. Unlike the Indian restaurant, here they served no real purpose apart from making the place seem a bit more "festive."

Hasslein the bartender leaned against the cash register, arms folded, surveying the meager crowd, waiting for someone to empty a pint. The Christmas lights reflected off his shaven head. It was just after ten, and he knew the place wasn't going to get much busier than this.

"So some guy rushes in and fills you up with bad dope about the setup," Rocky was saying. "That pretty much the story?" He and Hank were seated at the end of the bar. Behind them, an oval window looked out on Third Avenue.

"Pretty much, yeah. This week they say they hafta move the radiators to do some damn thing or another."

"Move the radiators."

"It's what they say, yeah. Radiators and the tub. I stopped asking questions a long time ago." He scanned the crowd. Sitting a few stools down from them was a gray-haired man in a loosened tie. A half-empty glass of red wine sat before him. His elbows rested on the bar and he was clutching his head in his hands. His lips were moving but Hank could hear nothing. The guy was in there every night, head in his hands and mumbling away. Hank had learned from Hasslein that he was a law professor. "You know," he said, turning back to Rocky, "for years I didn't come in this place. Thought it was a dyke bar."

"Wondered that myself, from the outside," Rocky said. "I've had trouble enough like that." He took his own look around the place. "Yeah, but a dyke bar this sure ain't. Less these are all really ugly dames." He sounded disappointed.

"Nah, they call it Trog for other reasons." As Hank watched, the gray-haired law professor reached into his shirt pocket and withdrew a pen and a piece of paper the size of a matchbook. He flattened the paper on the bar and began writing in microscopic script. There was no reading it from where Hank sat, but from the look on the man's face it was obviously something of grave importance.

When he was finished, the professor replaced the pen in his pocket and carefully folded the paper several times into a neat square. He popped the paper into his mouth and washed it down with the rest of his wine.

". . . So I says to this guy, I says, 'That tune don't play here, Jack'—ya got me here?"

Hank turned back to Rocky, who'd apparently been telling a story. "Mm-hm."

"That's why I'm here. I need this Gowanus Beastie thing. It's an easy single-o. I'll make a pile, and it'll get Blount off my fuckin' back." Effortlessly, he slid off his stool and into his pitch.

"*Ladies!* And gentlemen!"

Everyone in the bar stopped talking and turned to stare. Hank recognized the particular timbre of Rocky's voice from the warped recording playing outside his tent at the Meadowlands.

"*This* is not a show for the faint of heart! The Gowanus *Beast*, ladies and gentlemen! Alive and inside! It's the most *vicious*! And *terrifying* creature . . . *Ever!* To walk the face of the earth!"

As he improvised his bally, he gestured using his cigar like a cane, pointing it at an invisible crowd in front of him and an invisible banner above and behind. He seemed to be in a trance.

"*See!* With your very own eyes! The murderous *monster* that brought the Big Apple to its *knees*! . . . And it's alive inside, ladies and gentlemen . . . *Alive! Alive! Alive!*"

He stopped and climbed back onto his stool, ignoring all the watery, bloodshot eyes staring at him down the length of the bar. His face was flushed, his own eyes brighter than Hank had ever seen them.

"See why I need to catch this thing alive?" He was out of breath and took a sip of his bourbon. "I tell ya, Hank, this is it. Nobody ain't seen nothin' like this since my last Wild Man of Borneo."

Hank, having at that moment tipped his glass to his lips, coughed, spraying beer onto the bar. "Christ," he sputtered, wiping his mouth and mopping up the bar with some nearby paper napkins. "How long ago'd you have one of those in the act?"

Rocky shrugged. "Dunno, five, six seasons back."

"And you weren't lynched? Jesus, Rock, and the quacks say *I'm* the one with Asperger's."

"Asperger's." Rocky thought for a second. "I hearda that. Ain't that just a fifty-cent word for 'asshole'?"

"That's what I'm told, yeah. But back to this wild man show. No one ever gave you the business for putting a colored guy—"

Rocky stopped him. "*African . . . American.*"

"What're you, my wife now? Fine, whatever. For putting this dusky blackamoor on stage with a bone through his nose and a fright wig?"

"Not a peep." Rocky shook his head. "But it was a pretty . . . ah . . . It was a well-focused tour schedule that season. 'Sides, who's gonna punch a midget? But a live monster? That's TV. *That's* big time." He clapped his rough hands. Everyone at the bar looked again. "So how we gonna catch it?"

It was about time, Hank thought, to tell him before this got out of hand. He took another drink.

"Don't mean to burst your bubble there, Rochester, but you might do better to recycle your wild man act. Just sayin'."

Rocky looked at him suspiciously. "What the fuck are you talkin' about?"

After taking a deep breath, Hank told him. "There's no monster out there, Rock. It's just people bein' stupid. You'd be chasin' your own ass, trying to catch shadows. Waste of time. It just doesn't exist." Not wanting to be a complete pisser he added, "Good to see you, though, gotta say."

This wasn't what Rocky wanted or needed to hear. His cold little eyes fixed on Hank. "You're just after this thing for yourself, ain't'cha?"

Hank clapped him gently on the shoulder and nodded to Hasslein for another round. He was getting the impression they'd be there for a while. "No, Rock, I'm not. What the hell would I do with it anyway? Set up my own single-o and take it on the road? You know how I am with traveling." He gave Rock an earnest look. "It just doesn't exist."

Over the next few minutes he laid out the whole story.

"Even if it *did* exist, and even if you *did* catch him, it, whatever it is, and put it on stage, nobody would believe it's real. It'd play like the Girl-to-Gorilla show. Wouldn't it just be easier to gaffe it? Get some guy in an ape suit or shave a baboon. Or save yourself some dough and use the old Creature from the Black Lagoon from the wax museum."

"*Hey.*" Rocky looked deeply offended. "Whaddya think I am, some kinda shyster? Blount made it clear I need a live act. And that Black Lagoon mannequin's been repurposed one too many times already."

He decided not to tell Hank about his chat with Helga from the Girl-to-Gorilla show. Instead he stared into his drink for a long time. Then something flashed. He sat up and turned to Hank, a growing, hopeful smile on his face.

"What if you're wrong?" he asked. "Long as I've known you, you been fulla shit about everything. So why not now?"

Having figured the whole stupid question was over and done with, Hank wasn't paying attention. "Hm?"

"Oldest sucker bet in the world. You only think it ain't real 'cause you ain't *seen* it."

"Yes, yes, yes," Hank returned to his drink.

"Now don't go lookin' at me all crosswise, Leroy. I know what I'm talkin' about. We need to go hunting." Something bad was churning away in Rocky's head much faster than Hank could keep up with it, and he didn't like the sound of it at all. "We'll need a net. You know any fishermen or, y'know, fishermen supply stores around here? There's gotta be, right?"

"No."

Rocky paused and studied Hank's face. "I detect a certain lack of enthusiasm for the undertaking at hand, here, Salamander. That's the wrong attitude."

The dead stare he got in return told him nothing except that he was alone in all this.

Someone from the other end of the bar had slipped a few more bucks into the jukebox, perhaps for no other reason than to drown out Rocky and Hank. A psychedelic number by Richard Delvy came on.

Rocky took a drink, set his glass down, and rested his hands on his knees. "Okay, lemme tellya story. Got this from a guy I know. Old newspaperman out west. Investigative type. Big kahuna. He told me this one night at a bar like this one." He stopped and cleared his throat. He reached into his pocket, pulled out his black half-cigar, blew the lint off the tip, and stuck it in his mouth. Nobody at the bar said a word. Hank waited patiently through all the preparations, wishing, by god, he could have a smoke.

"Now, imagine it, fifty rattlers loose in Albuquerque—or any other city," Rocky began. He grabbed the cigar from his teeth so he could properly gesture with it. "The whole *town's* in a panic, got me? Deserted streets, barricaded houses . . . They're evacuating the kids. Every man is armed. *Fifty* killers on the prowl." He paused for another drink and then wiped his mouth with his sleeve. "So one by one they start huntin' 'em down. They get ten, twenty. It's *building.* They get forty . . . forty-*five.*" He was gesturing with both hands now, his voice rising. "Then they get forty-*nine.* But where's the last rattler? In a kindergarten? In a *church*? In a crowded elevator? *Where?* Know what this guy tells me?" He didn't wait for an answer. "He says to me, he says, 'In my desk drawer, fan. Stashed away.' Only nobody knows it, see?" Rocky paused for effect, offering Hank an evil grin. Once it had settled in, he continued. "So then this guy, see—this reporter—explains the whole deal. The story's good for another three days, he says. Then when he's ready, he says, they come out with a big extra. *Sun Bulletin Snags Number Fifty!*"

Rocky raised both his hands and his eyebrows, too, waiting for a response.

"You didn't hear that from some reporter, you little liar, you stole it from *Ace in the Hole*."

Rock's hands and eyebrows dropped again. "So why didn't'cha tell me you heard it already, dickweed? Saved me some breath." The cigar went back in his mouth only half out of embarrassment as he spun to face the bar. "An' that ain't the point anyway. It's the *situation*. But you still shoulda stopped me."

Hank tipped his head briefly. "You seemed to be having fun. On the bright side, I know someone—an actual living reporter, by the way—who would really take that story to heart. Already has. You ever meet her, you should tell it again. But apart from that, no, I'm not gonna go buy a goddamn net to help you try and catch something that doesn't exist."

Rocky was suddenly angry. "So wha'd you call me for, askin' about gorilla suits?"

"Just checking out some possible explanations. First sighting was reported while you were still in town."

"Bullshit," Rocky said. "You called me because you knew I'd come up here, an' you wanted me up here 'cause you needed my help to find this thing."

Hank laughed dryly. "Guess it's an interesting theory."

Rocky leaned in, grabbed Hank's arm, and gave it a shake. "C'mon, get with the program, Rochester. Don't you see what this could be? This ain't just about savin' my ass. This could be your big break. You could finally make something of your pathetic life."

"So I'm told."

"And?"

"And," Hank said, reaching for his glass. "Who wants a big break?"

"*You* do," Rocky informed him. "Ya nickel-snatchin' bezark."

Twenty-four

It was a long night. Although the loosely defined crew of "handymen" had mercifully found no reason to invade their bedroom up to this point, the helicopters had started nightly patrols over the area, circling endlessly in the darkness, intense halogen beams roving the streets, tracking up to the rooftops, and making their way into apartment windows. Combined with the kids upstairs (who no longer seemed to sleep at all), Hank and Annie both awoke exhausted and puffy-eyed. The light coming through the bedroom window was dreary and helped only to highlight the thick dust floating and swirling in the bedroom air.

"I don't know if I mentioned this last night," Hank told Annie over three tablespoons of instant coffee dissolved in lukewarm tap water. "Rocky wants me to go with him on some kinda half-assed monkey hunt."

"Oh my god," Annie said, her cup clattering to the table. "*Rocky* suggested that?"

"Yeah, why?" It was a stupid idea, he knew, but he didn't think it called for a reaction like that.

"Isn't that some kind of Southern racist term for . . . ?" Hank was already shaking his head, understanding her confusion.

"No, honey. He wants me to come along and help him catch this imaginary monster. What you're thinking of is called—"

"I really don't want to know," she snapped, and he could sense it was not the morning to push it.

"All right." He took another sip of the fake coffee and grimaced.

"Do you know where he's staying?" she asked, in an effort to move the subject away from racist slang.

"Rocky? Dunno," Hank said. He could still hear the damn helicopters outside. "Never asked him. Probably with some whore. *Oh.* Don't know if I mentioned this either. I think I ran into Khalid last night on the way home."

"You think you did."

"Things were a little fuzzy."

"Wait a second," she said, frowning. "Which one's Khalid?"

He forced himself to drink more of the foul coffee, hoping it might clear his head. "You know him. The bum who's usually outside the grocery store. Big guy with the hair."

"Oh. Sure," she said. "But doesn't he prefer to be called *unencumbered*?"

Hank drained his cup, praying it didn't splash back up. As wretched as it was, it was still better than the shit he sometimes bought at Harry's newsstand. "Probably, but we all want a lot of things, don't we?"

"What was he doing way over by Trog's? Bit out of his range, isn't it?"

Hank stood. "Hell, I dunno. Maybe. But he's a bum . . . and to be honest, I don't even know it was him. All I remember is talking with some black guy for a few minutes. Figured it was him. Don't remember what I said."

Oh god, Annie thought. She didn't want to think about what kind of trouble he could get into out in the streets alone and drunk. Hank excused himself and headed toward what was left of the bathroom to rinse out his cup and brush his teeth.

"How are you feeling?" she asked after him.

"Right as rain," he droned back. "It's gonna be a peach of a day."

It was both a surprise and a relief that the cover stories in all of the dailies dealt with something other than the Gowanus Beast. It was the first time in a week such a thing had happened. Instead, they were focused on the disappearance of two Queens boys from two separate neighborhoods. The boys, ages nine and ten, had both gone missing on their way home from school. Nobody saw a thing.

It was less surprising when Hank opened the *Eagle* and found Stone on page 2, speculating not only that the boys had been snatched by the gay Gowanus Beast but that the creature itself was under the hypnotic control of an evil genius of some sort (she called him "diabolical"), who was using the monster to gather victims for his "nefarious homosexual experiments."

I should call and tell her old man Zabor's the one she's looking for, he thought, as he folded the paper and dropped it in the trash.

With an internal sigh he turned to the larger than usual stack of faxes waiting for him. Instead of the expected clog-dancing celebrations and mulch fests, he discovered as he flipped through them that at least half were overnight police reports. There were five pages worth for Cobble Hill alone, and six for Park Slope. It was unheard of for neighborhoods like that, where the biggest problems usually involved people who weren't recycling properly or had neglected to pick up after their poodle. Upon closer examination he noticed something else.

He'd been afraid this was going to happen. He set down the reports and picked up the phone.

"So in other words," Hank was saying five minutes later, "you got nothin' else for me."

"Oh, I got plenty," Lieutenant Crosslin replied. Behind him, Hank could hear the sound of voices shouting across rooms and into other telephones, doors slamming, papers shuffling, typewriter keys clacking, and squeaky shoes marching across tiled floors. He'd never heard that much activity at the Seventy-fourth before.

"But it's all Gowanus Beast crap."

"How long'd it take you to figure that one out?" Crosslin asked, before hacking loudly into the phone.

"It's really all there is." Hank flipped through the stack on his desk for effect. "Prospect Heights, Windsor Terrace, Brownsville, Bed-Stuy, everywhere. No family disputes, no love triangles. Nothing but monster shit."

"Mm-hm," Crosslin confirmed. "Snatched purse, simple assault, domestic dispute, missing dog . . . Beast did everything. Even a stolen pie. That came in yesterday. Dingbat comes home from the store, the apple pie she left on the counter was gone, so of course, y'know, that means a fuckin' *ape* snuck in her house and took it. Dame's got a big fuckin' dog, but oh no."

"That last one I believe," Hank said.

"You think Brooklyn's bad, try the other boroughs. Manhattan, Bronx, same thing. Fuckin' houseplant falls off a windowsill, guy calls nine-one-one, says the Beast is breaking in." He hacked another wet cough into the phone. "Weird thing is, Friday, Saturday night not a single D and D. Monster or otherwise."

"Guess people are afraid to get sloppy, let their guard down,"

Hank suggested. "Beast might sneak up on 'em. Which I guess is good news for Rebane's anti-booze campaign."

"It's not just the booze," Crosslin sounded frustrated. "Numbers are down across the board. Even when we do get something, we got nothin', 'cause the victims and the witnesses both are only seein' monsters. We got nothin' to go on. We can get security camera footage, right? Show it to the vic? And whaddo they say? 'Oh, no, that wasn't it—I was attacked by a big hairy thing.' Fuckin' crazy."

Something awfully clever occurred to Hank. "Jesus," he said. "With the numbers dropping, and a single perp responsible for all those crimes that do take place, you're on your way to the lowest crime rate in New York history. Don't even have to cook the books this time."

Crosslin snorted into the phone. "That's no bullshit, Jack. You think Commissioner Garrison an' the mayor aren't thrilled? Why'd you think they ain't said too much lately?"

"'Cept to slap me around."

"Yeah, boo-fuckin'-hoo. I wouldn't worry 'bout that too much, Kalabander. You're their best buddy right now."

It came to Hank after a moment's consideration. "Election's comin' up next year . . . And this is their ticket in."

"You're a bright boy, always on your toes, ain't'cha?"

"Try to be."

"Well get down off 'em. You're a half-assed crime reporter, not some fuckin' faggot ballet dancer."

If that was indeed the mayor's plan, Hank thought later as he began to ponder his follow-up story, it was only half working. He might have the crime rate to run with, but the local economy was another issue. More and more shops were remaining shuttered around his neighborhood, and those that did open were closing before sundown. Nutskin had mentioned that ad revenues at the

Hornet had dropped considerably, and that was likely the case everywhere else, too. Those businesses offering "Gowanus Beast" specials two weeks earlier no longer found them such sidesplitters. Both the Yankees and Mets had canceled their home night games and the big adult toy, trading card, and homeopathic medicine conventions were looking for venues outside New York. Even the psychiatrists convention had pulled out, which Hank thought was a terrible mistake.

As if to prove it, at noon he turned on a small radio he kept in his desk, inserted an earplug, and tuned it to Carl Goliath's call-in show. He had no idea why he did this to himself. Hearing the masses confirm what he always suspected about them only deepened his loathing. Turning the show on today was, likewise, a terrible mistake.

"*Good afternoon and welcome back to the Carl Goliath show, your voice of reason in the metro area.*" Goliath had a shrill and grating voice that dug into Hank's ear like an awl. Yet still he listened, he told himself (and Annie often confirmed), because he was an idiot.

"*. . . on AM all-talk radio. It's ten minutes after the hour here in New York City, and this afternoon we're talking about what everyone else is talking about—the Gowanus Beast who's been terrorizing damn near everyone in town, and what we as citizens can do to stop it.*"

"Oh, lord," Hank said aloud. Goliath was without question the most popular radio talk show host in the city, maybe even the country, even though his focus tended to be on government conspiracies, questionable medical theories, and his troubling obsession with Barbara Eden. At times Hank couldn't make the slightest bit of sense out of the man's popularity, and at other times, well, he could.

"*Seems you wonderful folks have all sorts of ideas about the*

Beast . . . Let's hear what Jake on Staten Island has to say. Jake, you're on the air."

"Thanks, Carl. Love the show. But lemme tell ya somethin'. If that thing comes near me, or comes near my kids, or even steps foot on my block, I'm gonna do to it the same thing I'd do to a—" This was followed by an unusually long beep, which continued until Goliath's abrasive voice returned.

"All right there, now, fellow Americans, I'm as liberal-minded as the next guy—hah!—at least when it comes to language. You all know how I feel about our nation's glorious First Amendment, but there are some things you just can't say on the radio. Who's next? Looks like Gloria from Canarsie."

"Hi, Carl. Unlike most of your other listeners, I've actually seen the Beast personally."

"You're saying he made it all the way to Canarsie without getting killed? Well do tell, my sweet."

Her voice was hesitant and nervous. It was impossible to tell if it was the result of the experience, or of being on the radio, or the early stages of Parkinson's disease.

"Well, Carl, it was two nights ago. My husband, Pete—Pete loves your show too—but he was asleep and I just wanted to catch the end of that show about the two doctors. Have you seen it?"

"I don't know, Gloria, but let's get back to the Beast."

"I love that show, and this was a real good one. The one doctor—the cute one . . ."

Hank heard a voice in his unoccupied ear that was no less grating than Goliath's.

"Heya, dollface, wanna date?"

There was a brief, muffled scream of horror from Becky's cubicle that still somehow came out like a question. From the corner of his eye Hank caught a flash of striped pants and a purple vest. He snapped off the radio, pulled the plug from his ear, and spun in time to see Rocky turn the corner.

"Hey wha'cha doin' there, one-digit? Confirming your suspicions of the holocaust to come?"

"Pretty much so, yeah. How'd you get in here?"

"Broad at the desk was filing her nails." He turned back to Becky, who was in the process of leaving. "Didn't mean to scare ya, toots."

"Becky," Hank said patiently. "This is Rocky Roccoco, a mongoloid I happen to know. Forgive him. He's a carny."

"Hello?" she said, not looking him in the eye as she stepped around him and headed for the lobby.

"High-strung chicks these days," Rocky said, his leer following her. When she was out of sight, he turned to Hank. "So *this* is where you work?" He gestured and looked around. "I thought you said this place still existed. Either you been bamboozled or I have. You been givin' me the impression you're some kinda hot diggity crime reporter."

"Yeah, well." In an effort to move along as quickly as possible he asked, "So where in the hell'd you stay last night? Annie was wondering."

"I dunno, with some whore. Like dancin' with the back of a fire truck," he said, as if only half-listening. "Man, you really *do* need that big break."

Twenty-five

Six-year-old Viera Venezuela didn't know why everyone was so afraid, just that they were. Some of her friends said there was a monster but she knew monsters weren't real.

It was early Saturday evening, and her mother had sent her and her father to pick up some things at the store for dinner. She had never seen people in her Bronx neighborhood moving so fast before. She grew nervous and clung more tightly to her father's hand.

She saw Diego Kronstadt, a man she knew was a friend of her father's. He was running with several other men but stopped and yelled something to her father. He said something about having a monster trapped in a parking garage. Then he told her father to come along and help them get it.

Her father shook free of her hand and left her behind as he ran to join Mr. Kronstadt and the other men. They all disappeared around the corner. She tried to follow him but couldn't run fast enough to catch up. In an instant, she was alone.

They said there was a monster, just like her friends had told her. If the grown-ups said it, maybe there really was a monster. That didn't sound good. Now she was scared.

Her first impulse was to cry, but her father told her crying was bad so she wouldn't cry.

The best thing to do when you're scared, she told herself, is to hide. If she hid, the monster wouldn't find her. She looked around for a good, safe hiding spot.

Most of the stores were closed, so she couldn't hide in one of them. There had to be a good hiding spot outside. Hiding behind a car or a lamppost wasn't good enough—it could see her. She needed a better spot.

She saw one over in the trash piled on the curb in front of the butcher shop.

She made sure no one was watching, then climbed inside the discarded refrigerator and pulled the door closed over her. The monster would never find her in there, and neither would anyone else.

"This ain't exactly what I had in mind when I said we were gonna go huntin'."

"Ah," Hank reassured him. "That's where you're wrong, my diminutive friend. You wanna be a successful hunter, you gotta think like your prey." He scanned the room. "He's here, believe me. Somewhere. I can feel it. We just gotta wait for him to show himself."

It was quarter after nine. Hank and Rocky sat at the end of the bar, which gave them a clear view out the two picture windows flanking the front door.

There was nothing fancy about the Gargoyle. It was dark, it was small, and unlike most New York bars of the day it didn't offer an array of forty different microbrews. This was good news for the bartender, Hank thought, who looked like he'd have trouble making a rum and Coke.

"This is better, ain't it?" he asked Rocky. "You gotta admit it. Better than being out there with the real animals."

"Yeah, fine," Rocky grumbled. "It's got air-conditioning at least. I'm just sorry Annie hadda work late. She's funnier'n you."

"And better-looking than you, Jo-Jo."

"Ah, shut your gopher hole."

Every ten or fifteen minutes, a cluster of half a dozen people wandered past outside, huddled close together, looking both wary and bloodthirsty. Apart from that, the streets were empty. It didn't take long to figure out they were hunting parties. They were carrying baseball bats and guns but looked like they should've been carrying torches and pitchforks.

At one point an ice-cream truck trolled slowly past, the tinny loudspeaker playing a mangled rendition of "Little Brown Jug." Ten or twelve people who didn't seem in the least interested in rocket pops or strawberry sundaes were walking alongside. Some of them paused to peer through the bar windows.

"Look at those jokers," Rocky said. "If I could get them out to the lot, I could suck 'em dry and send 'em away smiling."

"You do that, too?"

Rocky slapped at Hank's arm. "You got nothin' on me, Rochester."

They'd been at the bar for nearly two hours but had yet to see any sign of the Gowanus Beast.

"This is almost as good as the Son of Sam," Rocky said, watching another small posse pass by outside. At his feet lay a laundry bag containing a net he'd picked up at a flea market somewhere in Manhattan.

Hank nodded as he drained his beer. "I was almost gonna say at least with Berkowitz it wasn't just empty paranoia. People were actually getting killed." He set the glass down and gestured to the bartender before turning back. "Then I remembered people *are* getting killed. In the past two days three've been shot, five were beaten by yobs like these, and four either ran off rooftops or jumped in front of trains because they thought they were being chased by a monster."

"Weird thing I noticed today?" Rocky said. "Nobody has any facial hair anymore. You notice that? I noticed that. No mustaches, no faggy soul patches, nothin'. Jews, Moslems, everyone. I'll betcha fin the next group comes past is clean-shaven."

"Nah, no bet," Hank shook his head. "It's true. One of the ad reps shaved his beard off couple days ago. Found out he has no chin." His speech was beginning to slur. "Hey . . ." He put a hand on Rocky's shoulder and leaned in. "Hey, what are we doin' here? This is asinine." He kicked lightly at the bag containing the net. "You know well as I do there ain't nothin' out there." He inhaled sharply and a slow belch rumbled deep in his throat. "I know W. C. Fields said you're never supposed to wise up a chump, but that's exactly what I'm trying to do."

"And that," Rocky said, draining his own glass, "is why you'll fail."

Hank was quiet, idly sifting through the damp bills on the bar in front of him. He lifted his head. "Hey, Rock, you know about the Winsted Wild Man?"

"Connecticut, yeah. What of it?"

"Yeah, 1895. It seems there was this—"

Suddenly a raucous explosion of voices arose in the street outside. It was soon followed by more shouts and pounding footsteps.

Hank and Rocky looked at each other. Rocky grabbed his net. Hank took another swallow from his pint and they headed for the door, bursting outside just as a mad crowd of at least two dozen people rushed past them down the middle of the street, heading west.

"*They got him!*" several voices shouted. "*Down there!*" "*You see it?*"

Sirens wailed in the distance. Above them two helicopters, spotlights tracing the ground, were converging on the area.

Hank grabbed Rocky, who was about to follow them. "My god," he said.

Two blocks away, three adjacent buildings were ablaze, and a growing crowd of people gathered near the inferno. Wild cheers were punctuated with screams of rage.

Hesitantly, Hank headed toward them, keeping a tight grip on Rocky, who was trying to break away.

"Let me the fuck go, you bastard," Rocky snarled, twisting his body away. "It's *my* monster, see?" He craned his neck in an effort to bite Hank's wrist.

"Just shut up and calm down," Hank whispered, in the way he would to a misbehaving child, his eyes fixed on the scene in front of them. He was suddenly stone sober.

As the two of them advanced warily, Hank could see the mob had clustered around a single figure on his back in the street. All Hank could see were the man's black pants.

Individual voices arose above the mob's general clamor and the roar of the flames. "*We got the Beast!*" "*Where the hell are the cops?*" A woman shrieked back, "*Who needs the fuckin' cops?*"

Hank saw two men dash across the street to a construction site, grabbing loose bricks off a pile. One of the men, pale and thin, resembled the hippie candle maker Hank met at the street fair.

"Where the hell did they get those torches?" Rocky asked.

The sirens were drawing closer.

Hank released Rocky's arm and maneuvered around the group, trying to keep his distance from the burning buildings. As he remembered, these particular buildings had been condemned and abandoned for years and might well collapse.

He found a break in the crowd and, in the firelight, saw Khalid staring up from the pavement, his eyes darting across all the faces staring down at him.

"No," Hank whispered again as he began clawing through the tight throng toward Khalid. "Let him up, it's not your monster." His voice came out hoarse, hardly more than a whisper. Nobody was listening and, as the sirens drew closer, the crowd moved in more tightly, forcing Hank back.

"Stop it!" he tried to scream. "*It's Khalid!* You all know him!" But in horror and frustration he realized that his voice was no longer responding. His limbs were going numb as he tried to pull people away. In desperation he looked for Rocky's help but couldn't see past all the others who'd gathered around him. He began feebly slapping at arms and backs in an effort to force people away, but he felt frozen. *They can't be doing this*, he thought.

From the ground, Khalid caught a glimpse of Hank's horrified face and called to him, "*Hanky! Help me!*"

Hank tried again to tear through the crowd. "Stop it," he rasped, trying to force his voice out and above the rest. "He lives here! You lousy bastards, let him go!"

Behind him he heard a man say, "Looks like we got us here a *Beast* lover." The voice was unusually calm.

Hank started to turn. He wasn't sure what or who hit him on the back of the skull, but suddenly his face was pressed against the pavement among all the stomping and shuffling feet moving over and around him.

"*Careful, everyone!*" someone above him yelled. "*He might have that alien disease!*"

Hank heard Khalid screaming his name but could not move.

Three squad cars and two fire engines pulled to a stop several yards away. As the firemen hopped from their trucks, the policemen approached the quickly dispersing crowd. Hank pushed himself up on his arms, and then Rocky appeared beside him, helping him to his knees. "What the fuck did you say this time?" he asked.

"What's going on here?" one of the officers demanded, hand on his holster.

"We got him, officer," said a breathless, beet-faced man with frizzy brown hair and a blood-spattered Mr. Bubble T-shirt.

"Got who?"

"The *Gowanus* Beast, goofy!" The man pointed proudly at Khalid's twisted and broken body, which now lay alone beside the curb. Hank began limping over to him.

"We caught him lurking," a woman in a daisy print sundress explained. "And then we chased him down here. He ran into that building there." She pointed at the middle building of the three, all now completely engulfed in flames. The fire had already spread to a fourth. "And Joey . . ." She paused to look around. "Where's Joey? Well, anyway, he said we should smoke him out."

"But then before we could," the man in the Mr. Bubble T-shirt jumped in, shooting a glance at the woman, "the Beast itself set fire to 'em . . . I think he was trying to keep us away or somethin'. Hide his tracks, maybe."

"Then he came running out at us," the woman said. "An' that's when we got him . . . An' got him good."

The officer nodded as he dutifully jotted it all down in his notebook. "I understand," he said. "You just can't be too careful. You people did the right thing tonight."

Around them, firemen were hooking up hoses to two hydrants, cordoning off the area, and shouting instructions.

"We just had to put an end to all the horror," the woman told the officer. She looked up the street. "Do you think the TV will be here soon?"

Hank knelt down painfully over Khalid, who was still breathing. His eyelids were swollen and closed. His weathered face was coated in blood, his dreadlocks singed, and his shattered arms and legs bent at unnatural angles, but he was still breathing.

"Khalid," Hank whispered. "It's Hanky. They're gone."

Khalid's eyelids flickered open as much as they could with the swelling. It was only a crack but it was enough. "Hanky . . ." He breathed through torn lips and broken teeth. "Di'n do nothin', man. They jus' start chasin' me." His head turned slightly. "Whosa midget?"

"That's Rocky," Hank said. "He's one of us."

"Heya," Rocky said. "How's it hangin'?"

Hank reached down and tried to pat Khalid's arm reassuringly, but when he saw the spasm of agony on the man's face he retracted his hand. "Sorry."

"Hanky . . . ," Khalid whispered. "I seen heads, Hanky . . . *lottaf* 'em."

His body convulsed and he coughed. More blood spilled from his mouth and dripped to the pavement. It looked black in the glow from the fires behind them. His chest was still.

"All right, sir, I'm gonna have to ask you to step away from the suspect." Hank and Rocky both looked up to see one of the officers standing over them.

"Suspect?" Hank asked, his brow knotting. "But he's dead. They killed him."

"We'll need to determine that later, sir. First we need to bring him to the station for questioning and possible booking. Now if you'll kindly step back away from the suspect."

"But he's dead."

"Will you kindly stand back, sir?"

Not knowing what else to do, Hank and Rocky both took a few steps back and watched as two officers rolled Khalid's corpse over onto his belly, roughly pulled his broken arms behind him, and snapped on a pair of cuffs.

"You have the right to remain silent," the third officer said. "Anything you do say can and will be held against you in a court of law . . ."

Half a block up the street, the frizzy-haired man had reconvened the mob and the torches had been relit.

"All right, people," he shouted. "We found the Beast once tonight. Now let's go find it again!" With jubilant cheers they marched away toward Third Avenue.

A fireman dragging a hose charged past Hank, who finally recognized what was happening around him.

"C'mon, Rock," he said quietly. "I think it's about time we headed back to my place. I'm assuming you need a place to crash, right?"

Rocky nodded.

As the officers were trying to force Khalid's limp body into the backseat of their cruiser, Hank looked down. At his feet he saw a brick, still wet with Khalid's blood.

"If this is what the show's like," Rocky said as they slowly left the scene, "I don't even wanna know what the blow-off's gonna be."

"Ain't gonna be Miracle of Life, I can tell you that."

Behind them, a stray dog trotted unnoticed around and through the firemen. It paused where Khalid's body had lain and lapped at the blood that had run into the gutter.

By noon Sunday there had been some nine thousand reported sightings of the creature citywide, and 327 people (and one corpse) suspected of being the Gowanus Beast had been arrested. Fires burned from Coney Island to the Bronx. In Times Square, a woman visiting from Kenosha, Wisconsin, had been trampled to death at the Keenan Wynn Theater after an actor in *Hats for Sale!: The Musical* appeared onstage in a monkey mask, throwing the matinee audience into a panic.

The following morning, Mayor Rebane announced that, with the approval of state and federal authorities, he had called in the National Guard to help hunt down the Beast. During the announcement he noted specifically that, among countless other duties, troops would be posted in the theater district in order to ensure that Broadway remained "free of monsters and safe for tourists."

Twenty-six

Whaddya mean there's no record? It's your precinct. I checked when they were trying to stuff him into the car."

"Nope," Lieutenant Crosslin said. "Nothin' on file. I'm tellin' ya."

"Are you back on the junk or what? Don't fuck with me on this. There's gotta be a record. I was there." This was insanity.

"Hank, there's a lot goin' on, we're drownin' here. But I'm tellin' ya, no. Saturday night, homeless guy with dreads name of Khalid something, brought in all beat up? No. Zippo. That's the end. You try the morgue?"

"*Yes*, I tried the morgue. They never heard of any such thing either. The cops told me they were bringin' him to the station." It was another one of those times Hank really wished he could have a cigarette, just so he could stub it out angrily. "So what happened to him between Third Avenue and the station?"

Crosslin was quiet, and again Hank could hear all the activity behind him. He heard Crosslin muttering quietly to someone.

When he came back on the line his voice was louder and more deliberate. "Ma'am, I'm very sorry. No, we don't know where Julio is. But you—"

"Who the hell are you talking to?" asked Hank, who was sometimes a little slow on the uptake.

"*Ma'am*, please," Crosslin insisted. "You must understand that the city needs to save space, money, time, and manpower however it can. Especially now."

Both men were silent. Hank could feel himself grow cold.

"They dumped him."

"That would be correct, Mrs. Rivera." Crosslin was still talking more loudly than was necessary, as if making a bumbling attempt to communicate with someone who spoke little English.

But where would they have dumped him? Hank wondered. One of the burning buildings? No, that wasn't foolproof. If there was any kind of investigation they'd still find bones.

"They dumped him in the Gowanus," Hank guessed. It was the one place in the area you could be almost certain no evidence would ever turn up.

"I suspect if you just go check with your niece, Mrs. Rivera, yes, I'm sure you might find Julio's there . . . Yes, you have a good day, too, Mrs. Rivera." Crosslin hung up the phone. It took Hank a few minutes to remember to do the same.

I sure hope he's positive those calls aren't recorded, Hank thought.

He opened a new file and began typing as fast as his dry, stiff fingers would allow.

He had to admit he wasn't that surprised the next morning when Nutskin rejected his story about what happened to Khalid. To be honest, he might have rejected it himself. There was no body, there were no records, he and Rocky were the only eyewitnesses willing to talk, and there was no way he dared quote Crosslin—not even as "an unnamed source close to the case." In short, he had no proof of anything, even though he knew it all to be true.

Those weren't Nutskin's beefs, however. He was just pissed that it wasn't the Gowanus Beast follow-up story he'd requested. It was also, as he put it, "a real bummer." Hank would've argued for it more forcefully but he simply didn't have the energy. And if the story did run, Rebane finally would have reason to come down on him.

There was one other possibility, however distasteful.

He picked up the phone and called Stone, telling her he had something she might find interesting.

Stone explained she was working on a lead and asked Hank to meet her in an hour at the Fifth Street entrance to Prospect Park. "By the green cat statue," she said.

From there they strolled to a small playground just inside the park and took a seat on a dilapidated and creaky bench. Hank mopped the sweat from his face. Two nannies on the playground occasionally kept an eye on a single three-year-old as he played on a swing that emitted a repetitive metallic squeak. Hank tried to ignore it as he laid out what happened to Khalid, point by point.

"But you have no solid evidence for any of this, apart from what you claim you saw and some cryptic hints from a junkie cop."

"If you wanna look at it that way." He was wincing with every squeak.

Stone shook her head. "No, there's nothing I can do with it then."

"Oh, just hold on," Hank said. "Having no evidence has never stopped you before. You use episodes of old TV shows and fuckin' Rue Morgue as evidence. You claim that the first guy who was chased off the roof—Michael what's-his-name—died of fright, when you know damn well the coroner's report said just the opposite. You draw connections between things that have no connections and get away with it. It's all phony. You know it, too. But you're tellin' me I got nothin' to work with?"

She tousled her red hair. "Hank, I love you dearly, you know that." There was a hint of condescension in her voice. "You helped me get where I am today. But there's a difference. I cover the Gowanus Beast story from every conceivable angle. But what you got there isn't a Beast story."

The muscles in Hank's jaw started to quiver. "What are you talking about? That's why he was *killed*. This *is* the Gowanus Beast story."

"No, it's not." She raised an annoying finger at him to make a point. "Let me give you an example. I'm here today to meet with a mother and her six-year-old. Last Friday, the kid says, he played on these swings with the Gowanus Beast. See? Now that's a story. Homeless guy dies and vanishes. So what? That's no story. That's one less bum stinking up the trains."

He both could and couldn't believe what he was hearing. "Wow," he said as he stood to leave. "Jesus, but you're a dick."

When Hank stepped back into the office, Blanche handed him an envelope.

"Afternoon, Mister Kalabander, if you must," she said. "Some creepy old guy dropped this off for you. Said you'd understand."

"Short bald guy in stripey pants, chewing a cigar?"

She looked confused. "No . . . another one."

"Great," he said, tearing the envelope open as he returned to his desk.

There were six sheets of paper inside. The top sheet was yellow legal paper. The note scribbled upon it had been written in black marker.

"Mr. K—I'm STUPEFECATED! What does Lord Jesus WANT?"

It was signed "V.S.I."

The remaining five pages were photocopies of the *Times* crossword puzzle. According to the dates, they had all appeared within the past month.

In order to assist in Hank's understanding, Mr. Isopod had circled a number of significant clues, as well as specific letters in the solution. These were connected with a series of arrows. From these carefully chosen clues and letters, Mr. Isopod had derived an anagram, which he had written at the bottom of each page. Each anagram, then, had graciously been solved in order to further assist Hank in comprehending Jesus' latest mash note.

UNCERTAIN NEWT STEPS read the message on the first page. GRINNING MAN ELIZABETH was on the second, SAND MAN SCREAM on the third, and VELVET SKIP ROPE on the fourth.

Hank didn't have time for this nonsense. He crumpled the pages without bothering to look at the fifth.

Yeah, I think I know what Jeebus is telling you, Mr. Isopod. He tossed them all in the trash can and rubbed his eyes.

Twenty-seven

Clothes Make the Monster

Former trapeze artist Laverne Miller, 62, of Bay Ridge has always been a classy dame who took great pride in her appearance. That stopped working to her advantage on Tuesday, when she allegedly painted her nails with bloodred polish and donned a rabbit fur coat before heading out to get her hair done. Longtime neighbor Pete Van Horn, 57, seeing a "hairy beast" with "bloody claws" stepping out of Ms. Miller's Eighty-eighth St. home, became convinced some harm had come to her, and so allegedly went after the creature with a handy shovel. He was soon joined by other neighbors who, it must be said, did a mighty fine job of subduing the ferocious monster. When she emerges from the coma, Ms. Miller will be charged with criminal impersonation, malicious mischief, inciting a riot, and weapons possession.

Calling Klondike Kat

According to several witnesses, three Gowanus Beasts wearing black hooded sweatshirts, baseball caps, and black jeans allegedly broke into Oleanna's Pantry, a gourmet food shop in Park Slope, shortly before midnight on August 5. The three Beasts allegedly stole bonbons, cheeses, and the cash register. Police say they'll "get to it when we can."

But Did He Pick Up After the Dog?

Five independent witnesses reported seeing the Gowanus Beast walking his Yorkie near the Pratt University campus early Monday morning. Police say they likely won't be getting around to this one any time soon.

That Doesn't Sound Healthy

Ceylon Al-Mahazred, owner of Dickie's Tropical Fish on Avenue X, told police that a "hulking, hairy, smelly beast" allegedly entered his shop late Wednesday afternoon, reached into a tank full of expensive Amazonian piranhas, and grabbed two. He then allegedly proceeded to shove the two man(hood) eating fish down his pants before leaving the store. In a detail that seems to conflict with most reports, Mr. Al-Mahazred insists that beneath all that hair the creature resembled a middle-aged Asian gentleman.

Hank sighed deeply after typing the last entry. It was all so useless, but what more could he do when nobody seemed interested in hearing the truth? After what happened to Khalid, his initial rage had faded to a sour, nauseating hopelessness. Still he had to try. That's what Annie said, anyway. But he had tried, and as Rocky predicted he'd failed.

"Hank?" a voice asked from somewhere above him. He looked up to see Becky's eyes and bangs gazing down at him from over the cubicle wall. "Can I ask a question?"

"Well," he said. "At least the inflection'll be right for once. Sure."

"Have you ever seen a movie called *Psycho*?"

He bit his lower lip, but briefly. "You're talking about the Hitchcock film with Anthony Perkins and twenty minutes of Janet Leigh, right?"

"I dunno?" she said, her head bouncing slightly as she shrugged. "All I know is it's real old? So I thought you might've seen it?"

Unsure whether or not she was trying to make a crack about his age, he chose to let it slide. He was too tired to take things personally. "Let's just assume we're talking about the same movie. Yeah, I've seen it. Why?"

"'Cause I've never seen it? And my girlfriend is a film student? And her professor said they had to see it? So she got it and wants me to watch it with her?"

"Oh," Hank said. "Well that's very nice, but I thought your girlfriend was a jazz musician. Played the flute."

"Nuh-uh?"

"Oh," Hank said. *Damn kids.* "Well anyway yeah, you should see it—it's really something. Especially first time you see it. You could never guess that Norman's mother's actually been dead for years, see, and it's him dressing up like her and killing people."

"Oh." She sounded deflated. "Okay . . . Thanks."

"No sweat." Hank returned to his computer as Becky's head descended below the wall again.

If he couldn't wise up the chumps by telling them the dark and damning truth—namely that they were chumps—maybe he could wise them up by telling them a friendly white lie or, better still, by convincing someone else to tell that friendly white lie for him.

"So here's what you do," he was saying.

He swallowed his anger about Khalid when he called Crosslin. He couldn't be mad at Bud. Bud was as unhappy as he was about what was going on, and moreover he'd gone out on a limb to let him know what had happened. If he'd been caught, he would've been out of a job and Hank would be forced to get his information from faxes alone or some goddamn snot-nosed cadet.

"Ya hearin' me? Pass it up the line and get the chief to float an official statement to the press saying the Gowanus Beast has packed up and left town. That's what they did a few years back, remember, with that ninja burglar nonsense. Worked like a fuckin' charm. Calls stopped the next day."

"For about a year," Crosslin reminded him. "Then it started up again."

"And so what did they do? They did it again. Said it was a gang of Armenian ninja burglars, and that they'd all been rounded up and deported back to wherever the hell they came from."

"They were Albanians. Nineteen of 'em."

"Yeah, whatever you say. But the point is, there hasn't been another sighting since. Now, changing the story was a stupid idea, you ask me, but it worked. It'll work the same way here, believe me. Tell 'em it's gone to, I dunno, Ontario or Sarasota. Like the ninja case, everybody'll be happy and nobody'll feel foolish—though they should."

"Even though this is comin' from a mug like you," Crosslin admitted, "it ain't such a bad idea. Let me bounce it around a fewa the boys. Problem is, a lotta these kids believe as hard as everyone else there's somethin' out there."

Moments after hanging up the phone it rang again.

"Jesus," he muttered before picking up. "Yeah?"

"You see? *You see?*"

He didn't recognize Stone's voice at first. She sounded hysterical. When he did recognize her voice, his first impulse was to hang up. "I see what?" he asked.

"They just found another one—a kid—raped and beaten to death behind a housing complex in Bushwick!"

"Well there's a surprise."

"It's behind Denham Houses."

Hank groaned quietly, rolling his eyes to Topsy. "You sound very happy about all this."

Stone clucked her tongue at his ignorance. "*Denham* Houses?" Hank was obviously a moron for not recognizing the name. "There was a sighting behind a Denham House a couple weeks ago. An old Spanish lady."

"Stone," Hank said, decidedly unimpressed. "There have been sightings everywhere. There was one on the observation deck of the Empire State Building last week."

"Maybe, but not with a dead kid."

"That doesn't even make any sense." He should've hung up when he'd had the chance.

"So *now* do you still believe this thing doesn't exist?"

"Yyyup," he said, wondering why he was even putting in the effort. "Accept it. It's just another raped and murdered kid. Or to paraphrase you, one less kid getting in my way on the sidewalk." He hung up the phone without waiting for her response. Yes, he was tired. Almost more than anything, he was tired of the office and the cubicle and the phone. Then he remembered what things were like outside.

Twenty-eight

As he rattled along in the half-full subway car, Nutskin's warning rippled through Hank's brain. Just as he was leaving the office the editor had stopped him and reminded him that he had an assignment and a deadline. "You must get me something, Kalabander," he'd said with those loose, cadaverous lips. "One way or another. Prove it exists, prove it doesn't. I don't care at this point. Just get me something. I'm serious."

Hank knew where he was going, but he couldn't say for certain why. He honestly had no idea what he was planning to do once he got up there, but at least it was something.

At the next stop, a thin young man in a yellow T-shirt and horn-rimmed glasses shuffled aboard at the far end of the car. He dragged a skateboard behind him with a piece of string he'd taped to the front. Atop the skateboard was a filthy blue milk crate. The young man carried a beat-up coffee can in his free hand. Physically, he looked perfectly normal. His clothes were clean, his features weren't disfigured, and from where Hank sat there seemed to be no visible prostheses. But when he opened his mouth to speak, the muddy, thick-tongued nasality more than hinted that something was off.

"Laneeze an' gen'muh, im you ah um'ploy, I'ne here na hep!"

As he drew nearer, Hank could read the hand-lettered cardboard sign taped to the milk crate: "Fud N Toonz." The crate was filled with ancient, dirty cassette tapes—Boz Scaggs, Oak Ridge Boys, Quiet Riot, Debby Boone—obviously picked out of other people's trash. Along with the tapes, there was also a selection of unwholesome, potentially dangerous sandwiches wrapped in newspaper.

The deal, if Hank was translating him correctly, was that if you were unemployed and hungry (or in need of some uplifting entertainment), you could pick something out of his crate. Otherwise you could make a donation to the cause.

When the entire image came together for him, Hank erupted into the first solid, true laughter he had experienced in a long time. At least until he started coughing.

As the young man passed with his skateboard, Hank slid a dollar bill out of his pocket and held it up.

The young man beamed crookedly and held out his coffee can.

"You got a hell of an act there, kid," he said, dropping the dollar in the can. "Take the suckers for all they got." Then he winked.

"Hammy burtnay!" the kid replied merrily with that same crooked smile before moving on. That made Hank laugh all over again.

He stepped aboveground twenty minutes later and got his bearings. He could never walk around Bushwick without feeling like he'd accidentally stumbled into the scrubby end of some industrial town in northern Indiana. Look any direction but west toward Manhattan and everything was low, squat, half crumbled, and forgotten. Making the atmosphere even more oppressive was the low cloud cover, which cast a dirty gray filter over his surroundings.

At least it matched his mood, he thought, as he headed toward the Denham Houses. After the retard had left, the realities of, well, everything came back. At least there was nothing noticeably burning up here.

The Denham Houses were easy to spot from a distance. Monstrous and faceless and brown, the buildings making up the complex ranged from fifteen to twenty-three stories, each seeming to grow out of the other like a cement tumor. City officials always came up with friendly and inviting euphemisms for places like this—"low-income housing," "inner-city renewal"—but you stepped inside and you realized they were nothing more than glorified roach motels. They even smelled like insecticide. In the lobby, in the elevators, everywhere.

Hank paused and flipped open his notebook. The cops had found the kid at ten the previous morning. They'd all be gone by now.

There weren't many people on the street at that time of day, but those he did pass cast him a suspicious look. As he walked by a fast food joint, six men drinking tall boys on the sidewalk stopped laughing and stared at him.

"Gentlemen," Hank said, giving them a nod as he passed.

When he reached the front of the complex, he decided it might not be wise to walk in the main doors and wander around trying to find a way out to the courtyard. He might run into a security guard and that probably wouldn't be good. No. Given the way these places were designed that wouldn't even be necessary. He looked up at the sky again. The clouds were getting darker.

Damn.

He began circumnavigating the block-long structure but had only turned the first corner and gone another half block when he saw the wide gap between the buildings loosely cordoned off with twisted yellow police tape. Beyond it was the courtyard. From where he stood he could see a few of the dumpsters. They'd found the kid in one of them, according to the police report.

He looked around. Yeah, there were no cops in sight. They hadn't even left anyone to stand guard. There were a few pedestrians and a few cars moving in both directions, but they'd never notice him. Even if they did, he thought, they'd probably take him for a plainclothes detective. The key was confidence. He stepped carefully through the broken iron gate, strode purposefully to the police tape, lifted it, and ducked beneath. Nobody said anything but he kept his ears open for any approaching sirens.

He had no idea what he was doing here or what he might be looking for. All the windows in the buildings facing the courtyard were barred and their dirty blinds were pulled. That was a help.

There wasn't much back there to see. Gravel, patches of dirt that might once have been grassy, lots of uncollected dog shit, a narrow blacktopped path taking a circuitous route from the dumpsters to the back door. A few sparse bushes sprouted from beneath the gravel but they all seemed near death.

Apart from the police tape, there was no indication that there had ever been a young boy's corpse back here, let alone a full-scale police investigation less than twenty-four hours earlier.

He looked around helplessly at the crack vials and torn trash bags on the ground. Soiled napkins, diapers, and crushed Styrofoam takeout containers. Hundreds of blackflies swarmed over the open dumpsters. This was pointless. What had he been thinking?

He walked around the dumpsters and decided he was going to head home. He looked at his watch and, in doing so, noticed something.

At the base of one of the dumpsters a piece of paper was half-buried in the gravel. Just a bit of trash, he figured. He'd toss it in with most of the rest of the garbage.

As he shook it free from the loose gravel (keeping a careful eye out for discarded hypos and used condoms), however, he noted something odd about it. It was about three by four inches and someone had written on it.

He felt a few light drops of rain on his head and hands as he studied the paper. It took him a moment to decipher the crude, unbalanced red letters.

I am the SON

I am the LITE

He is my FIVE

He is no

Hank paused and flipped the paper over hoping to find a rhyme for "lite," but the reverse side was blank. The paper didn't seem to be torn. In all likelihood whoever wrote it ran out of time—it looked like it had been dashed off quickly—or simply couldn't come up with a proper rhyme.

He would've discarded it as some incomprehensible bit of concrete poetry from a third grader, except for what appeared to be a brown thumbprint in the bottom left-hand corner.

He brought the paper closer to his eyes. It wasn't marker or crayon, that was for damn sure. If anything, it looked like the thumbprint was made of dried blood.

Hank realized that what he was holding might very well be a note written by the murderer. It was no imaginary monster that killed that kid. It was a regular old human. And a semiliterate one to boot.

Nice work there, officers.

He was about to slip the paper carefully into his notebook when he heard footsteps and heavy breathing behind him. He also felt a few more raindrops.

Turning, Hank found himself staring into the scarred face of a massive pit bull. The dog didn't move, and neither did Hank. Its mouth hung open, its pink tongue sliding in and out over its jagged teeth.

"Oh, hello," Hank said in a gentle voice. "Are you going to kill me now?" It was the only question that came to mind, and perhaps the most logical. In the distance he heard thunder, and the rain started to fall more steadily, but he didn't dare try to run.

As Hank's eyes strayed from the pit bull's brown muzzle and black eyes, he noticed the dog's nubbin of a tail was wagging. It also wasn't growling at him. He allowed himself to breathe again. "Well, okay then," he said quietly, balling his left hand into a fist and slowly extending it, still expecting the worst, but figuring he might as well get it over with.

The pit bull lunged for Hank's right hand and Hank yipped as the dog neatly snatched the note from his fingers and galloped away. At that instant a searing flash of lightning and a crackle of thunder exploded directly overhead. The clouds let loose and a torrential, oily rain poured down as Hank clumsily chased after the dog and that vital piece of evidence.

"Hey! Dammit!"

Arms outstretched, he followed the bounding animal around the dumpsters, through several patches of slippery mud, then back out between the buildings toward the street.

The dog, soggy note still clutched in its merry jaws, hopped nimbly through the gate and was gone. Hank slowed to a stop, standing silently in his muddy shoes as the thick rain came down, knowing he was beaten.

"Well, shit," he said as the rain began to fall even harder.

" . . . *ordered the immediate evacuation of Denham House in Bushwick, Brooklyn, last night. The evacuation was ordered, an unnamed NYPD spokesman confirmed, after evidence was discovered by one of the tenants that seems to indicate the Gowanus*

Beast had once again returned to the scene where, just two days ago, the body of little . . ."

"What the hell are they talking about?" Hank asked, suddenly regretting having brought the portable radio home so he and Annie could hear the news over breakfast. "I was just up there yesterday and there wasn't anything except that note and a bunch of dog shit."

At least two, maybe more, of the kids upstairs began stomping in rhythmless unison directly over the kitchen table. It was loud enough to drown out the radio and sent a light sprinkle of plaster down on Hank and Annie.

Neither said a word but they both placed their hands over their coffee to avoid contamination.

" . . . *resident of the housing complex told the* Daily News *that the evidence in question was a set of footprints near where the body was found. The footprints, according to experts, were much larger than human footprints, but had very small toes, almost like a dog's. This constitutes the first piece of physical evidence found in connection with the Gowanus Beast, but it only deepens the mystery of what, exactly, is terrorizing our city. It is unclear at this point when residents of the Denham Houses will be allowed to return to their apartments.*"

"Oh, fuck me," Hank said, setting his cup of cold instant coffee on the gritty table before grabbing the small radio and casting it over his shoulder.

"Marv!" Annie scolded. The radio smashed against a wall.

"What? It's not like I could do any more damage to this place. Aren't they taking that wall down tomorrow, anyway?"

"Not that one, no."

"Still think the landlord shoulda shelled out a few extra bucks and hired some wops or krauts from the get-go. These guys'll probably replace the walls with tortillas."

"Now just calm down," Annie said, knowing now was not the time to chastise him. "So I'm guessing those were your big footprints."

"Mine and the dog's, yeah." He shook his head. "Jesus Christ. You never think people can get stupider, then they turn right around and surprise you."

Annie took his hand. "You've gotta call someone and tell them. You can at least stop this part of it from getting out of control."

He made a face. "Call who? And tell them what? That I was tromping around a crime scene, found an invaluable piece of evidence, and then chased a dog who ate it?"

Annie tilted her head slightly, seeing the problem in this. "This is insanity."

"Something like that, yeah."

The red message light was blinking on his telephone when he arrived at his desk. He turned on his computer. Within a few seconds the screen was displaying the top wire service stories of the moment. After an update on the president's goiter and some twenty-two-year-old celebrity getting arrested for attacking a group of fans with a machete was the headline, "Brooklyn Monster Returns to Murder Scene—What the Bloggers Are Saying."

He ignored it and sorted through the papers on his desk until he found the written instructions Becky had given him for retrieving phone messages.

He hit the necessary buttons and waited.

"Mister Kal—Ka, um, Kal-a-ban-der. This is Rasheeda Williamson. Of the Divine Inspiration Church. Of the Blessed Congre-gation . . . With Jesus." Hank wasn't sure if it was the same woman, but if it wasn't she seemed to have similar respiratory

troubles. He poised his finger over the button that would make her shut up.

"*Mister Kalaban . . . der. We was very disappointed . . . That you did not. Take us up on our kind . . . Offer. To visit our prayer meetin' last week. That makes us think you. Are a very . . . bad man. That devil still out there. An' we strongly sugges' you make it. To our next meetin'. Or else.*" Ms. Williamson slammed down the receiver.

Finger still poised, phone still clutched to his ear, Hank blinked.

Twenty-nine

Although the (apparently cursed) Denham Houses were set ablaze shortly after the discovery of the Beast's footprints, further trouble was quelled when word spread around the city that the Beast had in fact been killed by a fearless NYPD officer in Forest Hills, Queens. The Internet was aflutter with rumors, but it wasn't until the six o'clock news that people all across the tri-state area were able to see an exclusive interview with the man of the hour, Sergeant Ted Dadburn, conducted by Channel Six's own Belinda Steeley, live at the scene.

The stout-hearted Sergeant Dadburn was standing erect, hands clasped behind his back, on the sidewalk in front of the small, white, one-story house where the horror and heroics took place. Behind him, investigators were carrying evidence (including a computer and a television) out of the home to a waiting NYPD van. It appeared that hundreds of curious onlookers had gathered outside the blue police barricades to watch and wonder.

"Sergeant Dadburn," the blonde and painfully cheery Belinda Steeley began. "At this moment you have millions of New Yorkers on their knees before you. So why don't you tell us what happened?"

"Well, ma'am," the stony-faced officer recounted, "we received a call at approximately two o'clock this afternoon from a neighbor saying there was some kind of disturbance at the home of Mr. Breck here." He twisted the upper half of his body to indicate the small house behind them. "The neighbor also reported that they suspected Mr. Breck was being attacked by the Gowanus Beast."

"I see," Ms. Steeley bubbled. "Yet in spite of the obvious danger involved, you responded to the call, arriving on the scene alone, is that correct?"

"That is correct, ma'am, yes I did." Sergeant Dadburn nodded briskly. "In recent weeks everyone at the precinct has been handling a lot of these monster calls, so they've become fairly routine."

"Mm, but not today," Ms. Steeley interjected with a giggle in her voice and a knowing glance at the camera.

"No, ma'am, not today."

"Tell us what happened next."

Around them, the crowds outside the barricades had started cheering every time an investigator stepped out the front door with another box. As the camera panned across the scene, a body covered with a bloody sheet was clearly visible on the front lawn.

"Well, ma'am, as I was stepping out of my patrol vehicle, the front door of the residence opened and out came what appeared to be an orangutan."

Ms. Steeley gave an understanding nod. "I notice, Sergeant Dadburn, that you referred to the creature as an orangutan and not the Gowanus Beast. Why is that?"

"Uh, well, ma'am," Dadburn explained, "as I said, it appeared to me to be an orangutan. I've been to the zoo with my son and daughter and we saw an orangutan there. And that orangutan we saw at the zoo, uh, very much resembled the creature I saw here today exiting the household. Also, over the last five years or so, we've received several complaints from neighbors concerning the smell coming out of Mr. Breck's home. Mr. Breck was well known in the neighborhood as the owner of a pet orangutan, and so I presumed that one and this one to be the same."

"And yet you shot it four times." The camera cut back to the sheet-covered corpse on the lawn.

"Can never be too sure, ma'am. Those kissy faces it was making didn't fool me. The orangutan at the zoo threw poop at us. Hit my boy in the head. They're unpredictable creatures, and I made the decision in that moment not to take any chances."

"But that was four hours ago, and since then you've been informed that this wasn't merely an orangutan, was it?"

"Ah . . . no, ma'am, it wasn't."

"But instead?"

Sergeant Dadburn's eyes flashed from side to side quickly. "According to Commissioner Garrison, ma'am, it was in fact the Gowanus Beast, and that prior to my arrival on the scene it had in fact shot Mr. Breck execution-style with a snub-nosed thirty-eight-caliber handgun."

"Horrifying." Ms. Steeley turned to the camera, still nodding. "So that takes care of that, thanks to the heroic efforts of Sergeant Ted Dadburn. It seems our long nightmare is over at last. This is Belinda Steeley for Channel Six News, reporting live from Queens."

Thirty

Now that it has been confirmed that the creature shot and killed by an NYPD officer in Forest Hills earlier today was in fact what we had come to know as the Gowanus Beast, the lives of all New Yorkers can once again return to normal. The fear is behind us. So I urge shop owners to reopen their stores, and people to go back to work, and everyone to step out in the evenings again to start taking advantage of all the fine nightlife New York has always been known for . . ."

"Well at least someone listened to my suggestion," Hank said.

"Shh," Annie said, pointing at the radio. "He's not done."

"Just to be on the safe side," Mayor Rebane droned on, *"I have consulted with the governor on this, and we've agreed that it would be prudent if we maintained the National Guard presence in the city, as well as the checkpoints across all five boroughs for the time being, until we're certain that . . ."*

Rocky had heard enough and snapped off the small radio. "Shit," he said. "Ain't that the way luck goes, though? It's bad for a while, then all of a sudden it gets worse."

The three of them were sitting around the kitchen table in Hank and Annie's apartment. The dark room was lit with candles and the tabletop was cluttered with plaster debris, bent nails, spattered paint, and empty beer bottles. Half a case of warm beer rested on the floor beside the table. Hank had swept a few paths clear, but for the most part it was unsafe to leave the table, especially in the dark.

After making Hank promise he wouldn't throw this one, Annie had picked up a new portable radio and the three of them had gathered to listen to the mayor's address.

Hank found the silence an opportune time to repeat himself. "Well, not to toot my own petard here, but I just want you both to know that this was my idea, and I think I deserve a little credit."

"For shooting someone's pet to death?" Annie asked.

"No," Hank said patiently and with no little pride. "For having Rebane come out and tell everyone the problem had gone away. Guarantee by tomorrow things'll start getting back to normal."

"Don't make me laugh, Jackson, I'll break my legs," Rocky snarled. "You forget I needed that monster to stay in business? An' some fuckin' flatfoot goes an' shoots it. Un-fuckin'-believable."

Hank looked at Annie and shrugged. "Do I even bother trying to explain at this point?"

"Might as well call Johnny Macabro, tell him to start movin' into my trailer," Rocky was muttering. "Asshole."

"Oh, c'mon there, shorty," Hank said before draining a beer and reaching for another. "You're a professional showman. We've talked about this. There are ways around it."

Rocky looked up, his eyes both expectant and suspicious in the candlelight. "Yeah?"

"An ape's an ape. Just get yourself a chimp, say it was the Gowanus Beast. Survived all those gunshots and escaped or what-not. You can make up some kinda wild story. A few props, a few pictures. Get a dame in the mix an' you're golden."

The expectation in Rocky's eyes quickly became contempt. "Whaddya take me for, some kinda cheap charlatan?"

"Of course I do. You're a showman, for godsakes, not . . ." He had to stop and think. "Jacques Cousteau. You got people to pay two bucks to see Monster McGee, King of the Sea."

Rocky shook his head. "What's everyone got against my bear? Just leave him outa this. Besides—" He removed the cigar. "That ain't it. I worked with chimps before. Ain't as glamorous as it looks."

Annie was finding she became uncomfortable whenever these two got together. Part of it, she knew, was the childish jealousies that arose when two old friends got together, the exclusion that seemed inevitable. Part of it, too, was seeing Hank change. He relaxed. The silent anger he seemed to carry with him everywhere faded. But through that, she had to admit again, she had learned more about him than she had in all their years together. That was worth something—though for better or worse she couldn't say. "So when did you work with chimps?" she asked Rocky.

"Apart from when Hank and I knew each other, you mean?" He opened another beer. "Ah, long time ago in Florida. A winter gig between seasons." He looked to both of them. "Had a little roadside chimp wrestling attraction. Rubes pay a few bucks, get to wrestle a chimp named Eddie. You pin him, you get fifty smackers. But lemme tell ya, ran that thing for three years and not once did anyone pin ole Eddie. Those chimps are strong, boy. Don't think I ever wanna work with one again."

He looked around the cluttered and dim table for his half-cigar. When he found it he blew the dust off the end, then brushed it with his fingers before replacing it in his mouth. "So that's that."

Across the table, Hank hadn't been paying much attention to Rocky's story, having heard it several times before. Something had occurred to him. As they sat there, he'd been keeping an ear to the open window. The helicopters were still up there circling, but at street level it was the first night in a week he hadn't heard gunfire and screams.

"I can't believe those bastards are leaving the National Guard in place," he said. "And these checkpoints, Christ, what were they even looking for in the first place? Gorillas? And now what'll they be looking for?"

"Do what I did," Rocky suggested, booting the laundry bag at his feet. "Carry a big net around with you. They won't give you any shit at all."

Annie started gathering together a few of the empties to throw away. "I just wonder, now that this is over with, if they'll finally start looking for the guy who's been killing those kids, or if they'll just say it was the orangutan and leave it at that?"

"Take a guess," Hank said. Annie could see him sliding again. "We got the answer with Khalid. No muss, no fuss. Saves time, effort, money, and manpower."

Part of his mood on his way to work the following morning could very likely be attributed to the hangover, together with a lack of sleep and the unending heat wave. Plus Rocky had told them the night before that he was leaving. With no monster to capture, there wasn't much reason for him to stay. He still had a sideshow to run, and he was afraid to find out what his crew had done to it in his absence.

Everybody he encountered that morning seemed to be in a mood. You'd think they'd be happy after the mayor's announcement that all was well, that they were free to live their lives without fear again. From the looks on their faces, however, they all seemed disappointed to learn the threat was gone. The train was silent, eyes were downcast, mouths sour. Maybe it was simply the prospect of returning to work after a week's impromptu vacation.

The mayor's announcement—and Hank's pivotal role in making that announcement a reality—should've added a bounce to his step. The best thing about it was that he no longer had to worry about that follow-up story. Being able to concentrate on the blotter would be a relief. But there had been so much ugliness over the past weeks. He had witnessed things in his own neighborhood he never thought he would witness short of a trip to Bolivia or central Africa. No one would ever be held responsible for what happened to Khalid or any of the others. He knew that, and it fed a despair that ran far deeper than any hangover. Looking at those dead, stained faces around him, he knew now what they were capable of doing when given even the cheapest of excuses.

He reminded himself again that it was over with. He'd actually played a role in stopping it, as he'd been hoping he might.

Somehow, none of that helped when he reached the top of the stairs at the subway station and saw the National Guard checkpoint waiting for him. There were five people waiting to get through.

In no frame of mind to stand in that heat to show his identification and be asked the same ridiculous questions, Hank looked for traffic, stepped around the guards into the street, and continued walking to the office.

"Hey!" he heard a voice shout. "Halt!"

Hank kept his head down but raised a hand and waved as he continued walking.

He heard what sounded like someone wearing chain mail

clanking up behind him. "Stop where you are, sir!" Whoever it was sounded out of breath.

When the shadow appeared in front of him, Hank looked up and saw a kid who couldn't have been older than nineteen pointing a high-powered rifle at him. This struck Hank as more ridiculous than frightening. Nevertheless, he stopped.

"Don't be an ass, Rochester," he said. "Put that thing down."

The rifle didn't waver. "We need to ask you some security questions, sir, if you'll come with me."

"Questions," Hank said with a sigh. "You have asked me questions every morning and every night for the past week. The same questions. And I have given you the same answers. If you don't know them by now, well, I'm not sure what to tell you. You might need some outside tutoring."

"You need to stand in line, sir." The youngster gestured him back toward the subway with his gun. "Now, please."

Hank stared at him with tired eyes. "I'm hot. You must be hot, too, in that helmet and that getup of yours." Hank looked him up and down. "I'm old, son. I'm tired. I'm hot. And I need to get to work." He and the guardsman continued staring at each other. "It's *dead*, haven't you heard?" Hank saw the gun barrel dip slightly. "So why don't you just dangle."

He took a step to his right and continued walking. The guardsman took a half step to block his path but Hank skipped around him. "You need to come with me, sir," the guardsman said, his voice weaker. "My commanding officer says you *need* to be afraid."

Hank continued walking, waiting for the first bullet to hum past his ear. He no longer cared.

He flinched slightly when he heard the crack. The bullet didn't whiz past his ear but a few feet over his head. He waved again but didn't stop.

Around him, other pedestrians were screaming and ducking into doorways and behind parked cars.

"*You need to be scared!*" he heard the guardsman yell.

Realizing he was still alive when he reached the corner, he felt his mood lightening. Maybe things were okay after all, though he wondered briefly if he should consider taking a different route home that night.

Thirty-one

What the fuck are you trying to tell me, here?" Crosslin asked. He sounded as tired as Hank had an hour earlier.

"I mean just that. It's over with. The mayor's speech. Sure am glad someone's paying attention to me. Thanks, by the way, for passing my suggestion up the line."

Crosslin groaned on the other end and began hacking. After the coughing subsided there was a moment of silence before Hank heard him spit.

"Hate to be the one to bust your balloon, there, Kalabander, but I didn't pass your idea up any line. Never told nobody."

"What?"

"Your idea was for shit."

Hank felt his neck muscles tighten. "It was apparently good enough for Rebane."

"That should tell you something right there. And he didn't get it from you. It was a shitty idea wherever it came from. We got fifteen sightings phoned in to this precinct alone *after* the mayor's big speech."

Hank was about to say something but froze. "What?"

"They're comin' in faster'n ever. Have you been out in the streets today? People are goin' fuckin' nuts."

"I thought they were celebrating."

"You're such a numbskull. Got it? Two of 'em say this thing can shoot laser beams out of its eyes. Another said it carries a magic fishing pole."

"That's a new one." His voice was quiet and calm. This wasn't the way it was supposed to work.

"Another dame says it made her pregnant after . . . wait, let's get this right." Hank could hear Crosslin rustling some papers. "Here it is. 'Impregnated her by touching her on the wrist.'"

"At least they're getting more creative."

"Thought you'd like it. Wanna hear more?"

Hank shook his head. "I'll just read the reports when they show up tomorrow." He couldn't believe this. "Jesus, am I the only one who listened to that speech?"

"Looks like it. I sure as hell didn't."

He hung up the phone and pinched the bridge of his nose. He was tired again. *At least Rocky'll be happy*, he thought. He didn't know if that meant he'd be staying in town longer or not. He honestly couldn't say how he felt the night before when Rocky said he'd be heading back to the carnival.

He would have to ask Rocky one question at some point. He'd come to town with only the one set of clothes—the striped pants, the shirt, and the vest. Yet they'd been washed at least once since he'd been in New York. Hank just wanted to know how and where he'd done it. Can't very well wait around a laundromat without any clothes on. But that Rock was a sneaky devil.

"Kalabander?"

"Garrh?" Hank snapped upright, startled. He half-spun to find Nutskin standing at the cubicle entrance.

"You have a story for me?"

Hank grimaced slightly. There went his silly theory that the story was no longer an issue. "Well," he said. "Yes and no. Yes, in that there's a story. And no in that you'd never run it."

Nutskin didn't look happy about this. He pressed his lips together, which, Hank noted, somehow made them stretch to nearly opposite sides of his skull like some kind of muppet. "Then you don't have one for me. Kalabander, you need to get me something I can use, and soon." His lips relaxed, perhaps from the simple exertion required to play a gruff newspaper editor for a few seconds. "It was quite a weekend, wasn't it? We've gotta get something out there. I trust you heard Rebane's speech."

Hank scratched behind his ear. "Yeah. I heard it, Shed. Didn't change anything, though. Seventy-fourth reports fifteen sights last night after the speech."

"All the more reason, then. You've got to get me something. I don't care what it is, so long as it's something I can use and fits the space. If you want to jump to the blotter space, that's fine. At least it should be a light week in terms of picks for Stephen. Lots of events are being canceled. I don't know if they'll be on again after that speech."

"They won't be," Hank assured him.

"Great, so there's something off your plate. Give you more time. I need it by Thursday."

"Mm-hm," Hank said. By this point his eyes were back on Topsy as he waited for Nutskin to leave.

"I'm serious, this has been hanging on long enough. It's one simple assignment, and if you don't come through by Thursday . . ." Those cracked and wrinkled flappy lips were really working now, Hank thought. "I might have to consider letting you go. I don't like to make a threat like that unless I mean it."

"Mm-hm," Hank said.

"You need to prove to me that you're more of a team player than you've been lately."

"Team player, yup."

Nutskin turned away. "Thursday," he said as Hank gave the finger to his back.

Becky appeared from around the corner.

"I'm sorry?" she said. "I heard all that? And I've never heard him threaten to fire anyone before?" There was worry in her eyes.

"Imagine. Guess I bring out the best in people."

"Do you know what you're going to do?"

He looked over at her, his face more expressionless than usual. Instead of answering a question he had no interest in answering, Hank asked one of his own, one that has plagued him for months. "Becky, I gotta ask you something about that voice of yours."

Thirty-two

It was nine-thirty Tuesday morning. Two blocks down the street from where Hank and Rocky stood, a group of ten people, some carrying torches even on that bright, hot morning, had surrounded a car at the stoplight and were rocking it back and forth.

The two men watched for a minute, then turned to the newsstand. "Heya, Harry," Hank said, slipping a dollar out of his breast pocket and laying it on the counter. "What goes on?"

He'd abandoned his practice of picking up the *Eagle* every morning. His last few dealings with Stone had cured him of that nasty habit. Instead, he tossed Harry an extra quarter and got the lowdown straight from him. If there wasn't a line waiting, Harry was more than happy to oblige, and in recent days the streets had been pretty desolate except for the lynch mobs, who usually weren't much interested in reading the papers.

"Well, let's see there, Hank . . . Couple neighborhoods in Manhattan're on fire, Kips Bay over on the East Side and SoHo, of all places."

"Washington Heights?" Hank guessed.

"Goes without sayin', don't it?" He wheezed out a laugh. "An' a couple militia groups or street gangs—not sure which—seem to've taken control of the Bronx, lord knows what they'd want with it. Almost all communication's been cut off, and they've barricaded the streets an' the bridges leading in an' out. Most of 'em, anyway. So nobody really knows what's goin' on there." He looked down at Rocky. "Who's the stump?"

Rocky removed the cold cigar from his mouth, stood on his toes, and held out a hand, which Harry shook. "Rocky Roccoco," he announced. "Professional showman."

Harry's eyes darted to Hank for confirmation.

"Rocky's an old friend. Stand-up guy," Hank told him.

"Wouldn't expect anything less. So anyway, that's about it for now, 'cept for the obvious." He nodded at the group down the street. "Things are still pretty quiet around here. In comparison anyway."

Behind them they heard the echoed crack of gunfire. Hank ducked and turned in time to see the mob roll the stopped car over onto its roof with a crunch of metal and glass.

"Yeah, I can see that," Rocky said. "Good to hear."

Hank watched the mob move on down the street and reached for his wallet. "Y'know, Harry, I think you can do me a solid an' sell me a couple packsa them smokes you got back there."

"I been thinkin', Hank," Harry said as he grabbed two packs of cigarettes from the rack. "I toldja before to watch your back 'cause the mayor was pissed at you. But if the business about you suggestin' that speech to him is true, he's *really* gotta be pissed at you now."

There were more gunshots in the distance, and another mob passed by a few blocks away.

"So what the hell happened, Harry?"

The newsie raised his hands. "You're askin' me? Maybe nobody listened. Maybe they don't like Rebane. Or maybe they just decided that havin' a monster around was more fun than *not* havin' a monster around. God knows."

"The devil might be a better guess," Hank said, darkly.

When Hank entered the *Hornet*'s office, the first thing he noticed was the strained and confused look on Blanche's face. When Rocky came in after him, she looked like she might start crying.

"Heya, Blanche," Hank said. "You're looking pained today. Rough time comin' in?" She only nodded slightly to her left.

Hank turned and saw the source of her distress. A corpulent man with a scruffy beard and small, round glasses was standing in the corner among the cardboard boxes and back issues.

"Isn't it a little warm for a cape?" Hank asked him.

"Ah, good Master Kalabander, I presume," the stranger said with an accent that was as much South Jersey as it was Oxford. "Thou art the very soul for whom I have sought, lo these many days." He offered a bow and a flourish of his purple velvet cape.

Hank, Rocky, and Blanche could do nothing but stare, dumbfounded.

"There is much dark word afoot thou hast apelike hominid trouble, and thereby may beist in need of the proffered assistance of thy humble servant to vanquish this accursed scourge . . . Forthwith. Um . . . I pray thee."

"Personally, no, I'm not having any trouble," Hank informed him. "But it seems a few million other people around here are. Why don't you go help them?"

He and Rocky had seen plenty on the way in to the office that morning. The angry mob tipping the car was just one small part of it. They had crunched through the glass of a hundred smashed windshields. Trash cans had been overturned, small trees torn from the ground, and red paint splashed on the front doors of dozens of homes. There was blood on the sidewalk and thick smoke filled the air. The last thing Hank needed was an insane fat dork. Especially one he recognized.

"I beseech thee that I may introduce myself," the man said with another flourish. "For I am known as Dr. Ernst Prell, from Cambridge, England."

Hank glanced down at Rocky, who looked like he was about to launch himself at the man's knees. He tapped him on the shoulder, signaling him to back off.

For the briefest of moments Hank considered holding off with the punch line until later, but he didn't have that kind of patience when dealing with jackasses (Rocky perhaps being the sole exception). He folded his arms. "No," he corrected the visitor. "Your name is Ernie Flibbins—better known to most of your classmates as Dingus, or Dirty Dingus—and you're from Trenton, New Jersey."

Something deep inside Dr. Prell broke and a momentary pain flashed across his face.

"That of which thou speakest remains but a remnant of another time, another life—"

"And you can drop the faggy accent, and save your thees and thous for your Dungeons and Dragons buddies. Dingus."

"*Dirty* Dingus," Rocky chuckled.

Prell winced again in annoyance, as Hank explained to Blanche.

"See, ole Dingus here and I went to the same middle school together, but he probably doesn't remember me because he was in the sixth grade when I was in eighth. But I remember him, all right. The beard can't hide it. He was a dork then too." He smiled at Prell. "Weren't you, Flibbins?"

"I never really cared much for that particular moniker," he said, the accent evaporating. "Putting 'Dr. Ernst Prell' on the cover sells a hell of a lot more books than that other guy ever could."

"So you named yourself after a shampoo?" Rocky asked.

"Rocky, now," Hank scolded. "We're all adults here, so let's can the jibes. Dingus here has obviously found an act that works for him, which is more than you can claim at the moment. So let me introduce you to, um, *Dr.* Ernst Prell, one of the most renowned cryptozoologists alive today. And Dingus, this is Rocky Roccoco, one of the most renowned sideshow impresarios alive today." He shook his head, hardly believing that such a pair of sentences had come out of his mouth.

Hank forced a smile. He might have a use for this guy after all. "Look, Dingus—Ernst—whatever you're calling yourself. Why don't you follow me, okay? We'll let Blanche here work."

As the trio made their way through the office, the entire sales department stopped what they were doing and stared at the parade. At that moment, Stephen Brand stepped out of his office en route to the bathroom, but he stopped cold at the sight of Kalabander being followed by a cigar-chomping midget and a rotund man in a purple cape. He backed into his office and closed the door.

"Kayfabe this fruit," Rocky whispered as Hank dumped himself into his desk chair.

"Never a word from this Mortimer Snerd," Hank whispered back. "Nothin' to tell anyway . . . Hey, could you go find two chairs?"

Rocky turned and saw Becky. "Hey there, hot stuff—"

"Rock. Stop it," Hank snapped.

Without a word Becky stood and stomped away. Rocky grabbed her chair. "Here's mine," he said.

When they were all settled around Hank's cubicle, he turned to Prell and said, "So . . . why in the hell are you bothering me instead of, say, someone at the *Eagle* or the *Times*? Apart from our history and the fact that there's no security in this building."

Prell, who clearly had no interest in reminiscing about their days at Aldo Ray Memorial, tried to cross his legs but quickly gave up. "I've been in the city for a while now, conducting my own investigation," he explained. "Of course I've been following the coverage, and in so doing I noticed that you were the only reporter in town with the common sense to cite my work in your story, which, coincidentally, remains one of the most accurate and insightful pieces written about the creature at hand." The accent was beginning to slide back into place but without the bad Shakespeare. "It wasn't simple vanity that brought me to you, however. If I'm not mistaken, you, sir, are the one who first wrote of the Beast."

"Yeah, bully for me," Hank said. *Why is it the only people who know that are thieves and crackpots?* "Photo on your website doesn't do you justice, by the way. I had no idea it was you until you showed up here."

Prell pretended not to hear. "And I assume you'll be writing something more about this phenomenon in the days to come, correct? If so, I may be of some assistance to you. I am, as you know, a bit of an expert in unexplained activity."

"If you think you're gettin' your mitts on this thing before me, you got another thing comin', Jack," Rocky growled at Prell.

"Rocky, now shush," Hank said. Last thing he wanted to deal with was a fight between a midget and a fat guy in a cape. Unless there was some money involved. "You two should get along very well, considering you both have a fondness for purple."

"Ah, shut your pie hole," Rocky said.

Prell ignored them both. "It took a bit of time to find you."

"Yeah, I'm surprised you got out here alive in that quaint, uh . . . garb. But in answer to your question, I am doing something new.

Due Thursday in fact. But . . ." Hank paused, pretending to suffer a flash of inspiration. "Since you're here, I figure it might be worth getting a few quotes from you."

"Happy to oblige, good sir," Prell said, with a sweep of his arm.

"I think I'm gonna retch," Rocky mumbled. This time both Prell and Hank ignored him.

Behind Rocky, Nutskin (having been alerted by Brand) poked his head around the corner, took in the scene, then ducked away quickly.

"So," Hank said, opening a desk drawer. After a moment's digging through loose paper clips, rubber bands, pencil erasers, ballpoint pens, pocket notebooks, and for some reason a wooden fish whacker, he pulled out an old and dusty portable cassette recorder. He checked the batteries and the tape, then hit the RECORD button. "In your experienced opinion, what do you think we might be dealing with here?"

Having slid into "professional expert" mode, Prell suddenly exuded a comfortably supercilious attitude. The ruffles didn't hurt. "I can tell you now it wasn't an orangutan, although there is a slim chance we might be dealing with a phantom kangaroo. The radically different eyewitness descriptions of the creature might support that hypothesis. The footprints as well, at least as I've been able to discern from the news photos." He looked briefly disappointed. "Sadly by the time I was able to get up to the Denham Houses to make plaster casts for myself—the police haven't allowed me access to theirs—the complex was on fire."

Hank wasn't even going to bother.

Prell looked back up at him, an inexplicable overconfidence in his eyes. "There are many more phantom kangaroo sightings every year than you could imagine, and certainly more than get reported by the mainstream media."

"Which would be approximately *none*." Rocky pulled the shrinking cigar stub from his pocket, brushed it off, and chomped down on it. Although he would never admit it, he was making mental notes.

Prell gave him a worried glance but continued. "More likely, however, we're dealing, as I said earlier, with a large, apelike hominid, known to laymen throughout North America as Bigfoot, or Sasquatch, or a skunk ape. These beasts have been sighted in forty-two of the fifty states—including New York—as well as throughout the world. So I ask you, sir, why not in Brooklyn?"

"The rents?" Hank asked. Then, guessing in spite of his outfit Prell wasn't much of a joking man, he backpedaled. "You're saying that you seriously think all these thousands of people have been seeing Bigfoot."

"Not *all* of them certainly. But I also wouldn't discount the possibility that several of them *have* seen it. And if even one of these people has seen Bigfoot, that means Bigfoot is here. It's not as absurd a notion as one might think. All the development, the shrinking woodlands, which are his true habitat. Consider that in recent years the black bears in New Jersey have become common sights in suburban kitchens, so why not Bigfoot?"

Having read most of the postings on Prell's website, Hank was ready for that one. "A couple reasons I can think of, actually," he said. "First, I've been hearing that 'development's gonna force him into the open' crap since the seventies, and it ain't happened yet. And second, no matter how much development is going on, I can't see it forcing him to leave the Pacific Northwest to settle in *Brooklyn*."

"I must say, you are a peppercorn, my good man," Prell said, not caring much for the unexpectedly resistant attitude. "I'll have you know I have tracked this creature from northern California to the

Arctic Circle, through Wyoming and Canada and Alaska, through the tar pits and the Hapsburg Caves. You want to know if Bigfoot's real, you talk to some lumberjacks the way I have. They'll tell you."

Rocky leaned in, a cruel leer on his face. "So you like hangin' around lumberjacks, do ya, Maryann?"

Prell was having a more difficult time ignoring Rocky, but he pressed on nonetheless. This was his show.

Outside there was a brief volley of gunfire, followed by a squeal of tires and the clatter of what sounded like trash cans hitting an iron gate.

"Have you forgotten," Prell said, sounding smug, "about the Smithtown Ape out on Long Island? You might say, Sure, Dr. Prell, but that was a century ago. What have you done for me lately?"

"I can pretty much guarantee I would never say that."

"It doesn't matter. Remember that there have been sightings upstate for years, and sightings right here in New York City, too, dating back to nineteen seventy-four. You, of all people, have to be aware that there have been multiple sightings of such a creature on Staten Island. They call it Cropsey there. It's not that big a leap to get to Brooklyn from Staten Island."

"For one thing," Hank countered, "Cropsey, according to legend, was an escaped lunatic, not Bigfoot. Plus those were all singular sightings years apart. In the past few days thousands of people claim to have seen this thing simultaneously all over the city. People are being *killed.*" He nodded toward the window. Whatever had been going on out there had moved down the street. "That never happened with Cropsey. Or any of your other Bigfoot sightings. Doesn't that seem to indicate we're more likely dealing with some sort of mass hysteria instead of, y'know, a skunk ape?" He paused again. He couldn't believe a lot of the crap that was coming out of his mouth these days.

"Well, Mr. Kalabander," Prell said and paused himself, then smiled. "That feeds directly into a theory of mine. You see, there are two kinds of phantom creature which have been known by the great mystics throughout the world for centuries now."

Hank rolled his eyes under closed lids so it wouldn't be so obvious. He had to get down to work, and he really needed a smoke. He was also afraid he knew where Dingus was headed.

"The first is a Tulpa, a mind phantom which, if the mystic is powerful enough, can take on physical form."

Hank had been right—he did know where this was headed, and he wasn't impressed. "Yes, yes, yes, I read about this on your website."

"I'm goin' for a cuppa mud," Rocky said, hopping down from his chair. "You want one, Salamander?"

"Large black," he said. "Be careful out there. People might mistake you for an albino chimp."

Rocky looked at Prell briefly, said nothing, and left.

"That's all right," Prell said. "In England I've developed a taste for tea, anyway."

"Fine. So what you're saying is that if a mystic imagines something—an albino chimp, say—and for whatever godforsaken reason believes in it hard enough, it'll become real."

"Essentially that's what I just said, yes."

"Right." Hank checked the tape recorder to make sure it was picking up all this horseshit.

"But as I was saying, the Tulpa takes on a physical reality but it always remains under the control of the mystic who conjured him."

"Mm-hm," Hank never should've asked.

"But *then* there's the Tulkin."

"I know, it was in the story."

With his well-prepared spiel up and running, Prell apparently had no time for interruptions. "A *Tulkin*, you see, is a mind phantom that not only takes on physical form but also becomes independent of the mystic or mystics who created it. If enough people come to believe that it's real, it becomes an actual creature with its own tangible, corporeal existence. It can go and do as it pleases."

Gorilla my dreams, Hank thought, but decided to hold that one back for the story. Maybe he could use it as the title Nutskin would change.

"And herein lies the rub. The more people who believe in the Tulkin, the more people who have a thought of the Tulkin in their consciousness, the more powerful it becomes."

"In short," Hank said, "they're like celebrities. If no one thought about them, they would disappear."

"Cor-rect," Prell said, attempting in vain to roll his *r*'s. He was pleased with himself—the teacher who'd finally gotten through to the dull child.

Hank folded his hands and took a breath. "Like I said, Dingus, I read about these on your site. Even cited them in that story for a simple reason. Namely, that it's one of the most ridiculous, and one of the *cheapest*, monster explanations I've ever heard." He stopped and thought about that, and as he did so his eyebrows rose sadly. "And as things stand, it's also the most logical explanation I've heard for what's happening here. So answer me this. What's the difference between a Tulkin and mass hysteria?"

There were screams outside and the sound of smashing glass. For an instant Hank wondered what Rocky had said out there.

"Oh, it's quite simple," Prell said. "When you say 'mass hysteria,' you're clearly implying a group of people who believe in something that does not exist. In the case of a Tulkin, we're talking about something that *does* and it exists because people believe in it."

Hank stared at him. "You've had a lot of practice, haven't you?"

"It's been my life's work for thirty years. There are things in this world, Mr. Kalabander—living, breathing things—that you simply could not imagine in your worst nightmares."

"Uh-huh. So, just for the record, this is what you think we're dealing with here. A Tulkin, in the form of Bigfoot, which people keep seeing everywhere because they're thinking about it."

"It's a possibility. One of many."

Hank sighed and cleared his throat.

"All I know," Prell said, "is that we're dealing with something very unique, and I won't know exactly what it is until I get out and gather more evidence."

"Yeah, well, I suggest you watch your step out there." Hank didn't feel like arguing this anymore. It was too damned hot to be sitting in this stuffy office talking cryptozoology with a guy named Dingus. "One last question, Dingus, then we'll wrap up."

"I really wish you'd stop calling me that."

"Relax, we're almost done. Just out of curiosity, how many of all those monsters you've chased over the years have you actually captured?"

Prell looked to the ceiling. He seemed to be counting in his head. "Well . . . none, really. Not captured, no."

"Okay, let me put it this way, then. How many have you actually *seen*?"

"Seen myself, you mean? Right there in front of me, one-on-one seen?"

"Yeah, something like that."

"I've seen and collected mountains of evidence—footprints, droppings, markings left on trees, even a hair sample in one instance, after a Sasquatch had apparently become entangled in some elderberry bushes."

"But you've never actually seen anything yourself, have you?"

"They're sly creatures."

"Yes, well," Hank said dryly, wondering where the hell Rocky was with that coffee.

Thirty-three

Later that afternoon, Brand dared a meek look around the corner of Hank's cubicle.

"Henry, can I speak with you a second?"

Hank continued typing. "If you got a gnarl of faxes, just leave 'em with the others." He gestured quickly with his left hand.

"This is kind of important."

Hank stopped typing, pulled the earplug from his ear, and snapped off the tape recorder. There was half a sandwich (ham and American on a roll) sitting atop an open paper wrapper. Next to it, a cup of lukewarm coffee. Rocky had never returned, so Hank had to take his chances dodging into the deli next door.

He spun in his chair. "I'm busy, but what? Nice sweater, by the way."

Brand's eyes were wide and fearful. He looked around. "Could we go into my office? Sherwood's at lunch, so we'll have some privacy."

Hank raised an eyebrow.

"*Please*, Henry. It's very important."

Hank groaned as he pushed himself to his feet. He grabbed his half-sandwich and followed Brand around the corner and down the short hallway past the sales reps. Once inside the office, Hank walked around Nutskin's desk, taking a seat in his chair. He took a bite of the sandwich and chewed in patient silence as Brand closed the door, which slowly swung open.

Brand closed the door again, giving it an extra shove. Still it didn't latch and as he took a step away it creaked open. The third time Brand used both hands to push it shut and pressed his back against it for good measure.

Hank continued eating as Brand took a step back and watched the door creep open again.

Undaunted, he scanned the room and, not seeing what he was looking for, went to his desk and wheeled his chair over to the door. Hank took another bite, then for the next minute and a half he stared unblinking as Brand attempted unsuccessfully to prop his cushioned desk chair beneath the doorknob. When he stepped away, the chair rolled a few inches and the door swung open yet again.

Abandoning the chair, he walked to the other side of the room and grabbed a small wooden coffee table.

Hank looked at his watch and popped the remainder of the sandwich in his mouth.

Satisfied, finally, that the table would hold the door sufficiently closed for his purposes, Brand rolled his chair beside Nutskin's desk and took a seat uncomfortably close to Hank.

Hank looked from the door to Brand but said nothing.

In a stage whisper, Brand said, "I'm sorry to take such precautions. I just didn't want anyone or anything walking in here while we were talking."

"Okay," Hank replied, then waited.

Brand took a deep breath to steel himself, as if he were about to tell Hank that his gerbil had died. "Henry, I thought it best to warn you . . . It's about Sherwood."

"He's finally going in for the operation?"

Brand took another deep breath. "Actually, it's about your job. Sherwood told me that he's not sure you're a team player. He told me you needed to get a story in to him by Thursday—that's the day after tomorrow—with some solid proof that the Gowanus Beast exists or doesn't exist."

"I see," Hank said.

"This is the bad part, I'm afraid." Brand paused and closed his eyes. "Because he also told me that if you didn't get something in by Thursday, well, you weren't a team player, and that he might . . . he might have to assign the story to someone else."

There was sudden relief in his face. He'd finally said it. He sat back in his chair.

"That's it?" Hank asked. "This is why you called me in here?"

"I—I'm sorry—I know these things are difficult but I thought it was important to let you know."

Hank put a contemplative finger across his lips. "Not a team player?" he whispered. "How damn long did it take him to figure that one out?" He shook his head and stood. "Thanks for the heads-up there, Dudley. Guess I'll get back to—"

"Henry, wait, there's something else."

Hank paused and turned his head.

"It's about this Gowanus Beast . . . You know all about it so I can tell you. See." He took that damn drama queen breath again. "It has me a little frightened. I'm just . . . *afraid* every day coming in here and every night going home. I worry about it all the time."

Hank studied the anxiety on his colleague's face. Brand seemed near tears. It was all too tempting.

"I'm just scared of . . . what it might do to me. I mean . . . I haven't seen it yet."

"Don't worry about it." Hank gave him a cheerful, reassuring pat on the arm. "You'll see it soon enough." He turned to leave but stopped when he saw the table blocking the door. "*Great*," he said with exaggerated frustration. "*Now* how the hell are we supposed to get out of here?"

That same afternoon a group calling itself Humans Opposed to the Oppression and Killing of Animals by Humans, or HOOKAH, staged a rally in front of City Hall, demanding that Mayor Rebane do something to ensure that no harm would come to the Gowanus Beast, whatever it turned out to be.

"Who's the real Beast?" they chanted, and *"People are monsters too!"* A woman with long, straight, unwashed hair held up a sign that read, "I Love the Monkey Man."

The protest lasted approximately seven minutes, which was not even long enough for the first speaker to receive a round of obligatory supportive applause. Members of the Lower Manhattan Protection Squad and the North Jersey Militia decided the members of HOOKAH were nothing but a bunch of dirty, bleeding-heart creature lovers and set upon them with baseball bats, golf clubs, metal briefcases, stun guns, and expensive designer purses.

Half an hour later Mayor Rebane finally decided things had gotten out of hand, leaving him no choice but to call in the National Guard—not to restore order to the steps of City Hall but rather to clear away the bodies.

Thirty-four

Hank put his shoulder against the apartment door and shoved. He expected the usual resistance, the usual scrape and crunch of new damage, but the door swung open easily.

"Annie?" he called warily. "You here?"

He heard her muffled voice respond from the bedroom. "So get this," he continued shouting as he approached the bedroom door. "So Pork 'n' Beans calls me into his office today . . ." His voice died away.

He looked around but something seemed different. The walls were still ripped open, the stove and fridge were still in the hallway, there were holes in the ceiling and the kitchen floor, and thick electrical cables and ancient, corroded lead water pipes were piled in the corners and poking out from behind doors. Everything he saw was covered in gray dust and thick hunks of plaster. Somehow, though, it seemed no worse than it had the day before—that's what made it so curious. There was no fresh destruction to navigate.

He was still looking over his shoulder when he opened the bedroom door. "So what's going on?" he asked. "Place doesn't look any more ruined today."

Annie had her back to him. She was standing over the bed, her shoulders moving. "They went home," she said.

"Yeah, but didn't they wreck anything today?"

"I mean *home* home, Hank, to the Dominican Republic."

For a second, this didn't fully register in Hank's brain. "Uh," he said, then closed his mouth. He remained standing in the doorway. "They just left us like this?"

"Mm-hm," Annie said, her voice tight. Her shoulders were still moving, her back still to him. Only then did he notice the open suitcase on the bed in front of her and the stack of clothing next to it.

"What the hell goes on here?"

She stopped packing and half-turned to face him. He could see her eyes were red, her face puffy from crying. "I have to get out of here, Hank. I can't live like this anymore."

He leaned against the doorframe and folded his arms. "Don't tell me you're afraid of this Gowanus Beast shit, too . . . So, what, now you're running home to mother? What is this, a fuckin' sitcom?"

The despair in her eyes was replaced with sudden anger. "You *know* my mother's dead. God you can be such a monster sometimes." She shook her head in disgust. "And no, I'm not running away because I'm scared. Just look up."

He did and saw a hole in the ceiling. That was new. Through it he could clearly see into the apartment above theirs. A child was crouched over the hole like a squirrel, staring down at him with wide brown eyes.

"One of the kids crashed through the ceiling today."

"Oh, you're kidding me. Was it hurt?" He scowled at the face above him and it vanished.

"No."

"Damn."

"But that's only part of it. It's not just the apartment." She swallowed and sniffled. "Three men with guns came into the store today . . . They suggested I close down."

"What?" He took a small and hesitant step forward.

"They said that now wasn't the time for people to be reading, and that I might be in danger if I didn't shut down."

Hank dropped his arm. "Jesus, Annie."

"So no," she said bitterly. "It's not some stupid monster I'm afraid of. I'm afraid of the people who're afraid of the stupid monster."

"Well that makes sense, then."

"You can't walk the streets because of the lynch mobs. Militias have moved in. Can't even go to the park anymore because hunters are up in the trees shooting at everything that moves."

"On the bright side," Hank offered. "Three hunters were killed by other hunters last week. And two by some Nip."

Annie, who wasn't amused, shook her head and looked at the carpet. "And it's not just all that. It's you, too, Hank. You haven't exactly been a comfort. All this is going on, and I don't know where you are. You're off running around with Rocky. The National Guard is shooting at you. You're trying to prove something, and I don't think you even know what it is."

"Better have some idea by Thursday or I'm out of a job, looks like," he mumbled to himself, ignoring two-thirds of what she'd said, hoping to put the whole subject of his failings as a husband behind them. "So if not your mother's where do you plan to go?"

She resumed her packing. One bag was on the floor, already filled. She was working on a second. "I'm going to stay with Paula until things get a little better here."

Hank frowned. "Who the hell's Paula?" To be honest, he was half expecting her to say she was going to live with Marv in Tucson, forgetting for the moment that he, too, was dead.

Annie shook her disbelieving head again. "She's my best friend? Known her for thirty-five years?" She waited for some sign of recognition.

Hank shrugged.

"Hank, Christ, we stayed at her house, remember? She's with the State Health Department and you kept asking her questions about the hantavirus?"

He shook his head. "I really don't, uh . . . no."

She stopped packing. "Talk about a sitcom. No wonder your first wife killed herself." She knew immediately it was something she shouldn't have said.

His body and his voice went stiff. "*What* did you just say?"

"Hank, I'm sorry, it just slipped out." She took a few steps away from the bed toward him but he raised a hand to stop her.

"No," he said. "Don't." He dropped his hand. "Who told you? Rocky?"

She shook her head. "He stopped by the store a few days ago and it slipped out." Her voice was quieter now. "But it's not like I didn't know before that. You kept the news clippings around."

Three inches to Hank's left, a golf ball dropped through the hole in the ceiling and bounced toward the wall. As Hank watched, it seemed to break the spell. She could see him relax. He dropped his head and put his hands in his pockets. "Maybe it's for the best, your going away . . . And maybe when you get back we'll get drunk and I'll tell you about it. Kind of a funny story, you look at it the right way." An open book of matches flittered down from the ceiling and landed at his feet. As he took a step to the right he heard giggles above him. "I'm going to kill them, you know."

"I know." She smiled sadly.

"So where does this Patty woman live again?"

"Um, Albany? You know, the state capital?" she said. "And her name's Paula."

"*Albany*?" There was sudden, violent disgust in his voice. The sharp increase in volume made her jump. "But Albany's a *shit hole*."

Thirty-five

He convinced her to take a plane instead of a bus, thinking it would be safer. A plane might crash and burn, but at least it can't be stopped and overturned by a fear-crazed mob of bloodthirsty morons. Things generally seemed to calm down across the city for an hour or two as dawn approached, so at five the next morning he called the only local car service still operating. Together they rode to LaGuardia Airport through warm, dark streets lit with bonfires, past the rows of ravaged stores and gutted homes. No one threw any gas bombs at the car, which was a relief.

Before she left him behind at the security gate, she kissed him, promised to call, and begged him to stay inside when he could. To that end, she'd left him her laptop to use at home. With the store closed, she wouldn't have much need for it.

She also considered for the thousandth, silent time asking him to come with her, to get out of the city and away from all this madness. But she knew what his answer would be and so never brought it up.

After seeing her off, Hank got in a taxi for the thrill ride back to Brooklyn. There was no reason to return to the apartment at that point. Might as well just head in to work, he figured, get an early start, even if he had no fucking clue what he was supposed to be doing anymore. He gave the driver the *Hornet*'s address.

Along the way he rested his head against the back of the seat and closed his eyes. He didn't need to see those war-razed streets again. Within a few minutes of closing his eyes, an unbelievably stupid idea began to gather form in his head. His eyelids flickered open, just as the burning sun was rising over the charred skyline, revealing another hideous day. He almost smiled.

"Kalabander, have you heard from Stephen?"

Hank considered Nutskin's question and looked at his watch. "Um, no? But I rarely do. Was I supposed to hear from him?"

"I don't know. He never showed up this morning, and he didn't call. I thought maybe he would've called you."

Hank's eyes drifted over to the grainy image of Topsy. "Well, Shed, it's early yet. Maybe he's hung and running a little slow."

There was something beyond simple employer concern in Nutskin's voice. "I've never known him to be hungover. Or late."

"Maybe he's out with the ad reps. I noticed they aren't here either."

"Ad reps are a dime a dozen. Those I can replace. The troublesome thing is that Stephen's not even answering his cell phone."

"Hm," Hank said. He still hadn't turned to face his editor. "In that case, maybe he's dead."

During Nutskin's ensuing silence, Hank's mind drifted to other things. Prell had left him a voice-mail message, asking Hank to go, as he put it, "a-monster hunting with a professional" that night. He'd deleted the message before the word "professional" was all the way out of Prell's mouth.

When Nutskin spoke again there was a tentative suspicion in his tone. "You didn't . . . *say* anything to him, did you?"

"Can't think of a thing," Hank assured him. That seemed to be answer enough.

"All right," Nutskin said. "I can't worry about Stephen now. Are you going to have something for me in the morning?"

"Yassah," Hank said trotting out his virtually unrecognizable *Amos 'n' Andy* impersonation. "Ah do believes ah shorely will."

Nutskin didn't seem to notice. "Good. And if you hear from Stephen, please let me know."

Hank waited until the footsteps disappeared around the corner. Once they had, he pulled a slip of paper out of his pocket and picked up the phone.

He met Rocky at Fourth Avenue and Tenth Street, on the sidewalk beneath the subway overpass. The streets were mostly deserted over there, except for the occasional stray dog or speeding taxi. There were sirens to the west. A check-cashing place and a small donut shop on the corner had both been ransacked and torched. All the stoplights had gone dark and nearly every trash can he passed along the way had been dumped in the street.

"You get a video phone?" he asked as he approached the small man in the purple vest who was waiting in the shadows. He dropped the cigarette he was smoking and ground it under his shoe.

"'Course I did. Everyone's got one nowadays."

"*You* didn't have one."

"I do now."

Hank thought about asking him where he got it but decided it was best not to know. Instead he reached for another cigarette. "Any idea how to use it?"

"Not the foggiest."

"All the better. C'mon, we're going on a hunt of our own."

It took them only twenty minutes to get what Hank was after.

"Never thought I'd ever say this, Salamander," Rocky told him after their snorting laughter had subsided. "But you are one childish egg. No way on god's green earth this is gonna work."

Hank looked down at him, surprised. "You should be ashamed, calling yourself a showman—and the very one who gave the world Monster McGee, King of the Sea."

Rocky was getting tired of all the cracks about his bear. The bear'd served him well over the years, and now suddenly everyone and his brother has some smart remark to make about it.

They walked in silence for a minute before Rocky spoke again. "What's the scoop Betty Boop?"

"Scoop on what, this?" He pointed at the phone.

"No. Annie. Dumbass."

"She ran off with your bear." Now was not the time, he knew—and perhaps there never would be a time—to bring up his first wife and Rock's big yap.

As they walked, the streets around them were beginning to wake up. Not everyone was part of a mob, but it looked like most everyone was scared. Every pedestrian they passed gave them wide berth and cast a wary look their way, which Hank and Rocky returned. In the distance there were more sirens and occasional bursts of gunfire. Behind them they heard a Manhattan-bound train rumbling slowly across the overpass. Even the train seemed anxious, Hank thought. The air was hazy with smoke from dozens of smoldering buildings. It reminded Hank that he'd need to pick up a few more packs of cigarettes by day's end.

As they walked, he kept his eyes down or straight ahead, fearing that if he looked up he'd see bodies strung from the streetlights. It was good, at least, to see that a few of these fools around them still seemed to be headed to work. They weren't too petrified for that yet.

It was another hot one, though. He was getting awfully tired of that. The whole city stank of piss and smoke and uncollected, rotting garbage. An image, like a movie still from a lost film, flashed through his mind for an instant. Another deserted street, narrower than this one. A hot night and a bad smell. Getting back to the office would almost be a relief.

Two blocks away from the Gemora Building Hank slowed to a stop outside a shuttered dry cleaner. Someone had spray painted G-BEAST GO HOME in red on the corrugated steel gate. Next to it, for no evident reason, someone else had spray painted a crude flower being watered by a giant erect penis. Hank raised an eyebrow at this, then turned to Rocky.

"When we get up there, you gotta be nice to Becky. We need her."

"So when've I not been nice? She's just another uptight skirt."

Hank removed the cigarette from his mouth and rubbed it out against the closed gate. "Rock, Jesus, she's a *les'ban*, haven't you figured that out yet?"

Rocky stared at him in disbelief. "She's a *dyke*?"

"Yeah."

"She sure don't look like a dyke."

"Well, she is, so you can stop wastin' your charm. Just keep your hole shut." Realizing the sheer impossibility of what he was asking, especially after revealing what he'd just revealed, Hank changed his mind. "Y'know, maybe you should wait for me out here. Or go do something else and I'll meet you later."

"What, I embarrass you?"

"Just go do something else. Are you still hunting for the monster or what? I can't tell."

"Maybe."

"Fine, then. Go do that, and watch your back. I'll call once I see how this goes."

He was relieved to find Becky at her desk. That was the first step. He'd have to play this one smooth. "Hey Becky," he said, leaning around the entrance to her cubicle. "Any sign of Brand yet?"

She shook her head, thumbs flying over the miniature keyboard in her hands. "No? And Mr. Nutskin seems really upset?"

"Uh-huh," Hank said. "Well, I have this—"

"He was acting really weird last night? Before he left? Like, freaked? He was standing on his desk and crying?"

"Okay, fine. I was just making conversation," Hank said, pulling the phone from his pocket. "I shot something here, and I want you to take a look at it, tell me what you see." As he handed her the phone he added, "I honestly don't know how to work these things myself, so you . . . just do what you need to do."

She gave him a curious look but took the phone and tapped a few buttons. He watched over her shoulder.

Something beeped. The image that appeared on the two-by-two-inch screen was out of focus, shaky, and shot in deep shadows, but what was there was unmistakable if you looked hard enough. About ten yards away from the camera a humanlike figure was crouched on all fours near the entrance to a parking garage. It was covered in thick black hair from head to toe. Its back was to the camera, so even if the image had been focused and stable it would have been impossible to see its features. Given the scale created by a nearby parked car, it would have to be six or seven feet tall when standing on its hind legs. It looked like it might be giving birth, or something.

When the hairy creature was finished, it straightened up and loped toward the camera on all fours, its piercing eyes obscured by the shaggy black hair hanging across its face. The image jerked violently as whoever was holding the camera turned and ran down the street, still filming.

In all, it was about forty-five seconds of footage.

Becky watched intently, and when it was over she looked up at Hank, that quizzical expression still firmly in place. "You wanted me to see, like, a Bouvier taking a crap?"

"A what?"

"A Bouvier? It's a kind of sheepdog?"

"To the untrained eye, perhaps, but in reality it's something much more important. And here's where I really need your help. You're a technologically adept youngster . . . can you take that footage there," he pointed toward the small screen, "and e-mail it to someone anonymously?"

She thought about it, then nodded. "It might take some time? But yes?"

He had absolutely no doubt it would work as planned, but he was still chewing his tongue anxiously forty minutes later when Louise Stone Jr. responded via the chain of untraceable electronic forwarding addresses Becky had set up.

"She seems excited?" Becky reported as she read the note. "She used, like . . ." She paused, carefully counting aloud. "Eight exclamation points?"

Hank snapped his fingers. "Bingo."

"She also wants to know?" Becky continued reading, "Exactly where it was filmed? Because she wants to go there right away and get a stool sample? That it'll be the first solid evidence since the Bushwick prints?"

"Okay." Hank leaned over her shoulder to make sure she did exactly what he told her. "Write back and tell her it was shot at . . . um . . . J.J.'s Park-Rite Garage in, ah, the Darrow Park section of the Bronx. But you're not sure what street it's on. That oughta keep her busy for a bit."

Becky glanced up at him. "But there is no Darrow Park section of the Bronx?"

"No, but she's a white girl from Connecticut. She doesn't know that."

For a while there, Becky was happy to play along. But there was concern in her eyes now. "But the Bronx has been . . . ?"

He saw her worried look. "The militias. I *know*. Just do it. It'll be funny, believe me."

WORLD EXCLUSIVE!!!
FIRST VIDEO FOOTAGE OF GB!!!
earlier today, the above footage, shot on a cel phone in the bronx, was obtained by STONE'S THROW! although the picture quality is not what we might have hoped for, this is still a momentous event, as it is the first time the elusive GB has been captured live on film. previous attempts to film GB have been thwarted by his apparent power of invisibility.

our experts are currently studying this film for clues regarding the nature of GB—though as you can see, it does have certain unavoidable corporeal needs! this in itself is a clue. more details to follow as they arise. earlier still photos of GB available by clicking HERE.

"Now," Hank said, standing behind Nutskin's desk as the two of them watched the footage on the editor's computer. "That was posted five minutes ago. In half an hour it's going to be all over the Internet. By five there'll be late editions of all the papers, and it'll be blasting from the TV by the time you get home." Standing behind Nutskin made things easier, he found.

"And your point being?" Nutskin asked.

"My point being, Shed. I shot that footage this morning. It's an Onassis takin' a dump—even Becky could see that. But it's gonna be pitched as solid evidence that this thing is real. Solid evidence, my ass. I followed that dog for ten minutes. You want proof this whole thing's nothin' but a media fraud? Here it is." He pointed at the screen again. "I could write the whole thing up, get it to you first thing tomorrow, hit the streets Friday, and blast all of 'em out of the water." He rapped the desktop with his knuckles.

Nutskin stared at the screen as Hank gloated behind him, awaiting his rain of kudos.

"Kalabander," Nutskin began slowly as he whirled his chair to face Hank. "The only evidence I see here is evidence of a man who is so bitter and so desperate that he's willing to grab someone *else's* hard work and claim it as his own. Does that sound like a team player to you?" His wrinkled, cracked lips twisted in a slow anger Hank had, thank god, never witnessed before. "And *worse*, to *denigrate* the people you stole from when you do it. It's proof of a terrible attitude, and quite possibly of a deranged mind. That doesn't fly here at the *Hornet* . . . Not a team player at all."

Hank was far too flabbergasted to react. This wasn't the way things were supposed to go. He had a real story (which is more than he could say half an hour earlier), but douchebag here seemed determined to ignore that. "Lemme go get Becky," he offered. "She helped—she'll—"

"Don't drag Becky into your dirty juice. I know how you work."

"Did you just say 'dirty juice'?"

"Just leave her out of this. You know what I think happened?" Hank's eyes darted around the room. "I—I think you missed a huge scoop and now you're trying to cover your own butt. You're the *opposite* of a team player, Kalabander. And if you ask me I think you need help."

Hank's unfortunate choice of words before leaving Nutskin's office included, but were not restricted to, references to dried Silly Putty, dead teeth, "swinging colostomy bags," assorted shellfish, and coprophagia. He returned to his desk unclear as to whether or not he was still employed at the *Brooklyn Hornet*.

"Hey guess what?" Becky asked, poking her head over the top of the partition. She seemed excited, in her way.

"Hm?" Hank said, looking up but not really interested.

"I just got another text from Louise Stone? And you know what? After that clip had been up for, like, five minutes? One of the cable news channels called? And they offered her, like, two million dollars for the exclusive rights?" Her eyes blinked a few times. "Isn't that great?"

Hank closed his mouth as it began to drift open. He simply nodded and lowered his eyes, focusing once again on poor, doomed Topsy, seconds before the fatal jolt of electricity.

Lucky bastard, he thought.

The phone rang, and without thinking he picked it up. "Kalabander."

"Heya, Muttley," Rocky barked. "How's the poop playin' out?"

"It seems, ah, that once again we're ten minutes ahead of our time," he said.

"All right, then. Hey, just ran into that Prell faggot. He's got an idea. Catchya on the flippy flop."

Hank had just replaced the receiver when the phone rang again. He picked up. "Whaddya want now?"

"Mister Kala-ba—ban-der?"

Oh, goddamn. He knew the voice.

"Kalabander," he said. "Rhymes with Salamander."

The woman on the other end sounded large and asthmatic. "Mister Salamander, this is Lucella Colely, from the Divine Inspiration Church of the, uh, Blessed . . . uh."

"Congregation," Hank said flatly.

"With Jesus. An' we are sick an' tired of you missin' our very impo'tant weekly prayer meetin' every week in these terrible times. If you don't make . . . Our next weekly prayer meetin', God help me we will come to your house an' . . ."

Hank leaned back in his chair and listened.

Thirty-six

Hank probably could have done better for himself than team up with a cigar-chomping sideshow impresario and a flamboyant cryptozoologist, but unaccustomed to finding himself in such a situation that's exactly what he did.

An hour after sundown Wednesday night—his marriage, his job, his home, and now quite possibly his life in jeopardy—Hank and his two hopeless companions ventured out into the burning city, dodging bloodthirsty vigilante gangs, bumbling and terrified news crews, and herds of overzealous National Guardsmen, all in one final effort to prove whether or not the Gowanus Beast was worth worrying about.

He knew full well the damn thing didn't exist. He had all the evidence he needed three or four times over. But after a day like he'd had, and with all the bars shut down, he simply didn't feel much like sitting in his demolished apartment that night.

Even if they did find an answer, and whatever that answer happened to be, Hank realized they were still left with one of two problems. If the creature didn't exist, how do they get the word out to a blind, deaf, and heavily armed populace so adamantly unwilling to accept the truth? And if it *did* exist, well, what the hell did they do then? Good thing Rocky brought his net along.

For his part, Rocky had already decided that, even if he didn't return to Blount with a live monster in tow, he could find a use for Dr. Ernst Prell, big swish or not. Prell was a man ready-made for the sideshow circuit. This business tonight, though, Rocky wasn't so sure about anymore.

"This is incredibly retarded," he announced. Both Hank and Dr. Prell ignored him. They could hear the regular report of small arms fire, but it remained several blocks away. To the north and to the east, the bigger fires lit the sky a filthy orange.

"Watch out for the dogs," Hank warned. "They move in packs and they're bad news. That first kid they found, he was probably chewed up by Gowanus dogs."

"They rape him too?" Rocky asked.

"I don't know why we're headed down here anyway," Hank said. "City had their own people swarming all over here two weeks ago."

"They didn't know what they were looking for," Prell informed him, with the supreme confidence of a man no one ever takes seriously.

Dr. Prell stopped and unpacked an ovular gizmo and strapped it to his hip. Some kind of electronic wand was attached to the device with a long black cord. Prell checked all his connections, then waved the wand slowly in front of him.

Rocky dropped his net bag and plopped himself on top of it. He and Hank watched Prell briefly.

"So what the fuck are you doin' there, Dingus?" Rocky asked. "Some Harry Potter shit?"

Prell continued waving the wand, intermittently noting the readings on his machine. "I'm testing the immediate atmosphere for ectoplasmic residue," he explained patiently. "I only have a range of thirty feet, depending upon the prevailing conditions, but ectoplasm sticks around for a long time. If he's a spiritual entity by nature, as I suspect, and if he's been moving around in this area, which is near where the first sighting occurred, then I'll likely find something."

Hank looked around at the houses to either side of them along the narrow street. It seemed familiar but not in any way he could identify. It might've been one of the streets he walked down that night the trains screwed him up. He had to have been around here someplace. He almost remembered a construction site and looked around for one but saw nothing. No sawhorses, no caution tape, no orange barrels. He was probably wrong. Wouldn't be the first time.

"You don't wanna stick around here too long yourself, Dingus," he said to the preoccupied Prell. "Not just on accounta the dogs. One of the neighbors is liable to turn you in. Or shoot you."

Rocky made a face. "Talk about stickin' around, this place stinks to high heaven. I worked with some goats in my day—one had two faces, one had six legs—and those fuckers, I'll tell ya, stank somethin' fierce. But they ain't got nothin' on this place."

Prell nodded and shut off his ectoplasm doohickey, apparently having collected all the data he needed for the moment. Rocky hoisted his bag and the trio forged on, with Hank keeping an eye and ear open for fast-approaching devil hounds.

A few blocks later they stopped again, this time near the east bank of the Gowanus at the foot of the Union Street bridge. Prell needed more readings. "We're getting closer," he said ominously, surveying the area. "We're in the Forbidden Zone."

For once, Prell wasn't simply being overdramatic. The warehouses around them were dark and lifeless, but the canal seemed to emit an iridescent green glow all its own. Light from the few working streetlamps along the length of the bridge was reflected by the oil slicks, smearing rainbows across the water. Clouds of blackflies floated a few inches above the surface.

Even if the term "Forbidden Zone" had yet to be trademarked by the city the way "Ground Zero" had, the stretch three blocks deep on either side of the canal had been unofficially evacuated by both residents and industry. Few people—not the militias, the National Guard, nor the most reckless and mercenary of the vigilante groups—dared enter the area, and so, as a result, no one could say for sure what went on there. There were hushed tales of strange lights and stranger sounds, of unholy blood rituals and growing pyramids of skulls.

Hank, admittedly, didn't see any of those things. "Tell me, Dingus," he said to Prell's back as the good doctor waved his wand about. "You say you've been conducting an investigation in the city for weeks now, but you never came down here before? That ain't very, um, scientific."

"To be honest," Prell said, adjusting a few dials, "I wasn't one hundred percent comfortable entering the Forbidden Zone alone. I needed a reliable team."

"Pussy," Rock muttered from the curb.

"Hey, Prell," Hank called to him. "You ever end up taking Mr. DeKeyser for geometry?"

"My parents pulled me out of school before that on account of the bullying," he said. He froze, staring at his gauges. "Wait. I think I'm picking up something here."

"Probably just a sulfur cloud," Hank said, sniffing the air.

"Nah, that was me," Rocky confessed.

Prell was hitting assorted buttons on his whachahoogie when Hank asked, "So . . . Ernst." He paused and stifled a belch. "You really make a living doing this? I mean, who pays you?"

"American Pussy Association," Rocky said, kicking idly at an empty half pint at his feet.

Prell pointed his wand toward the unhealthy sky and checked a reading, yet he still seemed to be thinking of the best way to answer Hank's question. "There are book royalties, of course," he said. "And the website brings in some small income every month, especially with sales of the stuffed animals." He kept his eyes occupied so he could avoid looking at Hank.

"That's enough to live on, then? Sounds like you do a lot of traveling."

"Yes, well . . . to finance the field expeditions I have other sources." He tried to keep his voice even, but a small quaver had crept through.

Hank sensed a sore spot and promptly inserted a thumb. "So you have a trust fund is what you're saying?"

He'd already fallen too far out of character with Kalabander, he thought. He never expected to be recognized—and from middle school, of all places. For an instant, he let it all fall away. "I'm the floor manager at a Pottery Barn in Secaucus." The moment it came out he knew he'd made a horrible mistake. This was as close to a class reunion as he ever intended to get.

Rocky burst into hoarse, damning laughter, while Hank coughed uncontrollably and slapped his thigh. When he'd recovered sufficiently, Hank shot Rocky a look. "Rock, now, it ain't like you never did anything you weren't proud of."

"Speak for yourself, Rochester." He turned back to Prell, his nostrils flaring in an effort to contain his derision. "You *finished* yet, Dingus? We got a cleanup in aisle three."

Prell took one more look at his readings, then hit a button on his wand.

"Here, yes." He wanted to be Dr. Ernst Prell from Cambridge again.

"So where next?"

Prell brushed back his cape and put his hands on his expansive hips. "At this point the logical, and most promising, location . . ."

Hank had a bad feeling that he knew exactly what Prell was going to say, and he didn't care to hear it.

". . . is on those ledges down there." He pointed to the canal itself.

It was exactly what Hank was afraid he was going to say. He also suspected that Prell's plan was in no small part an act of revenge.

Rocky shoved himself to his feet and peeked over the side of the bridge to the narrow cement ledges perched a few feet above the surface of the water. He shook his head. "You know what, Dingus? I can see just fine from here, and there ain't nothin' down there 'cept some dead potted plants."

"Ah, my dear Mr. Roccoco," Prell said, allowing the character to take control again. "Sometimes the most important piece of evidence may be as tiny as a single hair, a broken branch, or a microscopic drop of dried blood. It might very well be completely invisible to the weak vessel of the human eye."

"Yeah," Rocky whispered to himself, "I'll give you some dried blood, ya tubba guts."

"Gentlemen," Prell declared pompously with a sweep of his cape. "Let us drive onward. Adventure awaits."

Much more nimbly than Hank ever would have expected from a man of Prell's girth, the cryptozoologist swung a leg over the aluminum guardrail to the ladder leading down to the ledge.

Hank looked at Rocky and shrugged. "Least the dogs can't get us down there."

"S'pose." Rocky seemed less than convinced, but he slung his net over his shoulder and clamped his cigar more firmly between his teeth.

"Good thing that's not lit," Hank pointed out. "One stray burning ash, this whole damn place would go up. C'mon, I'll give you a boost over." He bent his knees slightly and held out his arms.

"Just don't even think it," Rocky said, waving a hand in Hank's face and stepping around him.

It took a few minutes for all three men to make it down to the ledge, which was roughly forty feet long and eight feet wide. It struck Hank as dangerously narrow. It also seemed much closer to the water than it had appeared to be from the safety of the bridge.

"So . . ." Hank asked doubtfully. "Whaddo we do now?"

"Very simply," Prell replied, "we comb every inch looking for physical clues of the Beast's presence here. It is my suspicion that he considers this area home—or someplace near here, anyway. The site of his origin and a continued place of refuge."

"Uh-huh," Hank said. "And, ah, what leads you to that conclusion, exactly?"

Prell sucked his teeth at the simplemindedness of his fellow researchers. "Because he's called the *Gowanus* Beast, silly boy. Not the Central Park Beast or Chrysler Building Beast but the *Gowanus* Beast. You see? It's really quite simple." Prell pursed his lips in victory. "Now, if we find nothing here, we move up and over, then down to the next ledge, where we repeat the procedure."

"Jesus Christ."

"You two start at that end down there." Prell pointed away from the bridge. "And I shall begin at this end back here. We'll meet somewhere in the middle."

Hank asked, "What are we supposed to be looking for again?"

"Oh, anything that might belong to our boy. Anything out of the ordinary. Hair, droppings, half-eaten food, markings of some kind. The usual."

"We're looking for shit?"

Hank was starting to think staying at home might've been the wiser choice after all. He also wondered how Ms. Stone's quest up to the Bronx to find Brooklyn dog poop was going.

Let's see if that two million bucks'll help her up there.

As they separated toward their assigned ends of the ledge, Hank called after Prell. "Hey, Ernie, tell me. What made you get into this racket, anyway? Pottery Barn push you over the edge?"

"Oh quite the contrary," Prell replied, smiling. Hank immediately regretted asking the question. Not only were they closer to the water and the stench down here but they were closer to the flies as well. He was starting to wonder what kind of damage these chemical fumes might be inflicting on his lungs and brain.

Maybe that's what's driving everybody nuts, he suddenly thought.

"It began in the nineteen seventies, back when we were in school," Prell went on. "As you may recall things didn't go well for me within the institution. Fortunately the free thinkers reigned in the popular culture before the professionals moved in and ruined everything. With shows like *In Search Of* and all those Bigfoot movies. Writers like Charles Berlitz and Erich von Däniken. They showed me a world still full of mystery and wonder. Remember? So at an early age it was that world I chose for myself."

"Yeah, I think I remember the kids at Aldo Ray calling you Sasquatch," Hank said. Rocky, who didn't care, moved to the far end of the ledge and, he hoped, out of earshot, where he began looking for monster crap.

Prell's story ceased abruptly. "Enough sentimental reminiscing. Let's get on with it." While he admittedly preferred "Sasquatch" to "Dirty Dingus," he still didn't care for the reminder. They had work to do now and couldn't waste time with pointless blather. He turned and spat into the water. Then he froze, and for a moment Hank was afraid Prell was going to collapse—and, if he did, how in the hell would they get him up the ladder? It was almost as if he'd entered a trance state. Hank hadn't known Prell long or well but he could see the change.

Prell's eyes refocused and he chuckled weakly.

"This is still incredibly retarded," shouted Rocky, who hadn't seen Prell's seizure.

"Yes, well," Prell said. "We should get on with things." He pulled out his electronic wand and hit a button. The dials on his machine glowed orange and white. "I am quite enjoying this, I must say." A whisper of his fake accent was creeping in again as he more fully embodied "expert in the field" mode.

Hank was walking toward Rocky but he paused when he heard Prell's remark. "What, the stench and the flies?"

"No, I mean what this creature has created. I enjoy seeing people feeling fear, anger, anxiety. They're real emotions. Things most of these people probably haven't felt in years. Do you realize how many UFOs are spotted over this city every *month*? Yet nobody says a word. But this? This is fantastic."

Hank sighed. If he paused to listen, he knew he'd still be able to hear gunshots and sirens and screams. "I think I know what you're sayin' there, uh, Ernie. It must remind you of a big sale at Pottery Barn. I just wish these emotions didn't cause people to set so many fires and stomp my friends to death."

Prell cleared his throat. "I'm speaking academically, of course." He made a minor adjustment on his machine in order to avoid Hank's gaze.

"Of course. So why don't we get this over with, okay?" Hank switched on his flashlight and turned it to the far end of the cement ledge, where Rocky was sitting, arms folded, on his net bag.

"Remember, boys!" Prell yelled behind him. "Any decent monster hunter knows his prey will always do the unexpected!"

Yeah, like not existing, Hank thought.

"He must save up those gems for times like these," Rocky said.

"He's a man with some serious problems," Hank replied when he knew Prell was far enough away. For the seventh or eighth time in recent weeks, Hank had to ask himself one question. If he was so convinced this thing was nothing but the product of a crippled collective imagination, that it was nothing but human fear and superstition and stupidity all rolled together and run amok, what in the fuck was he doing out here on the Gowanus? Moreover, what in the fuck did he think he was looking for?

Hell if he knew. He was an idiot, that's why. "Get off your ass, Rochester, let's get this shit done with so we can go home."

"Came out here to catch a monster," Rocky bitched as he stood. "Not find goddamn broken branches. How in the hell'm I supposed to sell tickets to see that?"

The green-black sludge below them seemed to be barely moving at all. There was no breeze, nothing to blow the stench out of that long cement canyon they were in. Hank heard a dog barking somewhere above him and paused. Yes, if they had to be in the Forbidden Zone at all—asinine as he felt saying that—maybe it was better to be down on the ledge. With his flashlight, he pretended to carefully examine a dead and twisted tree someone had placed down there. The trunk was stunted and gnarled into an unlikely posture and the branches were knotted together. Upon examination, he noticed that some of the branches still carried dead leaves, while others, at some point, had been evergreen. *That can't be good*, he thought. It occurred to him that maybe it was the first step in the city's plans to beautify the canal. Or maybe it wasn't the first step—maybe this *was* the park they kept talking about.

Rocky, meanwhile, who'd had enough himself, was making only the weakest effort to even pretend he was looking for evidence, marching along the narrow ledge double time, swinging the beam from his own flashlight left and right at his feet.

"Wait just a second," Prell said in an echoed stage whisper up ahead of them. "What have we here?"

Both men stopped and looked to see Prell in silhouette looking over the edge and into the water. As they watched, he began lowering himself to his hands and knees in an effort to get a better view of something. They stood where they were and continued watching as Prell snagged his left foot on his cape, lost his balance, and, with an extravagant Shakespearean yip, rolled off the ledge, dropping ten feet into the canal, narrowly missing a cluster of blackened wooden pilings. The fecal water parted for an instant when he hit, then swallowed him whole.

A moment later his head reappeared, eyes closed, mouth open and shrieking, arms flailing and splashing like a harpooned sea cow.

"Jee-*zus*," Rocky said.

There were no ladders leading to the water, no way to reach Prell with their hands alone, and nothing on the barren ledge except that dead and unnerving tree.

"*Grab the net!*" Hank shouted as he jogged down to where Prell was thrashing and howling and gargling the poisoned muck.

"*Haaalp!*"

"Christ, tell him to shut up," Rocky called to Hank as he ripped the net from the laundry bag and toddled over to where Hank stood staring helplessly into the water. He unfurled the net off the side of the ledge, across Prell's head and arms.

"Grab that, fatso!" Rocky yelled.

Hank snatched up a handful of the net himself. Seeing it outside the bag for the first time, he turned to Rocky. "Is this a *volleyball* net?"

"All they had," Rocky explained, wrapping his hands in the netting for a better grip. "It'll work fine."

Prell was wailing and thrashing and likely didn't hear any of this, but still he managed to tangle his fingers and hands in the net, twisting his body around and holding tight.

"Thank god there's no current here," Hank said as they began heaving.

It was impossible to guess how long it took them to drag Prell, writhing and bellowing, from the Gowanus, but eventually they slid him, bellyfirst, onto the ledge. Prell continued screaming. He tore free from the net like some comic book supervillain, planted a thick, soft hand on Hank's chest and roughly shoved him out of the way, fumbled for the metal ladder, and flew up the rungs and over the guardrail before running down the middle of Union Street, face covered with both hands, still screaming.

Back on the ledge, Rocky and Hank were silent for a long time, listening as Prell's shrill cries faded into the darkness, blending with the howling dogs, the gunfire, and the sirens.

"He moves pretty fast for a wet fat guy in a cape," Rocky observed.

Hank was staring up the ladder. "My guess is it's all the shit in the water. He's . . ." He thought for a moment. "He's probably melting up there right now."

Rocky, who had been trying to gather his net back together, snapped around. "You zoomin' me?"

Hank looked down at him. "It's entirely possible. In fact you might want to forget about that net. You won't have much of it left in a few minutes anyway. This shit'll eat through steel."

Rocky dropped the net. "We gotta go get Dingus! Now I *really* need him for the show. C'mon!" He took a step toward the ladder.

"We can look if you want," Hank said. "But we won't find him.

Especially if anyone up there finds him first. Why is it, Rock, that every time we go out something horrible happens?"

Before Rocky could come up with a smart-ass answer, something caught Hank's eye. In the deep shadows just under the bridge—near the spot where Prell had been looking—was the edge of a blue plastic tarp. He couldn't believe he hadn't noticed it before. It was covering something and it was held down with cinder blocks.

"Oh, goddamn," Hank said quietly, as bits of another incomplete memory came back to him. More stills from a forgotten film he'd watched once while drunk a long time ago.

He was talking to someone on a bridge. Maybe this one. An old man, but that's all he knew about him. It was dark and there was a tarp involved. A tarp and an Italian monkey. That's all he could remember. There was something awful about it.

"Jesus."

"What?" Rocky demanded, obviously impatient to get moving.

"That." Hank pointed at the tarp. In the dark it was impossible to read a shape in the folds of its surface. He didn't want to know what was under there, but he had to know. Then what? If it was another disemboweled kid, what do they tell the cops? And how do they explain what they were doing down there on the canal?

"Come on," Rocky said. "What about Dingus?"

"He'll be fine . . . I just gotta see what's under here. Just make sure I don't fall in while I'm at it." He moved to one of the cinder blocks and nudged it off the tarp with his shoe. He really did not want to see a small, bloody arm when he pulled it back. He took a few steps and kicked another cinder block away. That should be enough.

He glanced at Rocky, who was thinking the fumes must've gotten to Hank already. He bent, grabbed a corner of the wrinkled, stiff plastic, and yanked it back to reveal an assortment of old busted-up bicycle parts.

Hank exhaled heavily.

"Hey, great snag there, Popeye. You need some new handlebars for your Schwinn? Let's get the fuck outa here."

Hank stared down at the rusted frames and pedals and bent tires. "Yeah," he said. "Let's go home." He pulled a cigarette from his pocket, lit it, and dropped the burning match into the canal. He closed his eyes and waited. When the whole damn mess didn't go up in a billowing orange fireball, he opened his eyes, nodded, and headed for the ladder.

Thirty-seven

For the first time he could remember, the gate on Harry's newsstand had been pulled down. The deep scorch marks on the corrugated metal as well as on both sides of the stand gave Hank a clue as to what had happened. Wherever he is, Hank thought, Harry will undoubtedly be blaming the mayor's cronies and thugs.

He didn't know if the smoke he smelled in the air came from Harry's place specifically or was drifting over from the rest of the burning city.

Unopened bundles of newspapers were stacked up in front of the stand. That they were still being published and distributed said something about civilization. Then he saw the cover of the *Eagle*. Next to an intentionally unfocused photo of a large black dog taking a crap was the headline "Stone-Cold Proof!"

As he stepped around the side of the newsstand to survey the damage he noticed the padlock on the door had been broken and was hanging open.

Hank looked around, then wondered why he was bothering to look around anymore. Nobody cared. He slipped the lock off the latch and the thin makeshift door creaked open. He took a step inside. The cramped interior was dark but the warm light filtering in through the open door showed him what he had expected. The place had been stripped clean, and what hadn't been taken had been smashed.

The walls were black and the flames had burned two holes in the ceiling. Hank was amazed the place was standing at all. The industrial-sized coffee pot in which Harry had made that dreadful sludge of his for decades was on its side. It looked like a vengeful coffee lover had beaten it with a baseball bat. A well-trampled issue of the *Economist* lay torn and singed on the floor but all the porn was gone. Much to his surprise, there were still two packs of smokes at the bottom of the rack, their plastic wrappers only slightly melted. Not his brand, but now was not the time to be picky. He slipped them into his pocket.

It could've been worse, he was thinking as he stepped back outside, closing the door and replacing the lock. He had been afraid he was going to find Harry in there, or what was left of him.

As he turned to head into work, a group of twelve or fifteen people marched past him in formation, singing. Hank couldn't decipher the words but it was sung to the tune of that old commercial jingle "I'd Like to Teach the World to Sing." Each of the marchers carried an eight-foot pike, and stuck atop each pike was a raggedly severed human head. A number of people had stopped along the sidewalks to cheer them as they passed. It was like a Veterans Day parade for the new age. Hank quickly scanned the sagging, bloodless faces of the dead for anyone he knew but recognized no one.

As he watched them go, he thought of Khalid's final words to him: "I seen heads."

"Yeah," Hank whispered, before continuing into the office. After the previous day's meeting with Nutskin, he wasn't sure whether or not he had a job anymore, but he figured it was better to pretend he did until someone told him otherwise. Likewise, he had no idea what he intended to do about this story Nutskin was expecting that morning, but again he figured it was better to pretend he did.

He was surprised to find the *Hornet*'s office locked when he arrived. After pulling out his keys and unlocking the door, he was even more surprised to find the lights out and Blanche's desk unoccupied. Blanche was always there. It was clear the rest of the office had been abandoned as well.

He looked at his watch. It was ten-thirty. This was all very strange. The *Hornet* was supposed to hit doorsteps the next morning. Where were people going to get their coupons?

He turned on all the lights and went to his desk, where he found an envelope addressed to him. Flipping it over, he saw there was no return address and no stamp but the handwriting seemed familiar.

Inside was a note from Vernon Isopod and a photocopy of the previous day's *Times* crossword puzzle. The puzzle had been solved, and Isopod's note instructed Hank to read every other letter on the right-hand column of the solution from the bottom to the top.

Honestly not having anything better to do at the moment, Hank flattened the photocopy on his desk, flipped the envelope to the blank side, and grabbed a pen from his desk drawer. Using his finger as a guide, he worked his way up the right side of the puzzle, jotting down every other letter.

When he was finished he looked at the string of letters and saw there was only one way to parse them coherently.

BEAST COME HOME

Hank rolled his eyes. *Well, that was two minutes' worth of entertainment*, he thought as he crumpled the note, the puzzle, and the envelope together and dropped them in the trash can.

He called Crosslin to try and find out if the people behind the head parade had filed for all the necessary permits, but there was no answer over at the Seventy-fourth. Hank let it ring nine times before hanging up.

Unsure what else to do with himself at that point, he searched his desktop, found a few stray press releases that, at least date-wise, still seemed pertinent. One was for a vacuum cleaner demonstration, another for a children's scavenger hunt in the park.

"That'll end well," he said as he began typing them up for an entertainment editor who might or might not be dead and a paper that might or might not still exist.

He had to admit, though, he didn't mind the quiet. He even pulled out a cigarette and lit up as he worked. For once, that cubicle felt like a world where he belonged.

At quarter after twelve he heard the office door open and close. There were footsteps. Hank couldn't remember if he'd locked the door or not. If so, this was someone with a key. If not, well, it could be a housewife from Brighton Beach with a hatchet and a pike. He began looking around for anything that could conceivably be used as a weapon.

"Heya, Rochester! You dead?" a voice shouted from the lobby.

"*Only halfway,*" Hank shouted back as he opened the drawer and emptied his fistful of thumbtacks.

A moment later Rocky turned the corner. "Just what I figured," he said. "I wake up, you ain't there. The fuckin' world's comin' to an end, so you musta gone in here like an idiot. You don't even know if you still gotta job."

"Looks like I'm the only one who does." He couldn't help but notice that Rocky was still carrying that damn laundry bag even though he'd abandoned his volleyball net at the canal. "So what's the scoop?" He nodded at the bag.

Rocky tossed it on the floor and went for Becky's empty chair. "Clothes."

"But you didn't bring any clothes, 'cept what you got on."

"These are mostly yours."

"Oh," Hank said, looking at the bag. "All right . . . Why, um, do you have a bag full of my clothes?"

"Ah," Rocky said. "Time for me to hit the trail. This monster bullshit's a waste o' time. It's over. Last night by that cesspool with the jerkoff—not you—proved that."

"That's what it took? I've been tellin' you that for two weeks." Although he dared not say so aloud, Hank was strangely and quietly saddened to hear Rocky was leaving.

"Besides," Rocky went on, "gotta make a jump to some high grass dates in Pennsylvania. I been in touch with my crew, an' those poor fuckers are lost without me."

"But you still need a show, right? Blount'll be expecting something. Hey, I know where you can get a big dog. People seem to buy that pretty well."

Rocky pulled the ruined cigar stub from his mouth, looked at it, then tossed it into Hank's trash can. He reached in his vest pocket, extracted and unwrapped a new one, bit off the tip and spit it on the floor, then stuck it between his teeth. "Dogs I can get," he said. "Dogs I don't need. Got a light?"

Hank handed him a book of matches.

"Anyway, Blount can kiss my ass."

"So . . . you think you're gonna be back around again next summer?"

Rocky struck a match and held the tip of the flame to the end of the cigar and puffed until it glowed. That was new, Hank thought, and reached for a cigarette of his own, suddenly wishing any of the bars in the area were still open.

"I dunno," he said ruefully. "There still gonna be a city here next year?"

"Good point. Let's assume there is."

"Still dunno. I been thinkin' about that. People just don't wanna see freak shows no more."

"What the hell are you talking about?" Hank snapped at him. "Whole goddamn *country's* a freak show. Look out the window here."

"That's just it, Shirley," Rocky said. "It's all around 'em for free, so why pay to go in a tent? 'Specially when you got no real freaks to show 'em?"

"Didn't stop Barnum—and hasn't stopped you either."

"Ah," Rocky said, reaching for his cigar and blowing a series of perfect smoke rings ceilingward. "Different time, different era, different people." He puffed some more. "We're dinosaurs, you an' me. Y'know, parta me really wanted that fuckin' ape. I wanted to believe it was real an' that you were jus' bein' difficult. That mighta changed things. Not just a live show but somethin' *real* like that. Know whaddimean? Like Bonnie an' Clyde's death car—that drew 'em in. But I think my time's about up in this racket." He looked for a place to tap his ashes, found nothing, and tapped them on the floor.

"Y'know, I'm sorry to hear that, Rock. From one dinosaur to another. Ten minutes ahead of our time, or ten minutes behind—either way we're royally fucked."

"Ain't it the truth? It's time for somethin' new. That's why I think I'm gonna try a spook show next season."

"You mean like a haunted house? People always dig those."

Rocky scowled at him. "No, *idiot.* I mean a *spook show.* You've been to a spook show."

"You mean a minstrel show? That'd getcha some press for sure . . . Also getcha hanged."

"*Nah. God!*" Rocky raised a hand as if to smack him. "A spook show. You know, a theater number? Bring out Dracula and Frankenstein? Fake lightning an' rubber spiders? Audience plants? Christ."

Hank fought back a tiny, wicked smile. "Okay . . . like the Johnny Macabro show that was gonna replace you, in other words."

"No, and that's the point. Mine'll be a million times better . . . *idiot.*"

Hank smiled and reached for another cigarette. "You know, Rock, I'd've thought after all these years in the carnival, you'd have a more colorful term in your lexicon than 'idiot.' Something like . . ." He raised his eyes in thought. ". . . I dunno, 'tabwanker' or 'shottlecrim.' Maybe 'jobbernow' or 'moonpie.' I like moonpie."

"'Idiot' works just as well, and you know what I'm sayin'." He looked at his watch. "Well, Rochester, you know how I am with these things. I think I should roll. Gotta catch a bus to Lord Knows Where, Pennsylvania. Long as nobody's torched the Port Authority yet."

Hank decided to forget about the clothes. They'd never fit Rocky anyway. "Well, as ever Rock, it's been an adventure." He pushed himself to his feet and handed Rocky the laundry bag.

"Not mucha one, really," Rocky said, hefting the bag over his shoulder. "But if Annie ever comes back, tell her it was a pleasure."

"If she comes back I'll do that, ya short shit."

"Oh. And you ever run into Dingus tell him if he's interested in seein' a real Chupacabra he should track me down."

"He'll be disappointed, I think."

"Yeah, probably. But I bet he pays to get in first. Besides, if this spook show comes together, I might have some use for him. He'd make a decent talker, don'cha think? Scare the shit outa them kids. That stupid cape's a nice touch. An' if he's half melted, all the better."

"Will do."

Hank left the office with Rocky, figuring there was no reason for him to stay. At the front door of the building they paused.

"An' as for you, Salamander, well . . ."

He left it at that and stepped out onto the hot sidewalk, his cigar clamped firmly and defiantly between his teeth. Watching him go, Hank thought that if it had been anybody else walking away in hopes of getting not just into Manhattan, but up to the bus station in Midtown, he would've been more than a little concerned—especially if they were carrying nothing but a bag of someone else's clothes. But no one was gonna fuck with Rocky Roccoco.

Thirty-eight

Hey, *Joey*! Go get Eddie an' tellimta get ovah here. Tommy an' Frankie, too!"

Given the condition of the body, there was no telling how long it had been lying unnoticed in the corner of the empty, garbage-strewn lot. The eyes had shriveled within the sockets. The blistered flesh had turned a dusty, spotted black and was constricted so tautly across the skull and away from the teeth that it had actually torn in places. The same was true of the hands, the dark, hard skin splitting in places to reveal the yellow bone beneath. Dogs apparently wanted nothing to do with him, as the clothes, while ragged, hadn't been shredded the way they usually were after the dogs were through with someone. There were a few holes and some scorch marks on the man's purple cape, but it was still knotted neatly and securely around his gray, ulcerated throat.

The condition and smell of the corpse didn't seem to matter to the members of the Carroll Gardens Protection Council, who pulled it out of the lot and onto the sidewalk, where they chained it to the rear bumper of a yellow cab they'd confiscated three days earlier. It was Eddie's turn so he got behind the wheel, and for the next hour they dragged the body through the narrow streets of the neighborhood honking the horn in proud celebration of their latest victory in the ongoing war against the Gowanus Beast.

For nearly three hours, Hank had been roving like a shark, warm beer in hand, from one seminavigable section of the apartment to the next, eyes rarely straying from the exposed wires and pipes and beams of what was left of the ceiling. There were at least two sets of tiny pounding feet up there and, after what Annie had seen, he was doing what he could to avoid being directly underneath either of them at any given moment. They moved to one end of the apartment, he sidled to the other.

Through the open front windows, he heard another hooting mob working its way down the street, accompanied by the smash of another car window and the jubilant crack of semiautomatic pistol fire.

There was an advantage to having no electricity at night, he thought. It made his place less of a target. But even the safety of being inside was tenuous, with the constant threat of a five-year-old crashing through his ceiling at any moment.

He nearly screamed and dropped his beer when the phone rang. He kept forgetting that somehow the phone still worked.

He moved back toward the kitchen table, stepping carefully around the coils of electrical cable and half-empty bags of Redicrete.

He slid the phone closer to him across the gritty tabletop and picked up the receiver. "Yeah?" he asked tentatively.

"Hi, sweets."

"Annie, hey." That was a relief. He shook his beer to see how much was left. "How are things up at what's-her-name's?"

"Things are fine here, but I'm worried about you. Nobody's reporting anything out of New York anymore. Last reports said that gangs were starting to tear down transmission towers because the monster was feeding on the signal."

Hank sniffed, then belched. "Yeah, that makes sense. So what's the rest of the country saying about us?"

"Most people seem to think it's pretty funny. But people in Austin, Chicago, Toronto . . . they're starting to report monster sightings of their own."

Hank smiled slightly. "Goddamn copycats. Anyway, not much more to report." Several voices in the street out front grew suddenly loud and he waited for them to subside.

"Are you okay?" she asked. "I'm worried about you."

"Me? Ah, I'm always fine." He took a drink of flat beer. "Rocky split back to the carny yesterday."

"All the more reason to be concerned," she said. Then she was silent. "Hank . . . I'm seriously worried about you down there alone. You have trouble taking care of yourself even when civilization *isn't* collapsing."

"What, you think I'm gonna do something stupid?"

"Probably less so now that Rocky's gone, but in a word yes. No offense, but I'm thinking of coming back home."

There was a sharp, concussive explosion that rattled the window over the table.

"Yeah, uh, honey, I don't think that's such a hot idea right now."

"What the hell was that?"

"Ah, no big deal. I think some jarhead found himself a stash of grenades. But they've all been at least three, four blocks away, from the sound of it." He remembered what she'd said. "Still, though, I'd feel much better if you just stayed where you are for the time being." As he spoke, he leaned over and pulled the blinds, just in case one of his neighbors had a night-vision scope.

"Hank?" There was still too much concern in her voice. "There's something else."

"Whoop, hold on." He drained the bottle, set it aside, and reached for another in the warm cooler at his feet. He only had five left. That would be his next mission outside. And while he was at it he'd see if he could get some gas or kerosene—something to turn all these empties into Molotov cocktails should it ever come to that. "All right, then," he said once the new bottle was opened. "So what is it? You and this broad decide to go all lesbian?"

Somehow she was able to ignore him. "There's something that's been eating at me. It's irrelevant but I keep thinking about it."

The lesbian follow-up was teetering at the end of his tongue, but he stashed it away for later. He could hear the hesitation in her voice. *Oh, wha'd I do now?* he thought as he pulled a cigarette from his pocket and lit it. "All right?"

"I guess I started thinking about it that night you were out with Rocky, when you mentioned that maybe you ran into . . . What was his name? The bum you knew?"

He winced at the memory. "Khalid. The one they killed."

"Khalid, right. You mentioned you ran into him that night but weren't sure."

Hank tried to recall. "I don't really remember that but I'll take your word for it. Was I drunk?"

"You were out with Rocky."

"Okay."

One of the kids upstairs stopped running and began pounding his or her heels like a drum machine directly over Hank's head. He flinched as a fine rain of plaster dust sprinkled down across the table and his head.

"What was that?" she asked.

"Upstairs," was all he said. "So what about that night?"

She paused again, and he hoped the connection held out long enough for her to get to the point.

"Do you remember what night it was we first went out with Rocky?"

"You mean the night we went to the fair?" Hank had always been a little shaky with dates, and in recent weeks they'd become less important than ever. "Hold on, there's a calendar around here under the rubble someplace. It's on there."

He ground out the cigarette, laid the receiver down, and began flipping through a stack of dusty, paint-spattered papers on the side table. Beneath the unpaid bills, passive-aggressive letters from the insurance and credit card companies, and glossy, four-color Chinese takeout menus, he found it, flipped back to July, and saw the seventh had been circled in red with an exclamation point next to it. (He'd done that.) He gave her the date.

"Okay," she said. "Now what night was the first sighting of this thing? That guy you wrote about in Carroll Gardens?"

That date he did happen to remember, if only because he'd read it and typed it so many times. "That was the next day, the eighth, early on the eighth." There was a sharp scream outside, followed by another grenade blast. It sounded closer than the last one. "Yeah, honey?" he suggested. "You might wanna get to the point here. Soon."

"I know," she said. "I'm still just working it out myself . . . That first night with Rocky after the carnival, I went home early and you stayed at the bar until one or two."

"It's a little foggy but, yeah, I guess."

"You got home about four the next morning. You told me you got off at the wrong stop and walked."

"Carroll Street, yeah." It was starting to feel like a *Dragnet* routine. "I apologized for that already. There was this fucker—"

"Hank, no," she stopped him. "That's not my point. Did anything strange happen on the way home that night?"

"You want me to remember *now*?" he asked. "Christ, I didn't remember *then*." This was just stupid, he thought. Then he did remember something. "Oh, wait a second. Just the other night when Rocky and I were on the Gowanus with Dingus—"

"When you were what with who?"

"Never mind," he said. "Not important. But while we were there I remembered stopping and talking to a creepy old man on a bridge for a few minutes. It might've been that night, but I'm not a hundred percent sure."

"Anything else?"

He tried to think back, but once again it was like flipping through a series of fuzzy, unconnected snapshots. "Just the old man. Not unless running into some lampposts and traffic barrels counts."

"All right," she said. "Maybe this is going nowhere. You didn't see anything else?"

"Nope."

"Do you remember getting scratched on a fence?"

"Annie, *no*. Christ." This was all beginning to annoy him. "I have slightly more important things to think about at the moment."

There was a distant, rumbling explosion outside. Something much larger than a grenade.

"I'm sorry," she said, backing off. "It's stupid. I don't even know why I'm bringing it up now. It was just something I was thinking about."

"It's all right."

They talked a few minutes longer, during which Hank tried to convince her that yes, he had enough food to hold him awhile, yes he would be careful, and no she shouldn't think about returning to the city just now.

Someone began screaming as he hung up the phone. It reminded him of another scream. Not one he'd heard recently but one he might have heard that night while walking home. Screams no longer struck him as odd, but that one had. It echoed in his head the way it echoed through the empty streets and off the quiet buildings. He thought it was a dog but, no, it was definitely human.

Again he thought of the old man on the bridge but couldn't remember what they'd talked about. Damn that Annie for putting this in his head.

He heard two people laughing loudly outside. A man and a woman, it sounded like, but their laughter was more desperate and hysterical than it was joyous. Hank drained his beer and reached for another. That left him with four, he noted. The stomping and running above him continued, but he remained at the table. If they came through the ceiling, well, so be it.

In the darkness he felt his sweaty forearms. The scratches she'd mentioned were long gone. No, he didn't remember any fence. The old man hadn't done it either, he didn't think. He hoped not. The idea made him uneasy. Maybe he fell when he ran into that orange barrel. He couldn't remember getting up off the ground, but it might have happened. He did remember struggling with it for a second, though, almost as if it were fighting back.

He was raising the bottle when it came back to him that the plastic traffic barrel had arms. Soft, pale arms. They'd grabbed at him. Above the arms was a head.

His mind flashed to the framed family portrait in the Pierce living room. Standing off to the left was Mrs. Pierce's fat son Chuck, in his orange and white shirt.

There in the glow of the wavering streetlamp was half of the face in that photo. Older but still round and soft, and that night it was perched on top of an orange and white traffic barrel.

Hank closed his eyes. It hadn't been a traffic barrel at all. Traffic barrels don't flail their arms or scream like little girls.

Slowly, Hank began shaking his head as he reached for another cigarette. He struck a match and lit it, then opened the blinds. Outside, the nearby fires were reflected off the neighbors' darkened windows. "I don't fucking believe this," he said.

Above him there were three loud and brutal thumps, followed by silence.

Thirty-nine

It was about eleven o'clock in the morning by his guess. His watch had stopped.

Three houses across the street were ablaze, and there was no effort being made to douse the flames. The smoke had finally become so thick that he had to close the windows. It was probably safer that way anyway. It made it easier to ignore what was going on.

Demolished cars lay on their sides and backs on the sidewalk. There was furniture piled in the middle of the street. The only people who dared step outside anymore were the packs of monster hunters, who now defined a monster as anyone else who dared step outside.

At least things had been quiet upstairs.

Hank had found the one outlet in the apartment that was still working. Somehow the workmen had forgotten the one hidden behind the bookcase. He used it to recharge Annie's laptop, and for the previous five hours he'd been sitting at the kitchen table, typing. On the table next to the laptop a spoon jutted from an open can half filled with cold beef stew.

Confessions of the Gowanus Beast
by Henry Kalabander

In the article he set down everything as bluntly and honestly as he could, from end to beginning. Every move, every detail, every mistake and misinterpretation and failure from that night after the fair to, well, the collapse of Western Civilization, complete with historical analogues.

He had no idea what he'd do with it. Maybe give it to Nutskin, if he was still alive. Maybe see if Stone could get it in the *Eagle*, though she'd probably just slap her name on it. He'd have to decide something soon. He reached the end of the story, typed the last few words, and knew there was no more for him to say. It would, if nothing else, be a record for future generations.

As he was scrolling back to the top for another read-through, he heard the sound of a gunning engine and a shriek of spinning tires moments before he heard the exploding glass and the heavy crumple of metal. It sounded like a bad one.

He stood from the table and found his way to the front window, where he took a careful peek outside. It was a bad one, all right. The car was still upright but the front end was twisted at an unfathomable angle. It looked like it had slammed into whatever immovable object was hidden beneath the pyramid of discarded furniture in the street. The driver had been thrown halfway through the windshield, the impact all but decapitating him. The body hung there in mid-dive, the blood spilling freely into the street and across the accordion hood. Hank wondered if it was a suicide or if the driver simply wasn't expecting to find something solid buried under all that furniture.

As he watched, the front door of the building directly across the street opened.

A young couple—two kids, really, he guessed in their early

twenties—stepped outside, looked up and down the street, then dashed over to the wreck. They didn't seem in the least concerned that one of the houses adjacent to theirs was engulfed in flames. As the young man stood guard with a crowbar, the woman wrenched the nearly severed head free of the driver's body. When she had the head wrapped safe and tight in her blood-smeared arms, they darted back into the house and slammed the door behind them.

A gray loathing soaked through Hank's heart as he watched, yet at the same time a small, dark smile still crept across his face. Rocky was right the night Khalid died. He didn't want to know what the blow-off was.

You've seen the show folks, but now we've got a little something extra for you . . . Just step over to the side of the stage, pay an extra fifty cents, and take a peek through the curtain . . . We'll show you what you really are.

"Alive, alive, alive," he said softly. With a shake of the head and a wheezy laugh, he returned to the kitchen and the laptop, scanning one last time through the story that explained everything, making minor corrections and additions as he did so. When he was fully and truly satisfied that he had said all there was to say, he marked the entire document. Then without the slightest hesitation he hit the DELETE button.

Across the street, one of the burning houses slowly collapsed in on itself.

Acknowledgments

I would like to thank the following people for their assistance, encouragement, and assorted inspirations.

My remarkable agent Melanie Jackson and my editors Sarah Hochman and Michele Bové continue to believe and make all this happen.

Special thanks are due the great Don Kennison for editorial contributions far and above simple copyediting. James Taylor of *Shocked and Amazed!* magazine, Brian Berger, and John Graz have also made invaluable contributions to the story at hand.

Thanks are also due Philip Harris of ElectronPress.com; David E. Williams and Germ Books; Jerome Deppe; Ryan Knighton; William Bryk and Mimi Kramer; Raquel Rios; Leif Solem; Daniel Riccuito and Marilyn Palmeri; Linda Hunsaker; Priscilla Cohen; Erik Horn; William Monahan; Laura Lindgren and Ken Swezey; Derek Davis; John Strausbaugh; Luca Dipierro; Richard Dellifraine; Mom and Dad; Mary, McKenzie, and Jordan Adrians; Mike Kenny; TRP; Thomas Nola; and Homer Flynn. Elmer Bernstein provided the sound track.

I've said it before and I'll say it again. None of this would be possible without the constant support, humor, intelligence, and wisdom of Morgan Intrieri. She's the best there is, and not just because she continues to put up with my foolishness. I love her very much.

About the Author

Jim Knipfel lives in Brooklyn, where he doesn't believe a damn thing he hears.